SHE WAS NOT CRAZY, SHE WAS NOT LOSING HER MIND.

She sat there thinking, almost with admiration, how clever her tormentor was. She had little left of importance; almost every facet of her life that mattered had been tainted: her school, her job, her writing, her apartment, the man she loved. And her life itself. Control had slipped from her like silk through fingers. She would continue to function, to get through the hours and days performing her duties. But always she would be waiting . . . waiting for the next voiceless telephone call . . . waiting for—

THE OTHER ANNE FLETCHER

"Effective"—*Library Journal*

"The believing and doubting sides that are locked in battle in all of us . . . a novel you'll want to read."
—*Glamour Magazine*

Great Reading from SIGNET

THE *OTHER* ANNE FLETCHER

SUSANNE JAFFE

A SIGNET BOOK

NEW AMERICAN LIBRARY

TIMES MIRROR

PUBLISHER'S NOTE

This novel is a work of fiction. Names, characters, places, and incidents are either the product of the author's imagination or are used fictitiously, and any resemblance to actual persons, living or dead, events, or locales is entirely coincidental.

NAL BOOKS ARE AVAILABLE AT QUANTITY DISCOUNTS WHEN USED TO PROMOTE PRODUCTS OR SERVICES. FOR INFORMATION PLEASE WRITE TO PREMIUM MARKETING DIVISION, THE NEW AMERICAN LIBRARY, INC., 1633 BROADWAY, NEW YORK, NEW YORK 10019

Ø

SIGNET TRADEMARK REG. U.S. PAT. OFF. AND FOREIGN COUNTRIES REGISTERED TRADEMARK—MARCA REGISTRADA HECHO EN CHICAGO, U.S.A.

SIGNET, SIGNET CLASSICS, MENTOR, PLUME, MERIDIAN and NAL BOOKS are published by The New American Library, Inc., 1633 Broadway, New York, New York 10019

First Signet Printing, June, 1981

1 2 3 4 5 6 7 8 9

PRINTED IN THE UNITED STATES OF AMERICA

With special thanks to Claire Smith,
for her intelligence, encouragement, and patience.

1

Anne N. Fletcher sat cross-legged on the floor, unwrapping glassware from cocoons of newspaper. Cartons and crates littered the living room, dwarfing her; she felt insignificant against them and the task they presented. Moving was not fun, she decided.

She twisted a loose strand of brown hair behind her ear, and a sliver of excelsior drifted to the floor. She tiredly pushed herself upright; she had been unpacking since ten in the morning and it was now almost seven-thirty at night. She massaged her lower back; her hands, ink-dirty with newspaper print, came away with fistfuls of excelsior. Punchy with fatigue, she tossed the white packing material up in the air, and laughed out loud as it showered back down on her. Weaving her way through the obstacle course of her living room, she went into the kitchen to stare ruefully at the Buddha awaiting homage. Two of the three kitchen counters were piled with appliances and dishes, utensils, pots, trivets, trivia. The third counter had been scrubbed diligently and on it rested a typewriter. Periodically needing a break from the cartons and crates, Anne would come in here, look at

1

her Smith-Corona, satisfy her conscience as she fed her guilt.

She had to get to work. The article on "Feminism for the Managerial Woman" was due in two days, and she had not even begun. First there had been the packing, then the move, now the unpacking. She knew well enough that it was articles like the one due that had enabled her to leave her cramped one bedroom apartment on East 84th Street for this junior two bedroom floor through on the West Side. From impotent editorial assistant on a museum newsletter when she was twenty-two and ambitiously out of Mount Holyoke to her present status at twenty-eight as a free-lance writer who not only got called for assignments from the leading magazines but who was paid promptly as well had been a strenuous achievement; she could not now toss away her diligence as lightly as she had the excelsior. She did not blame her lack of enthusiasm for the article solely on the move, though. For several months now, all the real people she interviewed, the trendy topics she covered, failed to interest her as they once had. Six months ago she had begun work on her first novel, and it was her people and the situations she created for them that fascinated her. But it was an as-yet-unsold novel, and the movers had to be paid, a higher rent had to be met, and articles would continue to do that. She had to get back to work, she again told herself. Soon.

First, a shower, she decided. She maneuvered her way to the bathroom, her toilet articles still in the travel case she had toted them over in this morning. She glanced at herself in the mirror, and recoiled in mock fright. Newsprint shadowed her cheeks like a patchy beard, making the cheekbones seem more prominent than usual. Her nose, straight with a cleft at the tip that only appeared when she was tired, glared at her like a cracked promontory. If moving was not fun, she considered, it certainly was not good for one's ego. A shower was definitely nec-

2

essary. Perhaps if some of the glow was returned to her hair and skin, if her brown eyes could be found again underneath the crinkle of fatigue lines, she would feel good enough to do the article. She took her chin-length hair in both hands and pulled it away from her face and up, an unflattering style to her at any time. Impishly, she stuck out her tongue at her reflection.

"Ugly," she accused, smiling because she knew it was not true.

Anne Fletcher sat on her living room couch, her feet propped up on the chrome and glass coffee table she had bought on sale at Sloane's. The current issues of *Vogue* and *Harper's Bazaar* lay discarded alongside her. A crossword puzzle book was in her lap, but she made no move to open it. She was bored. She had nothing to do, nothing that interested her, and no one to do anything with even if there were something to do. She could call Janey, but too much of Janey was boring and she had seen her last night. Arthur was out of town, but she wouldn't call him if he were around; too much of Arthur was as boring as too much of Janey, and she had seen him last week. She supposed she could work on the manuscript she had brought from the office, but she hated editing juvenile stories and had brought it home only because it was expected of her. What she should do, she knew, was work on her novel, but she didn't feel like it. After all, what was there to work on except some ideas that she couldn't seem to move from her mind to paper?

Listlessly, she picked up the issue of *Vogue*, then put it down. She lowered her legs, and headed for her bedroom, her mind made up. She would play with makeup, paint her face an exotic mixture of colors and textures so that she would feel she got her money's worth from the new bag of expensive toys she had allowed the cosmetician at Bloomingdale's to convince her she had to have.

Sixteen years ago, at the age of twelve, Anne had decided that if she did not develop into an acknowledged beauty, she would do whatever was necessary to fool others into believing she really was one. To that end, she spent more on cosmetics and creams than she spent on food, for she had not developed into the beauty she wanted to be. Now she sat at the small vanity in her bedroom and creamed off the day's makeup. She did not like to look at her naked face; it was not the face she wanted. The hair, once brown, now rinsed with an auburn wash, hung thick, straight, long to her shoulders. She tended her hair as if it were a finely tuned instrument to be cared for and cherished with loving attention. That was where satisfaction stopped.

Anne Fletcher was pretty; only the most critical of judges would say she was less, but because she was not beautiful the way she longed to be—with classic features and strong bones, with a sensuous mouth and Sophia Loren eyes—she could not accept pretty. Her face was too soft, too unmolded, she believed. When she had been a child, her mother had called her "dumpling" and assured her that the baby fat would disappear with adolescence. But the flesh had never gone from her face, and the high cheekbones, the sculptured jawline had never arrived. No matter how many hours Anne would sit in front of a mirror, sucking in her cheeks, using her fingers to pull back her chin, the strong, classic bones would not come. Eyes round and deep and the color of emeralds in a fog were so extraordinary as to lure the looker into ignoring Anne's slightly pug nose, her lips that were just thin enough to give her mouth the look of perpetual annoyance. She played up her eyes with a variety of makeups, not realizing that she needed little for them to be outstanding. Without the heavy coloring, she looked at least six years younger than twenty-eight, with a soft sex appeal that would garner enviable attention. With the makeup, the lips became tighter, narrower; little puffs of flesh stood out on either side of a mouth that now seemed petulant, even mean at times; and her eyes, while still unquestionably lovely, were so arresting under makeup as to become a subject for scrutiny, and the wariness in them, the loosely reined anger, could not be mistaken. They were watchful eyes, not predatory in themselves but alert to what might be; they were the eyes of a cat who would never totally trust her master; they were the eyes of a girl guarding her soul.

Anne picked up one of the new bottles she had bought: SparkLite, a makeup base with specks of gold that was supposed to make her face shimmer radiantly. She was about to try it when the telephone rang. She had no phone in her bedroom; it was the type of compact apartment that anywhere else but the Upper East Side of Manhattan would be called a studio but clever builders had added a wall to make a sliver of a bedroom for which she paid too much. She got up from the vanity stool and was in the kitchen by the third ring.

"Hello?"

"Hi, Anne? How are you?"

The voice was male, and unfamiliar. Maybe it was that guy Jack, no Jake, she had met last Wednesday night at The Gingerbread Bar, she wondered hopefully.

"I'm fine. Is this Jake?"

"Isn't this Anne Fletcher?"

"Yes. Jake?"

"No. I must have the wrong number."

"Or the wrong Anne Fletcher." Her tone was light, without discernible disappointment.

She replaced the receiver and returned to the bedroom. She picked up the jar of SparkLite, put it back down; the makeup had lost its appeal for her. That was the second wrong number in as many days, she was thinking. Nothing unusual in itself, she knew, but yesterday's had also been for Anne Fletcher. As had many

5

she had received during the six years she had been living in New York, she now realized. She had never bothered to look up the name in the directory, probably because the other wrong numbers had not occurred with this frequency.

She went back into the kitchen and got out her Manhattan directory. There was an Ann-Trudy Originals/Ann-Trudy Fletcher listed at 1209 Broadway, several A. Fletchers, her own listing at 320 East 74th Street, an Ann Fletcher on Charles Street, an Anne N. Fletcher on East 84th. More bored than curious, she decided to try the one on Charles Street. She had no idea what she would say once someone answered. "Please give your friends the right telephone number?" No, of course she couldn't say that. Well, she'd think of something.

She dialed the number, and was about to hang up when the fifth ring was finally answered.

"Hello?"

Anne said nothing.

"Hello?"

"I'm sorry, I must have the wrong number," Anne muttered, and hastily hung up. The ancient voice, sounding in her ears like the rustle of yellowed paper, did not belong to a girl who received calls from young men.

She then dialed the listing for Anne N. Fletcher at 401 East 84th Street. The phone rang twice, then there was a buzz, a click, and a recording of an operator's voice came through.

"The number you have called has been changed. Please make note of the new number."

A flush of triumph unexpectedly filled Anne as she scribbled the digits on a note pad, and hung up. Acting on impulse, she dialed the information operator. She had to pretend to get the new number in order to see if she could discover whether the address had been changed as well.

"The address is still Eighty-fourth Street, isn't it?" Anne asked innocently. "I have to send a package there and I wouldn't want it to get lost."

There was a moment's hesitation, then the operator said, "The new listing is at twenty-five West Eighty-second Street."

"Oh, I guess she did move. Thank you very much, operator."

Anne hung up, studied the piece of paper in her hand with the telephone number and address of a total stranger. She still didn't know why she had bothered to get the address, the information meant nothing to her. At least now she didn't have to call, though. She had the explanation for the wrong numbers. With a move and a change of telephone, people who didn't know where the other girl lived might call the first Ann Fletcher in the book, which was the old lady. That would let them know immediately that they had made a mistake. Then they might try her number, which was what had been happening; even the telephone operator might give out her number first. Moving always created this kind of confusion. She had no doubt it would soon stop.

With her curiosity satisfied, boredom returned. She stared glumly at the telephone, willing it to ring. She wished that guy Jake would call, if that was even his name. She could not remember, and she did not particularly care, either about his name or that she had forgotten. He was a man, someone new to amuse her. It was at times like this that she could acknowledge the value of having a regular boyfriend; at least they were there when you needed them. Of course, she was quick to remind herself, they were also around when you didn't want them.

With little interest for the makeup, but with less for anything else, Anne returned to her vanity and Spark-Lite.

A thick red towel was wrapped around her wet hair, and an equally thick white terrycloth robe covered her body. Now when Anne looked into the bathroom mirror, she was relieved to see that she had not been indelibly imprinted with yesterday's headlines. She liked her face best the way it was now: without makeup, shiny with cleanliness. But she knew makeup was necessary, something to make her brown eyes a little larger; to pull the high cheekbones and too-prominent chin into balance with the fine straight nose and the mouth that seemed just a bit wide. Her mouth, ready to explode into expression, was a street tease on an otherwise patrician face, a surprising anachronism, a delightful one that removed the risk of describing her looks as aloof and intimidating. Washing away the grime and fatigue had done the trick; she was ready to work on the magazine article.

She headed for the kitchen, stopping to get a chair that would be the right height for the counter top. Her desk and her dining table still had the wrappings on, and so she had no other place to work. The telephone rang as she was inserting the first piece of paper. She reached behind her for the wall phone.

"Hello?"

"Anne?"

"David? Is this David Knowles?"

"I guess you're the right Anne Fletcher."

"What?"

The man, an international banker she saw three or four times a year, told her about the wrong number.

"That happened last night, too, with a photographer I sometimes work with. But he didn't have my old number. Since I moved, there's supposed to be an automatic—"

"I forgot your old number and had to call the operator."

"Didn't you give her my address?"

"I forgot that, too," he admitted. "I said East Seventy-

or Eighty-something, I couldn't remember which. I have been out of the country a month, after all. It doesn't matter since I finally reached you. . . ."

She hoped she wouldn't lose too many calls to people less persevering than David, but she knew she was bound to forget to give her new number to everybody, just as she probably forgot to send change-of-address cards to some.

She turned down David Knowles's invitation to dinner that night, accepted for the following evening. He was one of several men she counted as friends, men she could enjoy and who could enjoy her without the high toll of unreasonable expectation. She liked having men as friends, needed them, in fact. They put the times both with and without a romantic interest in better perspective so that emotional dependence became choice, not necessity.

David did not know about her novel; none of her friends did, nor did her parents or her brother. She had told no one, suspecting that they would have laughed at her foolishness for attempting what so few people succeeded at, and warned her that doing articles for slick magazines did not make one a writer. She had used the same arguments with herself when the idea to do a novel had first come to her, after a particularly exhilarating interview with three female novelists. Despite the inherent negatives, she had begun to write, and now she had a four-hundred-page novel. She considered it utter fluff, escapist entertainment of the least literary merit—and she adored every word. Madison Avenue, boutique-land, the ladies who lunch, their men and their money and their moods—that was the story of *Honorable Mention.* She had had the temerity to submit it a week ago to Matthew Holmes, one of the best literary agents in town. Anne had presumed on a relationship that came from parties and lunches, and he had not turned her away.

Reluctantly, she forced herself not to daydream about

Matthew Holmes calling her to say her novel had been accepted by a publisher. Equally reluctantly, she forced herself to banish the thought of calling David back and having him rescue her from the night ahead. She had movers to pay, rent to pay, and so an article to write.

2

Arthur Dumont gave the cabdriver Anne's address on East 74th Street.

"That's only a coupla blocks from here," the cabbie pointed out.

"I know. I have to pick up someone there and then we'll go on," Arthur explained.

Despite the short distance, the cabbie managed to miss every light, but uncharacteristically, Arthur did not care. He felt too good, too rich, at least with promise, to let a few extra cents on a taxi meter ruffle him. He had returned yesterday from San Diego where he had successfully won an out-of-court settlement for his firm's client. It had been an admiralty case, and much was riding on it, personally. At thirty-three, Arthur was his firm's only maritime lawyer, and though there was not an abundance of such cases, he handled them all. The case in San Diego held more significance than most: July 1 would mark Arthur's fifth anniversary with his firm; this latest triumph should help guarantee that that occasion would be commemorated with a gift of junior partnership.

Arthur had started out as a tax attorney, but when he

was twenty-eight and able to afford his first summer share in Easthampton, one of the four other attorneys in the house had spoken to him about how much money could be made in admiralty law. And money was what Arthur wanted. Though he was newly hired by his firm that summer, they paid for him to return to school at night for specialized study, and while he still worked on a few tax cases, he became their maritime expert. He would be acutely disappointed if this expertise was not properly rewarded in July.

Arthur Dumont was doing exactly what he had dreamed and planned to be doing at his age, especially if he were named a junior partner. He had money to live and look well which, for him, meant money enough to live in the upper Seventies between Park and Madison avenues in a large one bedroom apartment with working fireplace and marble mantel, nine-foot ceilings, and furnishings through a decorator. It meant money enough to dress in supple suedes and real Shetlands, in the softest wool blends and the finest silks, thus providing him with the poise to feel comfortable in the right restaurants, in the Hamptons, with the right women. For Arthur, the right woman was not a secretary or teacher or social worker; she was middle management chic during the day, and liberated the rest of the time. In other words, for Arthur the right woman was manageably intelligent. He also had enough money now to play squash three times a week, work out in his health club whenever he felt like it, tote a Mark Cross attaché case, and own a Gucci backgammon board. These accoutrements—for such they were—had, for Arthur, the same effect as a nose job on a girl who always wanted to be pretty. Before the nose job, she has no self-confidence; after the surgery—regardless of how good it is—she sees herself differently, and gains a new poise that makes her pretty. With the clothes and the clubs and the Hamptons, the edges that growing up in Queens and attending Hofstra and New York University Law School had left Arthur with were polished away, smoothed out so that the roughness, like the girl's lack of confidence, suffered attrition from nonuse.

What the accoutrements had not done for Arthur was to aid him in developing individual style, personal taste. He was, so far, a trend-keeper. Perhaps, with the added security of a partnership, albeit junior, the other too would come.

Anne Fletcher was precisely the type of girl Arthur spent time with (he was not the kind of man to question too closely whether he *enjoyed* spending time with a particular woman). He liked Anne, believing that she represented the level of woman he should be with. He had met her at their health club, which meant she spent money and she cared about her body. She was not a secretary, but had the respectably and not threateningly intelligent job of juvenile book editor in a publishing house of quiet repute. She had her own apartment and a great queen-sized platform bed; thus, independent, adventurous. She was neither too young nor too old to be a difficulty; neither too beautiful nor too unattractive to make him uncomfortable. She did not use sex to stake a claim on him. They had a good arrangement—nothing heavy, he would be the first to say. A nice, mutually convenient, commitment-free relationship, as it should be.

He had been looking forward to tonight. Good dinner at that new Japanese place on East 50th, maybe a nightcap at one of the hotel bars, and then bed.

"That's a buck and a quarter." The cabdriver's voice was a pothole in Arthur's smooth thoughts.

Arthur glanced out the window, but there was no sign of Anne in the lobby of her building. "Keep the meter running. She'll be right here." Dammit, I told her to be waiting downstairs. He now felt the *plang* of every dime. When the meter read a dollar sixty-five, he banged on the plastic partition. "Wait here. I'll have the doorman ring for her."

Arthur slammed the cab door shut and strode the few steps to the apartment. The doorman was in the vestibule, talking on the intercom so Arthur opened the door himself, and began to pace impatiently in front of him.

"Hello, Mr. Dumont, how are you this evening?" the doorman finally greeted. Usually Arthur would enjoy being remembered and would exchange a meaningless word or two with the doorman, but not tonight with the meter ticking loudly a few feet away.

"Please ring Miss Fletcher and tell her I have a cab waiting."

"And what apartment would that be, sir?"

"Eleven D," Arthur snapped, irritated because the doorman knew Anne's apartment and was being deliberately difficult.

"Good evening, Miss Fletcher, this is Pete," the doorman said as the buzz on his intercom was answered. "You have a gentleman waiting down here, Mr. Dumont. Says there's a cab running its meter for you." Arthur glowered, reached for the intercom receiver, but Pete ignored him, unwilling to relinquish his moment of power in a seven-hour shift of subservience.

"Certainly, Miss Fletcher, I'll tell him." Pete turned to Arthur. "Says to let the cab go and come upstairs."

"I'd like to speak with her," Arthur said tightly, again reaching for the phone, but Pete was too quick for him.

"He says he'd like to talk with you, Miss Fletcher. Sure, sure, just a sec." Pete now offered Arthur the phone.

Arthur avoided eye contact with the doorman; the petty nuisance had been eliminated and was worth no further expenditure of energy. "Hello, Anne? What's wrong? I have a cab waiting and . . . well, sure, that sounds okay but . . . yeah . . . sure . . . okay, I'll be right up." Without expression, he handed the receiver to Pete who had been listening shamelessly. Arthur showed none of the irritation he was feeling as he walked back outside and paid the cabdriver over two dollars for a fare that should have been half. He brushed past Pete as he re-entered the building and went to the bank of elevators. He was not pleased with what Anne had done. Deciding to make dinner at home when she knew he had planned they go out more than displeased him; it angered him. He did not like being taken by surprise, especially by a woman. What she had done insinuated an intimacy that did not exist between them; if she did not understand exactly what the parameters of their relationship were, he would have to explain them more clearly.

Arthur forced a lid on his anger. Self-control was important to him; he had learned its value as an attorney, and attempted, often with success, to apply it to his personal life. The advantage was always his, he believed, if others did not know with sureness what he was thinking, and more importantly, feeling. It would serve him ill to let Anne see the effect her changing his plans had on him.

He walked down the carpeted hallways to her apartment, eager to put the evening back on course with a few well-chosen words delivered in the right tone of sternness. But he never had the chance. She was waiting for him in the open doorway of her apartment, wearing a filmy seafoam green caftan he could only associate with the cover of *Cosmopolitan*. The neckline was a deep vee, and the material so gauzy that the light filtering from the apartment shone through and around her, outlining her legs and the line of bikini panties underneath. He saw her like that and a vision of the platform bed flashed through his mind; he decided to save his lecture for another time.

"It's been so long," she murmured after kissing him deeply in the hallway. "I've missed you."

"Show me how much again," he said into her hair.

She did, pressing her body against his with a sensuality she usually did not display.

"I should go away more often," he said when she had moved out of his arms. She smiled and took his hand, leading him back into the apartment.

Anne made him a drink, and they chattered meaninglessly while she moved back and forth to the kitchen. Arthur really did not want to eat. Anne did not really want sex yet. So she let him kiss and fondle her in the kitchen, and he let her feed him.

"Dinner's just about ready," she said. "Why don't you open the wine and bring it in."

Arthur stopped nuzzling her neck and took the corkscrew and bottle. Anne watched as he expertly popped the cork. When she did it, she always got half the cork in the bottle and had to pour the wine into a carafe. She smiled at him, and told him how impressed she was.

Arthur shrugged. "One of my many small accomplishments," he said with mock immodesty. "I intend to show you a few others later," he added with a leer.

"I can't wait," Anne answered, "but I hope they're a little bigger."

"They will be if you keep talking like that," Arthur tossed back as he led the way into the small alcove that served Anne as a dining area.

"This is really very nice," Arthur commented, looking at how the table was set with candles and tulip-shaped wineglasses; at the basket lined with a cotton floral printed napkin that held chunks of French bread; at the napkins in their own rings; at the salad of endive, watercress, and chicory glittering with dressing. In spite of himself, he was pleased that Anne had gone to this effort for him.

"I'm glad you like it," she said, sitting down and placing a dusky rose polished cotton napkin that contrasted cheerily with the navy blue floral printed placemats, on her lap. "I never do this for myself, and it seemed like a nice way to welcome you back."

Arthur poured the wine, dry and white, and tasted his salad. "This dressing is delicious. Did you make it yourself?"

Anne nodded. "I hope the rest of the meal comes out all right. Tonight's the first time I've tried shrimp scampi."

"You mean I'm acting as guinea pig?" Arthur asked with not totally feigned alarm.

"Well, if it's no good, there's plenty more salad, and I've never ruined rice," Anne laughed.

They ate their salads and drank their wine in relative silence, a quiet that was as comfortable as the shimmer of candlelight and the warmth of the wine.

"I'll get the shrimp now," Anne said, standing up and taking away the salad plates.

She returned shortly with two plates of jumbo shrimp on a bed of herbed rice. The garlic and butter bubbled juicily, giving off an appetizing aroma.

"They look great and they smell great," Arthur commented. "Now for the most important test."

Anne watched expectantly as he bit into the first shrimp.

Arthur shook his head and smiled. "I can't believe how delicious this is."

"Really?"

"Really, it's great. Not too much garlic, just right. And the shrimp are unbelievably tender." Impulsively, he put down his fork and leaned over to kiss her lightly on the cheek. "Thank you," he said softly. "I'm glad you decided to do this."

"I'm relieved it came out okay. You might not be thanking me if it hadn't," she said, smiling. Then she asked him about his trip to San Diego, and he told her a little about the case as they ate.

"Let's wait a while for coffee, okay?" she suggested when they had finished.

"Sure. I'm stuffed anyway." He paused, then leaned toward her, hoping he had been able to put the right combination of interest and passion in the set of his lips, the fixed look in his eyes. "I missed you these past two weeks," he said gently, assuming she knew the words for the lie they were, assuming she also knew that they were the proper words for the mood, the moment. "I thought about you a lot," he added, reaching out and pressing her hand, his smile not getting as far as his eyes.

"Why didn't you call me then?" she asked, removing her hand seemingly to get the wineglass. Her expression was without guile or accusation. He had made a statement; her question, she believed, was the appropriate response.

But Arthur did not agree. He had been dating Anne casually for four months, seeing her once or twice every few weeks with no regular pattern. He never called her just to chat, only to make a date, and she had called him only twice, both times to cancel the date because she had been ill. Nothing had ever been exchanged between them, either overtly or tacitly, to give either cause to doubt the insincerity of his words.

In the past, like tonight, he had carelessly tossed out small niceties as another would put out candies in a dish: Take one but do not expect it to satisfy your appetite. Compliments and romantic pleasantries were spoken rarely and then casually to the women he knew, used to fulfill the barest minimum of expectations in what was basically a relationship of sexual convenience. It was not that Arthur was a callow manipulator of a woman's feelings. The women he knew returned the sentiments with equal meaninglessness. It was a pat on the head to a favored child, favored only for the moment. Anne knew this, and had always seemed to accept it.

Until tonight. Her question about his calling struck him as peculiar. In fact, the intimate dinner, the seductive dress, the musky odor of her perfume—all broke the pattern of their relationship. There it was again, Arthur thought; subtle maneuvers to get closer. He *would* have to stop her.

"You're different tonight," he began.

"Is that a positive or a negative?" Anne asked.

"I'm not sure. You're more . . . more . . ." He shook his head, embarrassed, unsure of how to approach the issue. "More something," he finished lamely.

Anne laughed. "Is Arthur Dumont, articulate attorney and glib ladies' man at a loss for words?" She poured him the last of the wine. "Is all this"—and she gestured to include the dinner, the lighting, the mood—"frightening you in some way?"

Arthur nodded, his smile uncharacteristically sheepish. "A little, I guess. It's not exactly your style."

"And what is my style?" Anne asked somewhat sharply. But the smile was still on her face, the innocence still in her eyes.

Arthur shrugged. "Well, not this intimate, I guess." He sat back in his chair. "You've never made dinner for me, for one thing, or set out to be quite so seductive."

"Is that bad?" The smile was gone now from Anne's mouth, and the innocence in her eyes had subtly segued into cold and controlled contempt, but Arthur did not notice.

"No, of course not," he quickly said. "I mean the seductive part, that's terrific. But changing my plans, the dinner and all, well, that is a little possessive, don't you think?"

"Possessive?" she repeated. "I certainly didn't mean it to be that. I just thought it would be nice, dinner à deux, quiet, at home, that kind of thing. If I had thought it would make you nervous or that you would misinterpret it to mean my getting possessive, I never would have done it, believe me." Her tone of voice revealed only an edge of defensive disappointment; it betrayed none of the hostility she was actually feeling. But her eyes were green gunsights of suppressed anger, trained hard on him had he cared to look.

"I'm glad to hear it," was all he said, and drained his glass of wine as if to put an end to the conversation.

Anne waited a beat or two, then conversationally asked, "Are you going out to the Hamptons this weekend?"

"Yeah, can't wait, too. You've got to come out there one weekend. You'd love it. The house is in the middle of—"

"When?"

Arthur laughed nervously to cover, in quick succession, his sudden awkwardness, confusion, irritation. "I don't know, soon."

Anne sat back in her chair, shaking her head slowly, so slowly that the wisps of auburn-tinted hair trailing alongside her ears did not move. Some of the contempt had trickled into her expression; her lips had grown tighter, the eyes glassy, candlelight and anger glinting off them like chips of mica in a sidewalk. She wanted nothing of this man, she was thinking. No commitment, no promises. She did not even want honesty. The trouble she had gone through tonight had been for herself, not for him. She had needed to do something nice for herself. She did not care what meaning he cared to attach to it; it was important only that *she* know why she did it. Yet she felt herself being inexorably drawn to a confrontation, driven to vent this hostility that had come unbidden, unexpected.

"You're so damn transparent, Arthur," she quietly accused. "You don't even make the game interesting anymore."

"I don't—"

"You don't what?" she snapped, her voice brittle, two

small white spots of heat flashing onto either side of her mouth, bracketing her emotions.

"I don't know what you're talking about," he muttered.

She laughed icily. "Of course you don't, so I'm going to tell you."

"Anne, look, maybe you've had too much wine. Let's not spoil what's been a lovely evening with—"

"Shut up, Arthur. Please." The words were a hissed command, and now when Arthur looked at her, he saw what had been there for many minutes: the green opacity of eyes watching him carefully, lips stretched tight like the strings of a bow into an expression of such ultimate distaste and disdain that he felt his heartbeat quicken with shock that he should be the target of such vehement emotion.

"You sit there so worried about your precious independence," she began, "your precious control of this so-called relationship. I can just hear the wheels turning in that ego-locked brain of yours: 'I hope she's not going to make a demand on me.' 'I hope she doesn't think I really care about her.' " Anne laughed, an ugly crackle that held no amusement, no delight, no invitation to join in the humor. "You throw out some of those barren bones I get so tired of, little ribboned packages you assume I know better than to open because I'm supposed to realize how empty the gift is. 'I missed you.' 'I thought about you.' 'You must come out to the Hamptons.' " She mimicked him cruelly.

"Anne—"

"I'm not finished!" she exploded. "You can sit there, with your empty words and your empty promises, Arthur, I don't give a shit, I really don't. Just don't expect me to deliver my lines on cue anymore. I'm tired of it. That's all. Tired of you believing I'm so grateful for the pleasure of your company that I'll accept your candy-coated crumbs like a beggar takes a used cigarette butt.

I use you too, Arthur, know that. If I'm a convenience to you, you're not even that to me. You're a diversion, and if there were a more interesting one around, you wouldn't find me so accommodating, believe me. A hassle-free relationship is what you wanted, and that's what you've got. Don't clutter it up with sentiment, Arthur, and don't give it the stench of your bullshit."

The silence vibrated like a tuning fork with the echoes of her outburst. Arthur did not trust himself to speak, to move. He watched her carefully, expectantly, but there was no more. The white puffs of angry flesh around her mouth were fading; dimension was returning to her eyes. She glanced away, down at the hardened grains of rice on her plate. There was nothing in his knowledge of her, or in their history together that could have prepared him for what he had just been witness to. It was as if he had been an audience of one, watching an actress play a role she had been rehearsing in secret. There was nothing of the Anne he knew in the Anne he had just heard. The actions, the words, the emotion were those of a stranger. He was not appalled or surprised or disgusted or even angered; there was a detachment to his reactions that startled him, then did not for so unreal was the performance that his response had to be similarly unreal. Emotional placebos were part of the game; she had always seemed to understand that. But tonight, because *she* had stretched the boundaries, because *she* had needed more and he had not been forthcoming, he had been accused and blamed for duplicity in a relationship that was based solely on that.

He could have told her this; he could have presented a monologue of innocence with courtroom aplomb and conviction. He chose not to waste any more of his time. Slowly, he pushed back his chair and started to get up. "I guess I better go," he mumbled.

At the sound of his voice, Anne's eyes darted up from her plate. It was as if she suddenly remembered he was there. "No, not yet," she whispered. "Let me make some coffee."

"I think it would be better if I just left."

"No, please, don't go yet." Her voice was soft, almost pleading, no sign of the former rage evident.

Arthur looked at her, saw the flush in the cheeks, the way her tongue darted out to moisten dried lips; the way the filmy seafoam dress rose and fell with each breath. Yes, he would stay, he decided. He would stay and he would fuck her. He would fuck her so hard and so good that she would cry for forgiveness and beg him for more of those candy-coated crumbs she so foolishly disdained.

"All right," he said, sitting down.

Anne tried to smile but managed only a weak parting of the lips. She went into the kitchen, busying her hands with the mechanical chores of pouring water, measuring coffee, taking out cream, sugar. Isolated phrases and words of what she had said screamed back at her and she trembled with regret. She dared not think about why it had happened, not now. There had been no reason, no provocation for the invective; it had sprung, unwanted, unannounced, from within her like a long-dormant volcano suddenly heaving forth lava it had grown tired of restraining. She could not possibly hope an apology would be enough; she did not know how she could begin to make up to him for what she had said—and did she want to? Yes, she had to until someone new became available.

She went back into the dining alcove, and quietly placed coffee and cups on the table. She poured for both of them before attempting to speak.

"I'm sorry, Arthur," she said, her voice hushed. "I don't know what came over me. I guess I was nervous that everything should be all right. And I think I was a little disappointed, too."

She noticed the arching of his brows, the coldness in his eyes, and she rushed to explain. "When I got home

23

from work today, a box of flowers was waiting for me. I was so excited—I haven't gotten flowers since . . . well, in a long time. They were the most beautiful jonquils, anemones, and roses—yellow roses." She glanced at him, her smile tentative. "I was sure you had sent them and I was so pleased. But the card wasn't from you, it was from someone named Dan, and I don't know any Dans. I called the florist's number on the card and they picked them up." She gave a short, thin laugh. "That can be kind of disappointing to a girl."

Arthur sighed, prepared to offer some solace in order to get what he wanted. "I'm sorry. I should have thought of doing that."

"No, don't be silly," Anne quickly assured him, ignoring the meaninglessness of both their gestures. "I was just explaining why I went a little whacko before. I didn't mean to imply that *you* should have brought flowers." With an effort, she forced warmth and sincerity into her expression. She reached over to squeeze his hand. "Forgive me?"

Slowly, he brought her hand to his lips and kissed it gently. He said nothing.

"Would you like a brandy?"

He shook his head, letting his eyes drop to her lips, then to the white flesh exposed by the vee of her dress. When he looked up at her face again, his smile was rich with insinuation.

Anne nodded with understanding. They would go to bed now, following the script, playing their parts. She had no desire for sex, but she would perform because it was expected of her; it was the apology of action. The thought flashed through her mind that she rarely had desire for sex with Arthur; it was done because to not do it would be to alter the dimensions of their relationship, make it more complex, perhaps more important than either of them wanted it to be.

24

"Bring the candles into the bedroom," she invited, standing up. "We've never done it by candlelight."

Arthur got up, candleholder in each hand, and followed her into the bedroom. He placed a candle on each of the two night tables attached to the platform bed, and then began to undress, methodically folding shirt and jacket and trousers across the vanity stool. Naked, he turned toward the bed, surprised to see Anne sitting on it, still fully clothed.

"What's the matter now?" he asked, the edge in his voice indicative of how close to the surface his anger was. "Changed your mind?"

Anne shook her head. "No, of course not. I was just waiting."

He studied her face, trying to discern a lie, but in the warm and gentle glow from the candles, he saw only two large green eyes challenging him with their desire. He sat down next to her, and Anne bent down, her mouth on his chest, her tongue flicking out to caress first one nipple, then the other. She used her hands not to touch him, but to support her posture, and when she lowered her head, her tongue not stopping its licking, its tasting, its arousing, and Arthur's hands buried themselves in her hair, pushing her down, pressuring her to continue, still she did not touch him.

"Get undressed, Anne," he finally urged. "Hurry up."

Slowly, Anne raised her head, and Arthur felt his stomach contract with lust at the sight of her wet lips, the moisture on her chin. He lifted her away from him, and she stood up. In a swift and fluid motion, she pulled the caftan up over her head. He reached out one hand to feel the curve of her waist, then used that hand to press her closer to him so that he could kiss the rise of her stomach, and touch the small, firm breasts.

"Take off your panties," he ordered, and she did, even as his hands continued to fill themselves with her breasts, her buttocks. He liked feeling Anne's body; there was flesh to hold, to knead; to never let him forget that she was female. Often she had complained that no amount of exercise in the world would firm up her buttocks, or enlarge her breasts, but he did not share her criticism. He enjoyed fitting himself into her curves, molding the softness; there was pleasure to be had from her body.

Arthur let go of her long enough for them both to get onto the bed, and then Anne again lowered her head to rouse him. She felt his hands caress her back, reach for her breasts, entangle themselves in her hair. She heard him moan softly; she tasted and smelled and felt his excitement, but could respond with none of her own. She was outside herself, standing by the side of the bed watching this other girl have sex. She was not there with her, as her, but an observer, dispassionate and disinterested; bored, in fact, and impatient. She wanted her back for herself, back where she belonged.

Suddenly, Anne felt Arthur's hands on her shoulders, pushing her away, making her stop. Her eyes were round and questioning, but then he had her on her back, forcing her legs apart, forcing her to feel. She tried to stop him—with words, but his mouth silenced her; with her hands, but he pinned them above her head. He moved inside her, bruising her, chafing her, driving her to respond. He had never done this to her before, never really *fucked* her. She wanted to enjoy it; there was something deliciously brutal about what he was doing, brutal and exciting. But her mind would not let go of her body, and all her mind wanted was to have this over with, to have him gone.

She began to move, and what bruised seconds before began to slide easily. She was not deriving the enjoyment she could have, but it would be over, and he would not know the difference.

And moments later, if he did know, he did not care,

for both punishing or pleasing his partner were no longer important. When he lay back on the pillow, Anne reached for the comforter, and pulled it up to her shoulders. The gnawing emptiness in the pit of her stomach, the ache below, they would go away soon enough. She had fulfilled her obligation, she had played her part; it was time for him to leave.

"You didn't come," he muttered. "Why?"

Anne did not show her surprise. She was sure that she had pretended well, and that he had not noticed. "Of course I came," she lied. "How could I not come? You were unbelievable tonight."

He smiled. "Yeah, it was different. But I really didn't think you came. If you want, I could—"

"Arthur, you wouldn't have known if a stampede of elephants were coming at that point. You were sort of out of it, if you recall."

Again his smile, sheepish but proud. "I suppose you're right," he admitted. Then, "Well, catch your breath and we'll try for a repeat performance." Arthur was pleased with himself, so much so that he was willing for the second time to be an instrument of sex rather than of revenge.

Anne hesitated, then, "I'd like you to go now, Arthur. I'm really not in the mood for any more acrobatics."

He looked at her sharply. "What the hell is that supposed to mean?"

Her naked shoulders shrugged above the comforter. "Just go, Arthur. Please. It's been a long night." She did not feel that she was doing anything wrong, or rude. Arthur was no longer there for her, and so she had no longer to consider him.

Arthur did not know what to say or do. He felt he should speak his lines of the script: ask what was wrong, ask if she was all right; give and gain a small measure of false reassurance. Tonight's sex had been strange. He had been brutal, almost violent with her, and for him, it

27

had been more exciting than usual, but he suspected that he had not accomplished what he intended: to hurt her. Knowing what his motives had been, he now felt a pang of guilt, and wanted to ease his conscience by making sure that nothing was wrong between them.

But when he leaned on his elbow to speak to her, the expression on Anne's face chilled further effort at conversation. It seemed to Arthur as if she had turned totally inward like a piece of rubber flexed in reverse. Her eyes were open and unfocused on anything within that room, animate or not. Her mouth was drawn close, almost pursed, the little puffs of flesh evident on either side; her lips were pressed neatly together in serious contemplation, concentration inward; even her cheeks seemed sucked in so that her bones appeared higher, sharper. And the veins in her neck were taut as if rigidly supporting the effort her face was making in its interior deliberations. She was where he could not go; where neither she nor he wanted him to go.

He got out of bed and began to dress.

"Anne?" he called softly, standing by the bedroom door. "Anne, I'm leaving now."

" 'Bye." She did not get out of bed. She did not move her eyes.

"I'll see myself out," he added almost as a question, a plea for her to return to him if only momentarily, if only for the sake of the play.

"Thanks for dinner." He walked to the front door. "I'll call you," he said, loud enough so that she could hear. If she heard, however, she had long ago chosen not to listen.

Anne heard the door close, and made a mental note to be sure to get up and lock it. Soon. Later. Right now she wanted to wallow in the glorious sensation of relief that was surrounding her, flowing through her. She was alone again, and it felt good, so good. Alone with her pretty apartment and its pretty things; with her magazines and makeup and crossword puzzle books, her old friend the TV set. Alone with her thoughts.

She threw back the comforter and dropped her legs over the edge of the bed. Her legs, long for her body, were firm, almost muscular, the only part of her body she had no complaint about. She glanced down at herself, surprised and a little disappointed not to find any telltale marks from Arthur's brutality. She blew out each candle, and turned on one bedside lamp, blinking her eyes to adjust to the new, sharper light. She went to her closet and put on not the long, ruffled transparent batiste robe she wore for men, but her old terrycloth, the white now yellow like an old man's hair, the thickness now shrunken and worn out like an old woman's beauty. She stopped for a moment in front of her vanity, and bent down to look into the mirror. Not even her mascara had smudged, for all the ferocity of Arthur's activity. She had to have been very uninvolved for her makeup to have remained intact, she thought fleetingly.

She went and locked the front door, then began to remove the plates from the dining table to the kitchen. Now she could think; now she could allow herself the mental replay of the evening, and try to understand what had happened to her, and why. It was important that she understand because it must not happen ever again. She must have more control, a stronger ability to hide. But understanding was necessary, also, so that her novel would be rich with insight. At the thought of her novel, she turned off the water in the kitchen sink, and returned to the bedroom. She sat down on the bed, and opened the drawer to one of her night tables. Leaning back on the pillow, she began to talk into the microphone of her cassette tape recorder.

Arthur has left after what turned out to be a very strange evening. While the food was fine, I can't exactly say the dinner was a success. I got very peculiar, I guess that's a good word for it. I mean, I sort of flipped out, and started sounding like some kind of shrew, a bitch who was trying to make demands on a man. Maybe that's in me, I don't know, but certainly not with Arthur. At least I don't think so. Maybe I'm fooling myself, though. Why else go to all that trouble with the dinner. I never do things like that, and Arthur had said we were going out. Maybe he was right, maybe I was trying to close in on him—intimate dinner, good ambiance, sexy dress, the whole seduction bit. It was as if I wanted him to make a commitment, state his intentions. That's ridiculous, utterly impossible. If I wanted anything it was to get him to admit that I really don't mean a thing to him, and that's what's so crazy. I know I don't mean much to him, and he certainly doesn't mean any more to me, but the way I sounded you'd have thought I had decided he was Mr. Right, and my anguish was because I was his Ms. Wrong.

Anne shut off the machine, her smile of amusement at her words fading as she recalled how ugly she had sounded. She knew Arthur Dumont was not her Mr. Right. She didn't believe in such a thing so how could he be it, she reasoned. She had always prided herself on not wanting a Mr. Right, truly not wanting one, not just convincing herself of that so as not to be hurt by not getting what she really desired most desperately and deeply. She was not that painfully dishonest with herself. She again turned on the machine.

No, what happened tonight had nothing to do with wanting more of Arthur than he was willing to give. That would be something Janey would do. The way she talks about love is not anything I can relate to. She's always saying she'll know when it happens, as if it were a bruise that appears with discolorations you can't help but see and feel. That's as ridiculous as my wanting Arthur to make a commitment. She ought to know better by now, too. Look where her romantic foolishness has gotten her —six years in New York, and she goes from married men to her current predilection for detectives. Soon it'll be an out-of-work would-be poet or something.

Again, Anne flipped off the switch, her thoughts going back six years to a time that she did not want recorded on tape. Back to when she and Janey Ebersole had been roommates together at Northwestern, full of conviction that they would come to New York, and *The Times* would be forever grateful for the conflagration of wit, beauty, and talent they lighted in their offices. Conviction had given way to practicality, and Janey had gone to work as a copywriter on one trade journal after another, sleeping with men with no future for her; and Anne had reached her present status as a juvenile books editor who screwed too many men for lack of wanting a future with any of them. Anne shook her head with remembrance, a motion not of wry humor but of dismissal, tossing away the past and its dreams because it interfered too dangerously with the present and its truths.

I don't know why you're still out there, Janey, trying and believing. You have got to come to your senses and realize that all that time and energy is wasted, wasted! Spend it on yourself, become the person you want to be, should be. That's what I do. No way in the world am I going to care about a future with a man. My future is with me.

That's what makes tonight so difficult to understand. The flowers *were* a disappointment, no denying that. It's not that I'm jealous or anything of this other Anne Fletcher, that would be silly, I don't even know her, but I guess it hurt that they weren't for me, and a little resentment surfaced. Maybe it was just some of the old conditioning asserting itself. "You're twenty-three, Anne, time to get married." "You're twenty-five, Anne, twenty-six, twenty-eight, don't you think you should be married?" Well, Mom, if staying single means you'll be known as the mother of a spinster, I might do it, just for spite. [*She laughed.*] And Mom, you better get used to something else. The only lifelong commitment I'll ever make is to me becoming a terrific writer, the writer I know I can be.

She pressed the off button, an expression of bitterness settling grimly on her face. Two current best-sellers were on her night table, along with the most recent issue of the publishing trade journal. She picked up the two books and hefted them in her hands, as if their weight was the reason they were selling. She had read one almost to the end, had begun the other; she knew the trade journal's best-seller list from memory. She did not understand how, and more importantly, why these books were selling when there was not one redeeming literary quality about either of them except a fast-paced storytelling technique. It infuriated her that adventurous plots, some sex, a little glamour, that these hackneyed ingredients could, time and again, sell—and sell well.

Crap, it's all such crap. If it takes me a lifetime, my stuff is going to be literature and it will sell even better than this slick, unoriginal crap they call best-sellers. How dare these people call themselves writers? Do they suffer all day in a boring job the way I do, coming home at night too tired to do anything but relax a little? Writing is work, it's caring about your ideas, your words. They don't care, they don't struggle with themselves, wanting to write literature, the quality stuff that will be taught in colleges for years to come. Well, I won't compromise. I don't have to. I could write junk, and it would sell, too. But I won't. One day soon, I'm going to get a really extraordinary idea, but it has to be extraordinary, and then I will use you, dear tape diary, as a repository of material rich and original as you were intended.

Maybe I'll do it this summer. All I need is a little discipline and the right idea. Sit myself down at the typewriter and think until that special concept, that never-before-done theme comes to me, and it will, I know it will. I am going to be a great writer or I'm not going to be a writer at all. I will not compromise my talent by writing commercial junk like everybody else when I know I can be better. It's just a matter of time, that's all. And then people will be in awe of Anne Fletcher, they'll talk about me in whispered gasps of admiration for doing the impossible: writing quality that people want to buy. They'll quote me and interview me, and listen to my opinions, value them. I won't be like those hacks they laugh at, dismiss with no regard and no respect. Not for me that kind of attitude. One day soon, I mean it.

Meanwhile, I better remember to ask Janey if she wants to go to the Hamptons for a weekend. A couple of days at the beach won't stop me from writing. It's a good way to unwind, observe new situations and people. And if I wait for Arthur to invite me, I could wait a long time. Besides, he might get mixed up and ask the other Anne Fletcher by mistake. [*Laughter.*]

Anne turned the off switch on her tape cassette, and put the machine and microphone back in the top drawer of her night table. She turned out the light, and lay back against the pillow. Her face was totally relaxed, a complete contradiction to the strained inner concentration when Arthur had been there. This time with her diary was her form of therapy. Her moments alone with it were used not for introspection but for catharsis, to rid herself of frustrations and angers, hurts and hopes, freeing her to go on to the next day of dreams, the next night of disillusionment.

There was no feedback from the tape recorder; no support, sympathy, argument; no existence outside of what Anne gave it. And this was as it should be, for Anne Fletcher wanted a machine, a mechanism by which to record her struggle toward extraordinariness, her battle —against what she believed were the odds of silly friends, a boring job, shallow men, lack of time—to attain her due greatness. She did not think in terms of achieving: of thinking, acting, doing, but in terms of attaining, getting. She was single-minded in what she wanted to get, and support, sympathy, argument were unwelcome, unnecessary interferences on this single-mindedness. The tape recorder did not judge nor did it force her to get sidetracked by having to explain; it allowed her always to be right; it permitted her to answer to no one but herself.

CHAPTER

4

"Anne, honey, this is a terrific party. I can't get enough of those Danish. Did the Pillsbury dough boy bring them himself? I think he's so adorable, you know."

"Kevin, you're impossible when you're being fey."

"I know, hon, but I'm worse when I'm acting butch."

Anne shook her head in a gesture of amused hopelessness with her friend Kevin, a usually out-of-work actor who supported himself and his amyl nitrite habit by handing out fliers for massage parlors when he couldn't get a job demonstrating products in stores or suburban shopping malls. Kevin was one of about thirty people gathered in Anne N. Fletcher's apartment for Sunday brunch.

"You're looking wonderful, by the way," Kevin said offhandedly. "I like this new haircut on you." With almost professional expertise, he lifted a few strands of her layered, jaw-length hair. "I'm glad you're not beautiful," he added. "I might be terribly jealous, you know." And then he walked away, leaving Anne only a little regretful that she did not measure up to his aesthetic standards.

On this particular Sunday in mid-September, there

was not a great deal that could take the edge off her sense of contentment.

It had taken her four months of scouring and staining, scraping and polishing; four months of arranging and rearranging, and sometimes, throwing out so she would have an excuse to prowl the stores and buy. Her apartment would never be photographed for a decorating magazine. It was too eclectic; there was no pattern to the furnishings except what pleased Anne. But the parquet floor was waxed to an almost dangerous level of sheen and slipperiness; the windows glistened, seeming to deflect the raucous street sounds, bouncing children's cries and Hispanic patois back onto the street where they more properly belonged. The fireplace did not work but it was clean now, a repository for baskets of dried wildflowers instead of logs and soot. The Mexican rug was worn at the edges and too small, but the colors of hot sun orange and burnt earth belonged on the dark wood. The Spanish oak dining buffet had no place with the steel and glass dining table; it had been a find that Anne had not been able to resist, spending hours restoring its luster so that every crack glittered boastfully with age.

There were oversized and understuffed chairs, a worn green leather hassock that better belonged on Delancey or Orchard streets, but Anne refused to toss it because it had been her grandmother's; there were two steel and glass étagères, one holding some of her books and records, both housing her entire collection of various-shaped porcelain boxes. There were two ceramic floor urns, one white, one terra cotta, filled with silver dollar plants. She had waited patiently until they had dried, then painstakingly sprayed them silver. The effect was part ethereal, part funk, and she loved it.

The kitchen was her favorite room even though it did not have a window or a dishwasher or even a broom closet. But she had ripped up all the old linoleum and laid down imitation Portuguese tile, and it only popped up in one rarely trod upon corner. As a housewarming gift, she had allowed her parents to have all her counter tops replaced with butcher block. After bringing warmth and welcome to these two rooms, Anne had had little energy or money left for the bathroom or bedrooms. One small closet that was the junior of the two bedrooms she had turned into a work space. The other bedroom, and the bathroom, were both functional but much work would be needed before she felt as right about them as she did the living room and kitchen.

The idea for the Sunday brunch had come to her after the first post-Labor Day weekend had struck her as particularly uninspired. With schoolgirl habits still deep, she began her year in September, not January, and a party seemed the right way to start a new season.

Anne had needed the party for herself too, at least until two days ago. The summer had come and gone for her with little but wistful awareness that it was passing. There had been weekends with friends at the Hamptons, and weekends in the city by herself, working on deadlines. There had been men to have dinner with, fend a pass from, go to outdoor concerts with. But there had been nothing to excite or even genuinely amuse her. Her energies—physical, mental, emotional—had seemed to be invested in the apartment and in anticipation of word from her agent, Matthew Holmes.

Of course, she would ruefully admit, she had not been waiting for Holmes in order to find a new man. There simply had been no one whom she cared would call again, even when they did. The party—calling people, preparing food, shining and polishing—was her way of stretching out summer's sociability, and more important, readying herself for change, for a more receptive attitude.

Then, late Friday afternoon, Matthew Holmes had called to tell her that her manuscript had been accepted for publication by one of the leading hardcover publishers. Even with some small revisions, the book would be released early next year. Matt explained that publication was being somewhat rushed; a book originally scheduled had fallen through, and with some quick work, they'd be able to fill the empty spot with *Honorable Mention*. Now, nearly forty-eight hours later, Anne still could not get over the wonder of it, and the party, though not so intended, seemed the appropriate celebratory gesture.

After she had gotten off the phone with her agent, she had sat on her bed, grinning and crying at the same time. She had found herself remembering when she was in the fourth grade. Mrs. Ierardi had been her teacher, a lovely Italian woman who wore her gray-streaked coal black hair pulled into a severe bun that did not fully succeed in harshening the softness of her Latin features. One night Anne had had a peculiar dream, that all the girls in her fourth grade class held a contest, a doll contest, and she won for having the prettiest doll. The next day she had gone to Mrs. Ierardi and told her about the dream, and the next week, the class held the contest. Anne had won with her Missy Moppett doll. That contest had literally been a dream come true, and now, all these years later, it was happening again with her novel.

In the time since the phone call, she had gone about her life as if nothing unusual had occurred: Friday evening she went to her ballet exercise class and only managed to remind herself of Holmes's words twice—when the instructor scolded her for sloppily executing a *plissé*, and when she became momentarily bored. Saturday she had shopped and cleaned, almost forgetting her pleasure. But moments would come, unbidden; pockets of joy that buoyed her into smiles. Regardless of what happened afterward, these moments would be remembered and cherished; they were times of happiness, pure, absolute.

The only people who shared her secret were her parents. She called them Saturday morning, and they were, at first, speechless with wonder and pride. Then, as awe segued into parental rights, they barraged her with questions practical and earthbound. She told them she would keep them posted, and yes, they could tell her brother.

This afternoon, Anne had the fortuitous environment for an announcement, yet she hesitated. Of the thirty-odd friends and friends of friends here, at least six were writers of varying degrees of professionalism: a man who said he was a poet when asked what he did for a living; he had been published in a few obscure poetry journals, but his co-op and the $100-a-month garage bill for his silver Porsche came from Wall Street. There was a novelist by night, a French teacher by day; a magazine editor-in-chief who kept cartons of plays begun and never finished; a team of commercials writers; the ghost-writer of a Hollywood autobiography that had done moderately well as a paperback original.

Anne considered their feelings, their reactions; she did not want to hurt them, spoil their afternoon. For they would be envious, and understandably so, she decided generously. And her closer friends would resent her silence all these months. They would not truly comprehend that her secrecy had been protection, both of them and self. When the timing was better she would tell them, but not yet.

"Hey, I thought this was supposed to be a party. Why so thoughtful?"

"Karen, hi! I didn't even see you come in," Anne said, greeting one of her closest friends.

"That blond guy over there let me in. Who *is* he, and *what* is he besides adorable?"

"That's Kevin Langford. He's gay. Still interested?" Anne said teasingly.

Karen groaned. "An actor no doubt."

"I knew you'd recognize the type." Anne linked her

39

arm in her friend's. "Come on over to the buffet. I want to introduce you to some food."

Karen shook her head and smiled. "Cute, Annie. Did you just make that up?"

Anne shrugged. "A mere token of the genius I usually keep hidden."

"Please continue to do so. Keep it hidden, I mean." Karen was a tall platinum blonde with a body that was legs from neck to toes. She had had slight careers as first a photographic, then a showroom model, but found both excruciatingly boring for her frenetic personality. She switched to acting, and enjoyed it. She and Anne had met three years ago when Anne had been doing an article on breaking into the theater. Since then, Karen had almost gotten married four times, been up for lead parts as often, and always managed to end up in the cast of each season's hit comedy. Anne loved her for her acerbic wit, her vulnerability rarely revealed; Karen thought Anne one of the more intelligent things she had allowed into her life.

"I've brought someone with me," Karen told her, heaping a plate with food.

"Someone new?" Anne asked, always fascinated by her friend's succession of men, almost the way a herpetologist is interested in a new breed of snake.

"Not to me, unfortunately," the blonde replied in a voice throaty from three packs a day and projection across rows of theater seats. She looked around the room to locate the man she had arrived with. "I don't think I ever told you about him, probably because we were over so long ago and it wasn't worth telling to begin with. But he's a lawyer so I like to stay friendly. You never know, right? Where the hell is he, anyway?"

Anne knew her friend too well: she rarely bothered with an escort she wasn't sleeping with unless she intended him for someone else.

"Are you matchmaking again?" she accused.

Karen shrugged but would not meet her friend's eyes.

"Dan Foley should have stopped you for a while," Anne said, referring to a man Karen had introduced her to early in the summer; a man who had sent her flowers after the first date, and had confessed he was wife-hunting on the third.

"So Dan Foley was wrong," Karen defended herself. "How else will you know unless you try them all. Besides, I'm not matchmaking-matchmaking, I'm only introducing."

"Oh. Well, that makes all the difference, of course." Amusement glinted in Anne's eyes like a newly minted coin.

"You don't understand, do you?" Karen said with exasperation. Even as she spoke, her cobalt eyes were busily scanning the room. "For matchmaking-matchmaking, I'm deliberate in arranging a meeting. It's a setup and both parties know it beforehand. For introducing, I'm more casual. Hey, there he is. Come on." She grabbed Anne by the wrist and marched her over to the fireplace where a tall, dark-haired man was standing at the perimeter of an animated group.

Karen let go of Anne long enough to take possession of the man and bring him out of the background.

"Arthur, I'd like you to meet one of my dearest friends, Anne Fletcher. Annie, darling, this is Arthur Dumont, lawyer extraordinaire and a woman's delight."

Anne's eyebrows arched. "Well, that's quite an endorsement."

The man laughed with self-consciousness. "You know how actresses tend to overstate their case."

"That's absolutely not true," Karen protested. "I never exaggerate except to make a point." She smiled at them. "Now, if you two will excuse me, I'm going to circulate," and with a peck on the cheek for each, she moved away.

"She's something, isn't she?"

"I adore her," Anne said. "I'm surprised she's never mentioned you to me before," she added. "Karen's usually not shy about the people she knows."

"Well, we don't really see each other that often, and I guess I'm not as colorful as some of her other friends." He smiled. "She's never mentioned you to me either, in fact. I'm sure I would have remembered."

"Oh, please, my impact can't be that devastating," Anne said, disappointed with the age-old line.

Arthur was quick to explain. "I don't know about that yet, but I know another girl named Anne Fletcher. That's why I would have remembered."

"If it'll help you keep us straight, please call me Annie. I'll answer to that on occasion." Her smile was slight, brief.

Arthur heard her, but his mind was on the odd coincidence of knowing two girls with the exact same name. "Do you spell your name with an 'e' at the end?" he pursued. She nodded. "What a weird coincidence," he muttered.

Anne was losing interest in the conversation and the man. Because Karen had introduced them, she would give it a little longer, but only a little. He was attractive enough in a nondescript way; about five feet eleven, and athletically lean. Brown eyes that were neither warm nor particularly intelligent. Brown hair that she suspected had been blown dry to look thickly carefree. His face was fleshy now, but Anne could see it turning craggy, time removing the softness and deepening the planes and lines, if he kept in shape. Worth a few minutes more, she concluded.

"Have you had anything to eat yet?" she asked.

Her question jarred him away from the other Anne Fletcher, so unexpectedly brought to mind now when he had given her little, if any, consideration for several months. He had seen her sporadically during the summer. After that disastrous dinner, he had decided to run,

42

not walk away from her. But when he had been particularly horny and had not wanted to make an effort at getting laid, he had called her. Her availability was expedient, if not memorably satisfying. He wondered briefly how many other similarities were shared by these two girls besides their name. And him, he suddenly realized with a smile.

"Does food amuse you?" Anne asked, somewhat irritated by this man's boorish manner.

"I'm sorry, really. I guess my mind was still on that business of your name. And I'd love some food, but only if you'll have something, too. Like most hostesses, you probably haven't tasted a thing."

She smiled, and Arthur saw a certain aloofness melt into warmth. He could not help but smile back at her.

A walk of seconds stretched into minutes as Anne was stopped by friends who wanted to comment favorably on the brunch, or complain that they had not seen enough of her recently, or introduce her to someone they had brought.

"You're a very gracious hostess," Arthur commented when they finally reached the buffet.

Anne looked rueful. "I'm glad that's how it seems. I'm always a wreck before. My stomach gets a case of turbulence for at least a week." She turned to the table. "Now, what'll you have?"

Arthur did not glance at the food as he said, "Oh, anything. You choose." He knew he was studying this girl, pleased by her easy grace, and by the obvious endorsement of the people here. They seemed genuinely to like her, although he cynically assumed that at least one or two of the guests pretended friendliness for the sake of a free meal.

"Have you gone out with those three guys you were speaking with before?" he asked suddenly.

Anne handed him a plate, fork, napkin. "Coffee or bloody mary?"

"Coffee black, please." Then, "I apologize. That was rude of me."

"Was it?" She shrugged. "I just wanted to give you your plate before dropping it."

She filled her own plate, and they went to stand by a window.

"Now about that rude question," she said after they had eaten a bit. "Yes, I've dated those three, and also him," gesturing with her chin toward a stocky man with more hair in his bristly beard than on his head. "Why?"

"Why?" Arthur was stalling; he himself was not sure what had prompted him to ask the question.

"Why did you want to know?"

"I was impressed," he admitted.

"Because I have friends?" She was surprised.

"Because men you've gone out with are still your friends. That's pretty unusual."

"Well, not all the men I go out with want to stay friends," she assured him. "But if you like someone enough to date him, he should be likable enough to have as a friend, at least a casual one."

"I think that's the operative word," Arthur said. "Casual, both as a date and as a friend."

Anne was thoughtful. "I suppose. Otherwise, too many expectations set in, and from that it's a step away to disappointment." She glanced down at her plate, uncomfortable with the serious turn of the conversation.

"Does that mean you expect little to soften the disappointment?" he asked, a bit too sharply.

"Now, *that* is a rude question." Anne looked hard at him, the brown of her eyes deepening into sable but without any of its warmth.

"Not at all," Arthur replied lightly. "It was very natural after what you said."

"You're a very presumptuous man, and not completely pleasant," Anne said tartly, wondering how this innocuous social chitchat had gotten so out of hand.

Arthur felt relentless. It was a crack in the façade of social grace, and he was curious; what nerve had he touched? and why?

"Leaving my personality aside for a moment," he said, "you still haven't answered my question."

"And I don't intend to."

"What are you afraid of?"

"Afraid!" Anne retorted in a voice louder than she had wished. "I'm not 'afraid' as you put it, I am simply—" She stopped herself, and shook her head, as if by that motion restoring her poise. "This is ridiculous. I'm sure you didn't come to a party to squabble, and I certainly didn't give one so that I would have an opportunity to defend my ideas." She reached for his half-full plate, eager to be gone from his side. "I'll take this and let you meet some of the others." Her voice was low again, and cold, demanding distance.

"You're really angry, aren't you?" Arthur was somewhat surprised; it had been a game, a duel, both players to remain unscathed.

Anne hesitated. "Angry, no. Irritated, yes. You're too presumptuous and too arrogant. You offer me no disappointment now, I'm afraid, because I realize I have nothing good to expect."

With that, she left him by the window and returned the plates to the buffet table. She was seething, but outwardly not a sign showed as she circulated and chatted among the clusters of people. She loathed arrogance; it was, to her, as unpardonable a sin as dishonesty. And she had no tolerance of people, male or female, who felt the need to unbalance and strip another in order to gain a stronger grip on their own self-esteem. Arthur Dumont probably had never had a female as a friend, she was thinking. Her own ability to be with men sexlessly disturbed him, and so he had to challenge.

But even as she silently railed against him, she knew Arthur Dumont's question had not warranted quite such an overreaction. The truth was that he had touched upon an area of sensitivity, a vulnerability that she did not want exposed. Because what Anne expected of a man in anything but a casual relationship had proven to result only in disappointment.

She had fallen deeply, youthfully in love twice: once with her political science professor, once with a young man who had been interning with her older brother. She had slept with both, refused each in marriage. At the precipice, she would look down and out, past the bed to the patterns of constancy and tradition that would ineluctably set in like mold on cheese. And she would flutter with indecision, a movement as ephemeral, as fleeting as two extra heartbeats. And she would decide no, for they, like the men since, had loved out of need, not needed out of love; had been too steeped in their heritage of masculinity to find the strength to let her be strong. At twenty-eight, while her optimism had not faded, her sense of reality had sharpened. The man who would be friend and lover was the rare one, and if she did not expect it, she would not be disappointed in not finding him. For that reason, Arthur Dumont had been correct in his quick, and shrewd, assessment.

As the September sun settled far down in the sky, turning the west into a panorama of rouge-pot pinks and scarlets, Anne's guests began to leave, the scents of food and perfume and cigarettes lingering behind, reminders, remainders of their presence. A trail of hugs and kisses into the air and squeezes and "thank you," "call you soon," "terrific brunch" stayed behind, too. Then Karen was by Anne's side.

"Allow me to compliment you on your lousy party. Not even one fucking date," she grumbled. "Where'd you ever find such a bunch of losers?"

"It was easy, believe me," Anne went along. She paused, then, quickly: "Where's your friend Arthur? Why doesn't he buy you dinner?"

46

Karen's eyes narrowed. "He said you'd agreed to have dinner with him."

"What!"

"You didn't?"

"I most certainly did not. He didn't even ask me! Of all the outrageous, nervy—." She turned her head sharply away from Karen's penetrating gaze.

"It's exciting not to be bored for a change, isn't it?" Karen remarked quietly. "Sort of renovates the soul. Call you soon," and she was out the door before Anne could respond.

Her indignation was evident: her light tan was suffused with a flush of red that crept up from her neck; her eyes shimmered darkly. To anyone who did not know her well, she looked unapproachable with anger. But a small, so small, smile played about her lips, and a close friend would have spotted it. A close friend, like Karen, would have recognized it for what it meant.

There were only a few stragglers left, but he wasn't among them, she realized after discreetly glancing around. Then she saw him, coming out of the bathroom. She looked away quickly, feeling childish and intoxicated at the same time. How right Karen was.

"You are arrogant, presumptuous, nervy, and probably not at all nice," she stated assertively as soon as he was by her side. "And I won't have dinner with you tonight," she paused, then permitted a wide smile to light up her words, "because if I eat another bite I'll roll onto the street."

His response was a relief-filled grin. "May I at least stay a while?"

She nodded. "Just let me see the rest of the people out."

Arthur went to the now vacant sofa to wait. Like the rest of the apartment, the sofa was a reflection of taste, not an indication of style, but Arthur did not recognize this. Covered in beige polished cotton strewn with orange and lavender flowers, its cushions and armrests almost obscenely plump, the sofa was neo-art nouveau, and deliciously comfortable, as Anne insisted it be. She loved to sink into it at night, and wanted people who came to her apartment to feel the same sort of ease with her furnishings. The sensuousness of her nature was apparent throughout, in things that were meant to be touched and felt and seen and even smelled. If Arthur could not identify this quality, he could appreciate the comfort, and he sank back into the couch exactly as he was meant to.

He watched her as that grace, still easy and natural after hours in use, made the exits as warm as the welcomes had been. He liked her, a revelation that somewhat startled him, for he did not usually judge a woman by that criterion. There was nothing artificial about her, no image of magazine management, the term he privately applied to women like the other Anne Fletcher, women who were created from the pages of the slicks. Had he acted as arrogantly with them, their reaction would have been predictable: no reaction. Anne Fletcher might have gotten that opaque look in her eyes, but she would have said nothing, perhaps to take out her revenge later, in bed. But this Anne Fletcher—Annie, he decided, definitely Annie—reacted immediately and let him know. If that honesty was unexpected and disconcerting, it was also, upon mild reflection, pleasing. Here was someone, he suspected, whom he could not call at the last minute; who would require more gentle, at least more considerate handling than he was used to giving.

Of course, he thought, he could be completely wrong. Annie Fletcher might have much more in common with Anne Fletcher than a name. She, too, could take the route of passive resistance in bed, the way Anne now seemed to. And she, too, could prefer to talk about her secret ambitions for hours on end, the way Anne did about her writing. And maybe Annie Fletcher was a little too critical and unyielding; her sense of humor alive at another's expense. But he did not know any of this yet about Annie Fletcher, and he knew all of it about Anne, which is why one was so much more intriguing to him than the other.

"Whew, I'm wiped out," Anne declared, plopping herself on the sofa. She kicked off her sandals, leaned her head back, closed her eyes, then mischievously looked at him. "Alone at last," she whispered, grinning.

"Can I get you a drink, coffee or something?" he asked.

She shook her head, and said nothing for a few moments. Arthur waited, seeing little evidence of fatigue about her. Her white slacks and blue silk shirt still looked crisp; a smudge of mascara and lips now bare of lipstick, hair less full, but those were the only signs that she had been on stage for several hours. She was far from beautiful, he decided. Anne Fletcher was a prettier, sexier girl, her features more arresting. This girl, when not smiling, was Ivory Flakes good looks, undeniably attractive in an almost forgettable way. But when she smiled, when even just those eyes smiled, her appeal was incredible, more electrifying, sexier than he could have imagined possible.

"Finished?" she murmured.

He looked away. "Sorry."

She sat up. "No need. I'd be insulted if you didn't."

"Like loving to be annoyed by construction workers' comments, and being upset if they don't make them?"

She nodded. "You know, we've met, fought, made up, all in a few short hours. That's got to be the quickest relationship on record."

"Then we *have* made up?" he asked, caring about the answer.

"Well, at least long enough to have another fight, I would think," she teased.

"I was rude," he admitted.

"And arrogant. Please don't forget arrogant."

"But you overreacted."

"I did."

Silence, then suddenly they both began to laugh, an erasure of discomfo c and mistakes.

They began to talk then, Arthur telling her about himself, more than he normally did with a woman because she asked better questions, he realized. And without intending to, Anne told him about her novel.

"That's fantastic, terrific," he enthused, genuinely meaning it. "When will it be published?"

"Not till next year. I still have some work to do on it." She paused, then, "Uh, Arthur, I haven't told Karen yet so I'd appreciate it if—"

"I won't say anything," he assured her, "but why the secrecy? You should be shouting it to the world."

"Oh, I will, but I'm still not used to the idea myself. I can't quite believe it's really true."

"Well, thank you for telling *me*. I'm flattered." He waited a moment. "You know, it's unbelievably coincidental or ironic or *some*thing," and he laughed brusquely, "but that girl I was telling you about? The one with the same name? Well, she's in publishing, too. She edits juvenile books."

"Really? Do you know what house?"

"Amber Books, I think the name is."

"Oh, sure, I've heard of them. They do very nice stuff."

"I'm sorry to keep going on about this, but I can't get over it. Two girls with the same name, same field of work, and I know them both." He shook his head. "Incredible."

Anne did not know how to respond. She was not jealous, and only mildly curious. It did not seem particularly important to her.

"Do you get a lot of wrong numbers, or mail addressed to her?" Arthur asked.

"No, no mail, and not too many wrong numbers." She looked at him curiously. "This really has you hooked, doesn't it?"

He gave another short laugh. "I guess I'm becoming a little tiresome, but it's so uncanny." He leaned back, arm outstretched, his hand reaching toward her face. Gently, he traced the contour of cheekbones to jaw, then removed his hand; a gesture soft, replete with affection. Anne kept her eyes on his, unembarrassed, comfortable.

"You're very different from her," he said, and Anne sensed that he was almost talking to himself, comparing them not for her benefit, but for his, and so she did not venture to change the subject. For whatever reason, he needed to do this, as if to slot them carefully in his mind. "She loves a good time, lots of partying," he went on. "She hates her job, wants to be a writer. Like you."

"Oh?"

"Yeah, but I don't know if she'll ever do it. It's got to be tough to work all day and then try to write in your free time. She likes her fun too much."

Anne refrained from preaching about discipline and desire, or from pointing out that she liked a good time, too. She did not have to defend herself against a girl she did not know.

"She's not as self-possessed as you. She pretends to be, but she's not. Do you know what poise you have? She can't—"

"Arthur . . ."

He looked at her, and saw her. "I *am* sorry. I can't help it, though. It's just so—"

"I know, so incredible," but she smiled as she said it.

The sun had long since set. The children's cries and ethnic lilts had retreated from the street; the scents had diminished. Both of them understood that it was time for him to go.

He got up. "I've overstayed my welcome. You've got to be exhausted."

"A little."

He offered his hands, and she took them, letting him pull her to her feet. They walked to the door without touching. "Are you free for dinner tomorrow?" he asked, his hand on the doorknob.

She nodded. "I'll pick you up about seven, all right?" Again, her nod. Arthur hesitated, then brushed her lips with his. "I'm glad you let me stay."

She smiled impishly. "I'm glad you were presumptuous enough to decide to." Then, he left.

Anne stood by the closed door, a sense of satisfaction warming her like a bubble bath on a winter's night. She surveyed her living room, littered as it was with the refuse of party. She went to pick up a dead cigarette butt from the Mexican rug. Then she walked over to one of the étagères and lifted out a small round porcelain box, holding it gently as if it were a baby bird. She felt the smooth roundness, and smiled: pleasure, so much pleasure. The apartment, the book, perhaps a new man.

A new man. She said the words out loud, liked the feel, the texture of them, the possibilities they opened up. She wondered fleetingly if she would fall in love with Arthur Dumont, then hastily put the thought back on the shelf with the porcelain box.

Arthur Dumont did not get a cab immediately. He walked for a while, debating with himself whether to call the other Anne Fletcher. But he really did not want to see her, talk with her, have sex with her. He wanted only to compare her anew, almost convince himself of her existence. He knew he was being absurd about the entire thing. It was an unusual coincidence, period, and he was dwelling on it as if it meant something. He finally hailed a cab, and sat back, anticipating tomorrow evening, pleased with this other girl for getting him to feel that boyish eagerness again. She was different, more, somehow, than what he was used to. He briefly speculated, for the first time since he had been a freshman in college, if he would be enough for her.

CHAPTER 5

September slipped casually into October but the leaves on what trees there were in New York City stubbornly refused to turn color and fall away. They expected an Indian summer, demanded it more bullishly than the most demanding New Yorker. They hung on obstinately, waiting for first that rush of cool night air, followed by days of biting chill. They hung on, knowing that after the cold would come a respite, a period of sticky dampness, enervating heat that would taunt city dwellers with a reminder of what was, and what they would have to wait many long months for again. Indian summer in Manhattan: not unlike a woman.

By the middle of October, strikes were on, this year cabbies and elevator operators; children were being crossed carefully from street corner to schoolyard; South American, Japanese, and Arab tourists flaunted their wealth, spending flamboyantly and creating in New Yorkers what heretofore had been an alien emotion: envy. The leaves had given up their fight, and were floating willessly away as the sky darkened earlier, the air bit more painfully.

Paris is breathtaking in the fall, even the Parisians forget to be tight-hearted. And Los Angeles does have a fall: when the hills burn and the houses crumble, and the Santa Ana wind frightens life. It is autumn in the suburbs of Chicago, Detroit, Minneapolis when Sundays are divided between raking leaves and watching football games. But New York's autumn is particularly poignant, perhaps because it is so short-lived; perhaps because most city dwellers must again face their environment after a summer of escape. And what they see, for the most part, they like. There is something unique and totally charming about fall in Manhattan, as there is the unique and charming about a good con artist. You know you're being snookered by both, but you're having such a wonderful time it doesn't matter.

Too soon, the excitement of season openings: new stores, theater, ballet, opera; the delight taken in the change of fashions; the frenzied thrill of moving into a new apartment; the well-intentioned vows to keep exercising during winter; the pleasures of walking and bicycling with a light jacket on; the smiles of optimism in the singles bars, reserved only for fall—too soon, all gone as the days get shorter and darker and colder and bleaker and the nights get longer and lonelier and more desperate. New Yorkers, like moles, scurry back underground into protective custody of themselves. Gone with the length of the days and the fading warmth in the air is the challenge of new beginnings people feel in fall. Winter descends with maddening insistence, and the neat piles of refuse become windblown and are called garbage; the subways and buses stink of wet wool and frustration; skin turns sallow and junk food sells out of the supermarkets. Retreat, warns the weather, and New Yorkers, too sly to fight when they cannot win, obey, burrowing into themselves like dustballs in closet corners.

Thanksgiving came and went. Anne N. Fletcher spent it on Long Island with her family. Her brother and his wife drove in from Westchester where he had a developing practice as an internist. The Fletchers ate and celebrated with gusto, feelings of prideful achievement filling each of them. The only crack in the mellowness came after dinner. They were sitting around the Franklin stove in the Fletchers' family room, the one room in the house in which Mrs. Fletcher had acquiesced to Mr. Fletcher's wishes by making it comfortable instead of decorative. The group of five were occupied with a few minutes of quiet, the silence of well-fed contentment and indulgent self-satisfaction. Then Mr. Fletcher, beaming at his daughter, invited her to read from her forthcoming novel. With embarrassed laughter, she shook her head in refusal. The others took up the chant, the urge growing in proportion to the fading of her smile.

"Please stop," she finally said, all trace of embarrassment or good humor gone. Her voice was steel, the quivering blade of a rarely used épée. "I'm not going to do it."

"But why, darling?" her mother wanted to know. "We're all friends here, we're not going to make fun of you."

"That's not it. Words are meant to be read silently, at least the words in my book. This isn't a play but a novel," Anne stressed the difference.

They all agreed. "But this is yours, Annie. That makes it special," her father pointed out.

"No, and please don't ask me again," she told them firmly.

"Well, then, how about your next book. You can at least *tell* us about it, can't you?" her mother said, not bothering to mask the sarcasm.

Anne hesitated, but not long enough to arouse suspicion. "I don't have a next novel. I'm working on some new magazine assignments, finishing up the revisions for the novel, and—"

"Why on earth are you still wasting your time with magazines?" Her mother's voice had grown strident with annoyance.

Anne's sigh of impatience was not lost on anyone. "I still have bills to pay, Mother. When I no longer need to worry about those, I'll stop 'wasting my time' with the magazines." The words were spoken without rancor, but the sting was sufficiently obvious to get her mother to drop the issue.

Anne felt it was premature to discuss the fifty rough pages of her second novel. Premature, and somewhat bold. They were assuming, as was she secretly, that a new career had been launched, and it would forever be a matter of which would she next do, not what. She had not dissembled; she *was* working on a magazine article, but she had also begun another book. She could not tell them this, not yet. They must not suppose a star in the family; they must not secure her future so unquestioningly.

"If you're not going to talk about your work, will you at least tell us if there's anything new socially?" her mother said with exasperation.

Anne laughed, as did her brother and sister-in-law. "How come I'm getting it all tonight?"

"Because *I* got it last month," her brother told her.

Usually, Anne would dodge questions about her social life with the dexterity of an all-star halfback fending defensive linemen. She would assure her parents that despite being twenty-eight—unhealthily close to thirty—and not yet married, men still found her appealing enough to take to dinner or a show or an opening. She did not elaborate on the men, thus avoiding questions that might get her to reveal that one was gay, another lasted only for an evening, or that she had invited someone out to cover an event for a magazine. Anne did not believe that her parents worried about her not getting married; they thought it would happen because it would be against the natural order for it not to. Their concern was to whom and when.

Tonight she would have to yield ground; she had not given them enough about herself to ponder and discuss privately; they needed more and would insist upon it.

"Well, there is one man I've been seeing," she admitted slowly, catching the slight nod of approval from her brother.

"Anne, don't make us play twenty questions," her mother scolded.

Anne sipped from the mug of Irish coffee that had grown cold and bitter. "There's not much to tell. His name is Arthur Dumont, he's thirty-three, a junior partner in a law firm, tall, dark, and just handsome enough." She finished her recitation with a wink for her brother.

"And?" her mother prompted.

"Leila, how about another brandy?" Mr. Fletcher asked his wife, sensing his daughter's discomfort, and wishing to relieve it.

His wife shook her head. "How long have you been seeing him?"

"Since September."

Her mother's eyebrows arched as she exchanged a glance with her husband. "Often?"

Anne shrugged, and got up. She went over to the fireplace to warm her hands, which were not cold. Her back was to them as she spoke. "A couple of times a week. Nothing regular, though. Whenever we both have time."

"Sounds pretty serious, Annie," her father remarked gently.

Anne turned around. "It's nice," she said. "I don't know if I'd call it serious, but it is nice." She smiled. "And no, you don't have to meet him yet."

Appeased if not satisfied, the Fletchers turned to other

58

topics, creating conversations to which Anne did not have to pay attention. Her father spoke to her brother about football, her mother to her sister-in-law about safe subjects such as fashion and beauty.

"I'm going upstairs to make more Irish coffee. Anybody want?" Anne offered. With an order from her brother, she escaped.

As she prepared the coffee, she asked herself the question her father had asked; the question she had begun to ask herself more and more frequently: was it serious?

Since that Sunday in September, she and Arthur had reached a point that if they did not spend Friday night to Sunday and at least one weeknight together, it was either because he was out of town or one of them had business to finish. By many people's standards, she supposed that much time constituted if not a serious relationship, at least not a casual one. And yet, she was not really sure how deeply she felt about him; or, more truthfully, how deeply she was permitting herself to feel.

She liked him, certainly. She had admitted to herself about three weeks ago that she would very much miss him were he suddenly to exit her life. Yet something held her back; some invisible barrier existed between them that prevented her from having that total trust she needed above all else in order to love.

In the beginning, she had considered Arthur much as a teacher might look upon a bright student with a prankster's personality: the teacher would be helplessly charmed but the student never would be taken seriously. How could a teacher trust this student who seemed so careless of his gift of intelligence? For Anne, Arthur was the bad boy, charming enough to play with, too charming to trust. The arrogance evinced that first afternoon; the dangerous questions meant to test; the assumption of his appeal—all this was not defensive façade, peeled away with the security of familiarity to reveal vulnerability. It did not take many dates for Anne to realize that Arthur was a typical New York male: a category not without its negative traits. He was spoiled by women who never said no; he expected his success in everything, with everyone; he had style, and perhaps taste as well, but certainly undeveloped.

Anne had scrupulously avoided men like Arthur. A few experiences with them had convinced her of what she had strongly suspected: they did not like her, she did not like them. They were too ovine for her; following was their pattern, although being at the vanguard was how they saw themselves. And she was too unaccepting for them; she questioned, raised doubts, demanded self-appraisal.

She had not walked away from Arthur, though, nor he from her. They laughed together; he responded when she challenged; he challenged her. They understood their differences, and used humor and wit to both defend themselves and strengthen their arguments. And the sex was exhilarating. She responded to him as she had to no other man. It had embarrassed her at first. It was not that he was an exceptional lover, he once confided; he was an exceptional lover for her. She was warmed by the difference, and delighted that he recognized it. Even now, just thinking about them in bed, about the incredibly hard and masculine feel of the curve of his shoulders, the way his hands would yield, then demand, brought a tightening to her stomach, an aspiclike quivering in her thighs.

Neither, however, had yet spoken of love; neither had given over to the other the rights of possession. But in the privacy of her room at night, in moments like now, snatched away from people, Anne knew how close she was getting to relinquishing her safety hold. To continue as they were would be fun for a while longer, then it would get tiresome. A new plateau had to be reached or they would dissolve back into separateness. Gamble and give: the concept was frightening, and excruciatingly exciting.

Anne Fletcher spent Thanksgiving in a Greenwich Village restaurant, eating a bacon cheeseburger and French fries, and drinking beer with her friend Jane.

"We should have gone home for Thanksgiving, or at least I should have made a turkey," Jane was saying.

"Who stopped you?" Anne retorted unkindly.

Jane shrugged. "A turkey seemed like a lot of trouble for just the two of us at the time. Now I think it would have been fun." She paused, then: "Why are you in such a bad mood? Holiday glums?"

"I had a typical conversation with my mother this morning—shitty," Anne mumbled. "That woman asks the same dumb questions every time I talk to her. I don't know why I bother anymore."

"Because she's your mother, and she's the only family you have."

"I think she killed my father with her questions. He probably figured dying was easier to cope with than answering her all the time." Her expression was as sour as the words.

"Anne, that's horrible," Jane protested, aghast. "She means well, you know."

Anne's laugh was too short to be shared, and too humorless. "Since when? The only reason she asks me anything is to get information she can share with her canasta-playing friends. She doesn't give a shit about me."

"That's ridiculous," but Janey's voice belied the words. From college to the present, Jane Ebersole had heard about Anne and her family, and none of it had been positive. Jane had met Mr. Fletcher only once before he died, and her faded recollection of him was a large, walrus-shaped man too gentle for this world. Mrs. Fletcher never had seemed to Jane, on the several occasions they had met, to be the unfeeling creature Anne depicted her. But she did not doubt the veracity of her friend's stories: Mrs. Fletcher making fun of her daughter's flat chest; Mrs. Fletcher preening when someone said she and her daughter could pass as sisters; Mrs. Fletcher flirting with her daughter's dates; Mrs. Fletcher complaining that her daughter was not married, did not have a glamorous job, did not live an exciting life, would never amount to anything—anything, according to Anne, being a daughter she could boast about, puff up herself through. Janey felt sorry that her best friend did not have the special closeness she enjoyed with her mother. The only way she knew to help Anne was to let her talk out her anger.

"What happened this time?" she prompted.

"Who cares. The same old crap," Anne grumbled, signaling the waiter for two more beers. "She wanted to know about the job, so I told her how boring it is, of course."

"Didn't you tell her the good news?"

Anne looked puzzled. "What good news?"

"About the raise and the promotion to senior editor."

Anne snorted unbecomingly. "You call that good news? Look, the job is still boring and I'm still stuck in it, so what point is there in telling her the other stuff? She'll think I like it." She sipped from her beer, and her eyes were on the rows of liquor bottles behind the bar as she spoke.

"She wanted to know about my writing," Anne went on. "Now how many times have I asked her to lay off about that. If there's something to tell, I'll tell her." Her voice was thick with disgust, and the two white spots of anger were gaining prominence as frames to her mouth. "You know, you'd think she'd get tired of asking the same questions every time, but she never does. 'How's the health club?' 'Okay, but getting crowded,' I tell her. 'How's the apartment?' 'Expensive.' 'How's your social life?' 'Nonexistent.' " Anne refocused her attention on Jane.

"Finally she wanted to know if I had anything nice to tell her. Know what I said? I said, yeah, it was nice that we lived so far apart." She laughed, short, unpleasant again, no smile touching her face.

Janey did not respond, having learned a while ago that no response was expected or welcome. Anne was her closest friend. They had gone through college together; they had shared their first apartment in New York; they took vacations, spent holidays together. They held tenure in each other's lives, and with that came a familiarity so easy to abuse. Janey had learned that to let Anne's moods extinguish themselves was the safest way to avoid becoming a target of them. That was why she remained silent, watching her friend's face, waiting for the white spots to vanish.

This past summer and the fall had not been her best, Anne was thinking now. She had tried—she was confident she had—but nothing seemed to work out. She had gone to several business functions, hoping to change her attitude about the people in her field and the work she did. But when she read about the exciting high-priced auctions and the foreign book fairs and the movie deals on *real* books, she could feel nothing but contempt for her job and the people who did it. She knew she was capable of more, and so she went on an interview with one of the paperback publishers. They offered her the same salary but only an associate editor spot. She could not possibly take it; maybe if it had been a prestigious hardcover house, but certainly to take such a position with a paperback publisher would be a step down.

She had been more faithful to her tape recorder than to her typewriter. She had gotten as far as writing two pages but had thrown them out. She was determined that her first novel be a best-seller of quality dimensions, and that was the problem: she could not think of what to write about that would be both literary *and* commercial. She had several ideas but none seemed good enough to her. With winter settling in, and staying indoors more a necessity than a choice, she was sure she would have the time to write—and the right idea.

Socially, she knew she had exaggerated. She had been going out, but not that often and not with anyone worth talking to her mother. Arthur had dropped out of sight for almost three weeks after the dinner fiasco, and she could not really fault him for that. Then, toward the middle of July, he had called one night and invited himself over. They had gone to bed with little social preamble. He had called again two or three times after that, always at the last minute. Arthur did not mean enough for her to make an issue of his cavalier treatment. They used each other; she knew this and accepted it. Since September, though, she had not heard from him. She had called him once, back in early October, and he had alibied about being out-of-town a lot. Anne supposed that she would hear from him again sometime, when he needed a quick lay; and if he never called again, that would be all right, too.

There had been other men, of course; there were always men to be found at the bars, at Bloomingdale's on a Saturday afternoon, in a Soho café. She and Jane had gone to the Hamptons twice, and the men Anne had met there had lasted for a date or two in the city. There were men to keep her busy, and a job she did not like but that she did well. If her writing was not yet happening, it would, soon.

Then why be so negative with her mother? Why emphasize what was wrong when it would be just as easy to tell her what was right?

Because none of it was right *enough*, and she was tired of carrying the entire burden of dissatisfaction herself. She had spared her mother one grievance, though. She had not told her, in response to her questions about safety and precaution in the terrible sewer that was New York, about the invasion of privacy she had been experiencing for several months. She would achieve nothing by speaking of it. Her mother would say that wrong numbers and mix-ups with mail were hardly worthy of being called invasions of privacy. So it was not that Anne intentionally spared her mother; what she did was spare herself from having to explain and defend.

Soon after Thanksgiving, the first snow of the season fell on New York. The mayor made much of being prepared for it: the snowplows were ready, the sand spreaders equipped—the city would (mal)function as usual. Two and a half inches of snow came and went before anybody could claim an inability to get to work. But it was the first snow, a hint, like restless nights and migraine headaches, of the trouble to come.

6

Anne's fingers trembled around the business-sized envelope. She had never seen a copy of *Los Angeles* magazine, and this did not look like a subscription solicitation; it wasn't thick enough. Maybe someone had told them of her, about her being a writer, and they wanted her to do an article, or better yet, interview her. Her heart began to beat a drumroll of expectation in her chest. Yet even as she got excited, a part of her made a quick decision. She would allow them to interview her, if that's what they wanted; that kind of publicity could never hurt. She would not, however, permit them to abuse her talents. The only writing for her was a novel; no matter how great the temptation, she would not sully herself by writing for a magazine.

More composed, she sat down at the dining table and opened the envelope. She removed a check for $1200, a voucher that stated: "The NY/LA Connection—$1200," and a brief note from a Ken Samuels thanking Anne for the nice job she had done. The address on both the envelope and voucher was 401 East 84th Street. Instead of returning it to the sender, or checking their new address listings, the post office had automatically delivered it to her. This was not the first time such a mistake had occurred. As with the other wrong deliveries, Anne would reseal the envelope and give it to the postman in the morning, this time with a stern warning not to be so quick to give every piece of mail for Anne Fletcher to her.

But she did not replace the check and voucher immediately. The initial disappointment at discovering that she was not wanted for an interview was now curiosity; what was the "NY/LA Connection" and what did that other girl have to do with it that was worth over a thousand dollars? Maybe she could find a copy of the magazine in the library, but she didn't even know what issue to ask for. Maybe that other Anne Fletcher did research for them, or photography. Those were the only two possibilities that seemed logical, and acceptable.

Anne knew that the fee could not be for writing an article; nobody got paid that much by a magazine, and certainly not an unknown. Did they? The thought was so abhorrent to her that she quickly put the check, note, and voucher back in the envelope, as if removal of the evidence would erase that notion from her mind. But it niggled at her like an itch. A stone of angry resentment formed in her stomach. Her stride purposeful, she walked into her bedroom, sat on the edge of the bed, and took out her tape recorder.

It is December fifteenth and it happened again today. A check for $1200 came from *Los Angeles* magazine—for her. That's an awful lot of money and I can't figure out what it's for. It has to be for pictures, photographers are the only people who command that kind of money. She can't be a writer. That would be ridiculous. I mean, to pay an unknown so much. [*Laughter.*] I think I'd kill her if I ever found out she was a writer. It's bad enough that I still get calls meant for her and the post office gives me her mail. She could at least learn to spell her name differently, and didn't she ever hear of change-of-address cards?

Just for the record, let's see what's happened since she moved. In June, three wrong numbers, all men, and flowers delivered by mistake. July, a wrong number from a girl named Sarah. August, a picture postcard of the Eiffel Tower from an Ed. September was an alumnae bulletin from la-di-da Mount Holyoke, well, kiss my ass. One or two more wrong numbers. Then, a subscription renewal from *National Geographic* magazine and an invitation to speak at her college.

There's been nothing for a while until this check today. I'm really getting pissed off now. What's wrong with the post office that they can't get to work and find the right address? Okay, I'll be fair. Sometimes the address has been mine. I guess whoever sent the stuff just checked the phone book. Today's thing and the mail from her fancy-schmancy college were addressed to her at her old address on East Eighty-fourth, easy enough to confuse with East Seventy-fourth, I suppose.

I never used to get so much wrong mail, an occasional flier, maybe an odd letter over the years, but nothing like this. The post office should check—yeah, and you shouldn't open them. [*Laughter again.*]

Mount Holyoke of all places. I can just see her. Blonde hair, very straight, flat-chested and maybe a big ass from sitting on it reading crap like *National Geographic*. Jeez, she's probably still a virgin. Her voice is soft, shy, she gets her kicks vicariously through the lens of the camera. Either kind of unwashed and arty-looking or so scrubbed a man would be afraid to go near her for fear the starch would scratch. [*More laughter.*] Kiddo, you're really something. You hate her and you don't even know her. No, of course I don't hate her, but I am getting more and more annoyed. People move every day, it's no big deal, yet it's been over six months and these lousy screw-ups are still happening. [*The telephone began to ring.*] My luck, that's probably a call for her. Okay, I'm coming. Just a sec.

She turned off the tape recorder, and hurried into the kitchen. "Hello?"

"Hi, it's me."

"Oh, hi, Janey, what's up?"

"Nothing. That's the problem. I'm bored. Let's go to a movie or something."

"No, I don't feel like it."

"How about going out for a bite to eat then, or trying a new bar? Anne, I've got to do something, I'm going bananas."

"I thought you had a date tonight or a cocktail party," Anne said with little interest.

"No, that's tomorrow night. And it's not really a date. I have to have dinner with some people from the office who are trying to woo a big advertiser." She paused. "Come on, let's go out."

"I told you. I don't feel like it." Anne's voice was sharp, intolerant.

"You'd probably feel like it if Arthur Dumont or some other man called," Jane accused.

"You're right, I probably would," Anne agreed unkindly. "But since no man has called, I still don't feel like it."

"Where is Arthur anyway?" Janey asked, knowing that Anne and he had stopped seeing each other but wanting to sting back.

"How the hell should I know." The phone seemed to crackle with her acerbity. "He doesn't call me anymore, not even to get laid. And you know it, so stop asking me about him all the time."

Jane was not to be put off. "Why don't you call him?"

"Because I don't want to. Because I have nothing to say to him. Because if he wanted to see me, he could call me. Now, does that end the subject?" Anne knew she

69

did not have to be so abrasive with Janey, but the truth was that she *had* called Arthur—last week. She had told herself, and him, that it was a friendly gesture, a holiday greeting, but what had motivated her had been a desire for sex. Arthur had been one of three men she had phoned that night, none of whom had been available. He had made an excuse about leaving for Tucson or someplace early the next morning; she believed that, but not his promise to call after he returned.

"Not only does it end the subject, but forget any idea about going out. Your mood leaves a great deal to be desired." Jane laughed lightly to show that she was not hurt by Anne's tone nor did she mean her own words. "What's wrong, anyway? Something happen at the office?"

"Nothing worse than usual," Anne replied. "No, I guess this business that has been going on since the summer has gotten to me. I told you, didn't I?"

"You mean the wrong numbers and stuff?"

"Yeah." Anne hesitated. Then: "You know what happened today? An envelope came from *Los Angeles* magazine. Did you ever hear of it?"

"No, but it sounds like it's probably the West Coast version of *New York*. What about it?"

"There was a check inside for twelve hundred dollars. Twelve hundred bucks, can you believe it?"

"That's all that was in the envelope—just a check? No letter or anything?"

"Well, there was a voucher and a note from some guy saying what a good job she had done."

"What was on the voucher?" Jane wanted to know.

" 'The NY/LA Connection.' "

"The what?"

"You asked me what was on the voucher and I told you," Anne snapped, annoyed anew at the check, at the girl for whom it was meant.

" 'The NY/LA Connection,' " Jane repeated. "Maybe

that's the title of an article she did or something like that."

"Obviously," Anne remarked dryly. "What I can't figure out is how come so much money. The only thing I can think of is that she's a photographer. Magazines pay a lot for pictures, don't they?" There was in her last words an almost imperceptible hint of beseechment for agreement.

"They do," Janey said, "but that's not a lot of money for a writer, either."

"She's not a writer," Anne stated firmly.

"How do you know that?"

Anne ignored the question. "It's impossible."

"Why? Lots of people are writers." Jane's voice was innocent of guile or deliberate meanness. She knew Anne wanted to write; her remark was a statement of fact, not a way to wound.

"Of course lots of people are writers," Anne almost shouted, "but she's not!"

"I don't know what you're getting so excited about. I wouldn't be at all surprised if that money was for an article she wrote. Come to think of it, I remember hearing about an Anne Fletcher once, Anne N. Fletcher I think she goes by, and she had something to do with magazines. I'm sure that's it, Anne. She's a writer."

Anne did not speak. Her hand gripped the receiver with almost painful intensity. She breathed deeply, trying to slow the rapid beating of her heart.

"Anne, are you still there? Anne?"

"She is not a writer. Do you understand that? She is not a writer and don't you ever say anything like that to me again. Ever."

"I don't know what you're making such a big deal about. Why—"

"The only Anne Fletcher who's a writer is *me! Me!*"

"Okay, okay, just calm down," Janey said, confused by the vehemence of her friend's reaction. "After all, it's

71

not as if you've actually ever written anything. Besides, what if she is a writer? What has that got to do with you and your writing?"

"Everything. Nothing. Can't we get off this damn subject? I'm sick to death of this girl. Her calls, her mail, now this. I'm sick of it!"

Silence was Jane's reply; there could be no other. She found it difficult, impossible to believe that her closest friend could become so totally irrational about a person she did not know; it made no sense. There were zillions of people in the world doing things she wished she could do, but that didn't drive *her* off the wall. Somewhere there was probably even a Jane Ebersole with her own newspaper by-line, so what? If Anne wanted to write so badly, then she should write, and not get so unbalanced because someone else was—someone who just happened to have the same name. Maybe she would try to reason with her, but not now. Anne was in no frame of mind for logical discussion.

"I have to go now," Anne said abruptly.

"Are you okay?" Jane asked softly.

"You're wrong. I just want you to know that. You're wrong." And she hung up.

With mechanical slowness, Anne reached for a glass from the cupboard and let the water in the sink run until it was very cold. She drank until she felt that awful pulsing in her brain ebb, the banging of her heart ease. The white points framing her mouth began to fade, but her eyes did not refocus on her surroundings. They were seeing only what they chose to see.

She returned to her bedroom. She ran her fingers over the small digital Panasonic clock-radio on the night table. She looked at the dust, her chipped nail polish, the time of 7:37; she saw none of this. She sat on the edge of her bed, her queen-sized platform bed that had taken her almost two months to find at a price she could afford. She had wanted wood, not Formica; built-ins, not attachments, and she had wanted this because the picture she had seen of one in Bloomingdale's catalogue had astounded her with its sex appeal. She could be satisfied with no less. It would be an extraordinary bed for an extraordinary girl. She would be on that bed looking like a *Cosmopolitan* cover girl, wearing a deeply décolleté negligee of mauve chiffon, spooning whipped cream-covered strawberries from a crystal champagne glass into the sensuous mouth of a hirsute and almost-brutal looking man who was still glistening from their abandoned lovemaking.

It had never happened quite that way—never as pretty, or romantic, or sensual. And the mauve negligee had never been unwrapped from her mind. But such thoughts did not concern Anne now. *She's a writer. That's it, she's a writer.* The words echoed in her mind like a vicious curse.

7

Anne's head was bent over a printer's galley, her thick shoulder-length hair affording a frail veil of privacy as it cut off her vision from the traffic in the corridor. Her office window faced the brick and steel-gated windows of a transient hotel. Her office door faced the desks of three editorial assistants with constantly ringing telephones and clacking typewriters, and the frequently trafficked corridor that led to the lavatories. The outside wall of her office was made of glass so even with her door closed, there was no real privacy.

At the two-rap knock on the door, Anne picked up her head. "Hi, Sandy," she greeted, glad to stop her work.

The girl standing in the doorway came into Anne's office, and sat down in the one chair available.

"Felt like a break," the girl named Sandy said. "I'm almost finished editing the new Fischer manuscript. You know, we've been publishing her for what, three years now? The successor to Judy Blume, right? Meanwhile, six books later, the only ones calling her that are us." She shook her head, glanced at the galleys on Anne's desk. "What's that?"

"Crap," Anne said with disgust. She pushed the pages

to the side of the desk as if putting distance between herself and a foul-smelling object. "I wish I could find another job," she complained.

"You know how often you say that?" Sandy remarked. "At least twice a week. Why don't you do something about it if you're so miserable here?"

Anne looked at the girl with whom she was friendliest in the office. Sandy Bradlaw did not understand Anne's dissatisfaction, as Anne could not relate to Sandy's enjoyment of her job. How could anybody who considered herself an intelligent human being actually like dealing with children's books?

"I have been looking," she finally said.

"And? Anything?" Sandy prompted.

Anne shrugged. "Nothing. They wanted me to start as an associate editor so I told them no. Not at a paperback house."

"Why? If you hate this so much and you're offered—"

"I'm not going to take a step down," Anne snapped. "Would you?"

"Sure, if it meant doing what I wanted to do and getting out of something I couldn't stand. Besides, you're not stuck at that level. You can get promoted, you know."

Anne shook her head. "No. And anyway, if I get started on a new job when will I have time to work on my novel? At least I rarely have to take this place home with me at night."

"Hey, does that mean you've finally started?" Sandy asked. She had heard about Anne's writing and her novel for two years, since she had first met her. In the beginning, she had not quite understood Anne's insistence on not writing anything unless it was literature, nor had she agreed with her denigration of commercial books. Later, she had jokingly accused Anne of using every excuse possible to avoid writing because she was afraid that she *couldn't* write. Anne's reaction had been such venomous rage that the two girls had not spoken for three months, not until Anne invited her over for dinner one night, with no word of apology. Since then, Sandy rarely brought up the subject of adult writing, and never referred to Anne's ambition unless she instigated it into a conversation, as she had just now.

"Not exactly," Anne reluctantly admitted. Then, quickly, "But I'd never be able to do it if I changed jobs."

Sandy nodded in understanding, variations of the sub ject having become a commonplace. Anne would complain about the job, Sandy would suggest alternatives, Anne would find something wrong with each of them, every time. Sandy suspected that Anne preferred to point a finger and blame when she was unhappy; it was less risky than action. Many were the times she had heard Anne accuse a man of being weak, boring, unreliable, a lousy lover, smelling bad—*after* he had stopped calling. Many were the times she had listened as Anne blamed their boss—a kindly and fair man, Sandy thought—for holding her back and not promoting her into the adult division, though Anne knew that such a decision was made by that division's editor-in-chief, whom she had never approached.

Despite Anne's affliction with what Sandy called the "bitch and moan" syndrome, she liked her. Anne was great to go to the bars with, and Sandy enjoyed the sharp humor she exhibited at another's expense. It was mean, Sandy knew, but it was funny. She also, or perhaps primarily, liked Anne because there was something a little pathetic about her, and it bolstered her own self-confidence to know *she* was otherwise.

Anne prided herself on being different. Not different peculiar; different exceptional, she had once hastened to explain when Sandy had told her she was a chronic complainer. Anne had denied it vehemently, saying that being dissatisfied and striving for more were not the hallmarks of a complainer but of someone who challenged, who did not accept life blindly. The ordinary person accepted, the extraordinary defied, she had proclaimed with an air of pedantry. When Sandy had pointed out that pushing yourself where you don't belong was a dead-end challenge, achieving little, Anne had silenced her with the kind of haughty look of disdain one reserves for simpletons, and that had been the end of the discussion. But from that day on, Sandy had recognized that desperate need of Anne's, almost a compulsion, to be special as rather pathetic; it was a flaw that made Sandy more tolerant of Anne's moods and unreasonableness than she normally would be.

"By the way, I forgot to tell you," Sandy now said. "I saw Arthur a couple of nights ago."

Anne's eyes widened with interest, but all she said was, "That's nice," in a casual, unconcerned tone. So, he's back, she thought, and he didn't call—not that you really expected him to. Well, easy come, easy go.

"That's all you have to say, 'that's nice'?" Sandy said, surprised. From the two times she and a date had gone out with them, and from past conversations, she had assumed Anne cared about Arthur. But come to think of it, those conversations had been a while ago; maybe they weren't seeing each other anymore.

"What should I do, get all excited just because you saw some jerk I used to date," Anne said irritably. She forced a fraudulent smile. "Sorry, I didn't mean to snap, but I really don't care. Arthur's a nice enough guy but not my type. Too much take, too selfish."

Sandy shrugged. "Well, then I guess it won't bother you that he was with a girl."

Anne laughed away the quick stab of jealousy that pricked at her. She knew she did not care who Arthur went out with or that he no longer called her; proprietary rights had caused the reaction. "No, it won't bother me," she said. "Where'd you see him?"

Sandy mentioned a well-known Mexican restaurant.

"It was the weirdest thing," she said. "We were about to be seated when I spotted him. I went over to say hello, and he introduced me to the girl he was with."

"What's so funny about that?"

"Will you please let me finish?" Sandy said, relishing her narration. "He said her name was Anne Fletcher and I—"

"What?" It was a whisper, a breath that shuddered with disbelief.

Sandy nodded. "It's true. He said her name was Anne Fletcher and I said that was impossible, and the girl said that was really her name. She didn't seem too put off by my reaction," Sandy went on, as if just realizing that herself. "Maybe Arthur told her about you. I thought it was the funniest coincidence. Can you imagine—two girls with the same name and Arthur has dated them both. He must really get around."

A horrifying buzz went off in Anne's head, and she could feel the saliva die in her mouth. No, not this too, her mind screamed. She can't have him, she *can't*. I won't let her.

"What did she look like?" Anne managed to say, her voice sounding squeaky with desperation in her ears. But Sandy did not seem to notice, nor did she find anything unusual in the intense way Anne was staring at her, the green eyes rock hard.

"Pretty, I guess. I don't really know, I didn't stay at their table too long."

"Think, dammit," Anne hissed, her shoulders hunched, her hands gripping a pencil. "Think. Blonde, brunette, thin, fat, what? Tell me, Sandy. Tell me what she looked like!"

Now there was no missing the undisguised, uncontrolled hunger in Anne's voice, her posture, her face. Sandy shook her head and smiled smugly. "For someone who doesn't care about a man, you're incredibly interested in the girl he was with."

"Sandy, damn you—"

"All right, but I told you, I didn't stick around long enough to make a full inventory. She had brown hair cut in a layered kind of style, not short, not long. She seemed thin but I couldn't really tell since she was sitting down. She was pretty, not a knockout, but pretty. If it's any consolation, you're prettier."

"She wasn't a blonde, with glasses? Was she dressed in a plain white blouse? She was flat-chested, right? I bet she was flat-chested. She has to be."

Sandy laughed. "From what I could tell, she wasn't at all flat-chested. She was wearing a turtleneck sweater and she seemed to wear it well. Why did you think she'd be flat-chested or wear glasses? Do you know her?" Sandy asked with curiosity.

"No, no, of course not. I just thought . . . I was so sure . . ." Anne mumbled, not looking at the other girl. Then, with that same intense stare, she asked about Arthur.

"What about him?"

"How was he acting toward her? Affectionate, interested, bored, what?"

Sandy was losing patience. "Anne, I stopped by his table for a minute to say hello. I had a date waiting for me. I did not make a tour of inspection, only a friendly hello. I do not know how he was acting because I did not care to take notice. Now, is this third degree over?" She got up from the chair. When Anne did not respond, Sandy muttered, "See you later," and left.

Anne did not answer because she had stopped listening. She was locked away in a private hell where frustration smoldered, and jealousy blistered. Wherever I turn, whatever I do, *she*'s there, stealing from me, laughing at me. It isn't enough that she has my name. It isn't enough that she gets flowers and cards and calls from other men; she has to take *my* man from me now. *My man*.

And at this particular moment, Arthur Dumont was

Anne's man. She no longer felt casual about him; forgotten was the fact that he had never meant more to her than someone to fill up her time and her bed; lost was the certainty that he was not her type. All Anne could play and replay in her mind was that Arthur was seeing Anne Fletcher, and it was not her.

Her movements sharp jabs of nervous energy, Anne thumbed through her personal telephone directory for Arthur's office number, then she jotted it down on a piece of notepaper. She would call him, confront him with what she knew, dare him to explain away the outrageous disloyalty of his actions. For that was what Anne considered his dating this other girl: a betrayal. But he would never see it that way; he would placate her, the way Sandy had by saying she was prettier; he would not truly understand how deeply he had hurt her. And she was hurt; with the frustration and the jealousy was acute disappointment that Arthur could be so callow, so insensitive as to want *her*.

She dialed his number. His secretary told her he was in conference, and Anne left word he should call her.

For the next sixty minutes she sat at her desk, staring at the same galley pages, the red pencil poised in her hand but unmoving. Her head was bent over, her hair a shield, but even had someone come in, her self-absorption was so evident as to turn any visitor away.

At the end of the hour, she glanced at her watch, and realized it was lunchtime. He wouldn't call now, and just as well, she thought. This will give me more time to figure out exactly what to say to him. Maybe I shouldn't confront him, she thought; maybe I should wait to see what he has to say; taunt him a little and out of guilt he'll confess. Yes, the more she considered it, the more she liked that plan. There was something deliciously subtle and shrewd about it that appealed to her.

Two hours went by, hours when the rest of the office was out, and Anne thought with utter logic and clarity.

She told herself how ridiculous she was being. Arthur owed her nothing, certainly not loyalty. She took the full responsibility for her overreaction. She knew, foolish as it was, that her anger was not because Arthur was seeing another girl, but because that other girl was *her*. And then, as swiftly as the lucid thoughts had come, they disappeared, replaced with the conviction of betrayal, murky images to blame.

At three-thirty, the telephone rang.

"Hello?"

"Hi."

"Hi, honey. This is a nice surprise. Or did you call to tell me you're going to be tied up tonight?"

"Didn't you call this morning?" Arthur asked, puzzled.

"No. I was at my publisher's for most of the morning."

"You didn't call at around 11:30?" Arthur repeated.

Anne laughed. "No, I didn't call. Why would I say no if I had called?"

Arthur's laugh was self-conscious with confusion. "Well, there was a message for me that Anne Fletcher called and so . . ." His words trailed off as understanding dawned on him, swiftly followed by embarrassment. "Oh."

The silence at the other end told Arthur that Anne, too, had realized what happened. "I haven't seen her in months," he explained. "I don't know why she's calling me."

"I doubt it's for legal advice," Anne remarked dryly. "Why don't you just call her back and find out."

"No, I—"

"Arthur, call her back. That way we'll *both* be satisfied."

"You jealous?" he whispered.

"Maybe," Anne teased, a smile in her voice.

"Good. I'll see you tonight."

" 'Bye."

Arthur debated for a moment whether to call Anne Fletcher. He had nothing to say to her, but he supposed it never hurt to keep all options open. He and Anne, *Annie*, might not last forever; it might not always be this good with them, and the other Anne Fletcher was at least an available piece of ass. Yeah, he better call her.

At four o'clock, the phone rang, the ping ponging of her heart seemed louder in her ears. Five times the phone had rung; five times her chest had felt as if it were being stretched to bursting; five times it had not been Arthur, and she had, five times, exercised painful self-control by not calling him again.

"Hello?"

"Hello, Anne? This is Arthur. Dumont. I got a message you called."

Play it nice, play it calm, sweet, friendly. "Hi, Arthur, how are you?"

"Busy," came the curt reply. "Was there any particular reason you called?"

"No-o," she stretched out the word into a tickle, an invitation to play. "I haven't spoken to you in such a long time and I just thought, wouldn't it be nice to call Arthur and see how's he doing."

"I've been out of town."

"Oh, that's right. Tucson, wasn't it? Did you have a nice trip? Successful, as always?"

Anne could not see the puzzled expression Arthur gave the receiver, but had she, she would have been pleased. The conversation was going exactly as she desired: confusing him, throwing him just slightly off guard, lulling him into a sense of easy friendliness that would get him to confess his transgression. She smiled smugly, her red pencil doodling small, tight circles on the nearby note pad.

"I'm sorry," she quickly said when she realized Arthur

had spoken. "Someone came in for a second. What were you saying?"

"I said it was Phoenix, and it was okay." Arthur's voice held enough asperity for Anne to notice.

"Phoenix then. Isn't all of Arizona the same?" Her laugh was tinny. "So, how are you?"

"Okay, I guess. Busy as hell. You know how these business trips are, always lots to catch up on when you get back."

"But you've been back a while, Arthur. I would think you'd—"

"How'd you know that?"

Again, the tinny laugh. Don't confront him, let him tell it, let him admit it. But after an afternoon of self-control, after several hours of willing herself to act as if nothing were wrong, her energy was gone. She no longer had the ability to pretend, or to wait for him. "Sandy told me," she said quietly, traces of the teasing tickle gone with her willpower.

"Sandy?"

"Sandy Bradlaw," Anne explained.

"Sandy Bradlaw, Sandy Bradlaw," Arthur mumbled in recollection. Then, "Oh, right, the girl who works with you. We doubled with her a couple of times. I remember now," he said. "Yeah, I saw her the other night at Tio Pepe's. Great Mexican food. Best black bean soup I've ever had."

Anne gaped at the telephone in utter amazement. That's it? she thought. That's all he has to say about it? Her pencil began to jab the notepaper, hard lines forming inescapable boxes.

"She mentioned you were with a very pretty girl," Anne said. Admit it, damn you! Don't make me drag this out of you.

Again, she could not see the expression on his face. For now he was smiling with the understanding of why she had called. He could tell her about the coincidence of the other Anne Fletcher, he was thinking, but he chose not to. He owed this girl nothing; she was unimportant to him except as someone to keep in reserve, and there were plenty more like her if he needed that. Explaining who he was with did not appeal to Arthur; he explained when he wanted to or when he needed to; he did not need to with Anne Fletcher, and he certainly did not want to.

"Look, Anne," he now said, "I've really got to run. I'll call you soon. We'll have drinks, dinner—"

"That's what you said before you left for Tucson," she reminded him. "Do you make empty promises to all your girlfriends?" It was a stab in the dark, one last effort to get him to tell her. She would not accuse; he must admit. To put him in a defensive position, to force him to explain did not serve her purposes, for the day would come—she was sure of it—when he would run back to her, grateful if she would see him. Then, *then* she would have him where she could hurt him.

"It was Phoenix." Anne heard his sigh of impatience. "And this time I mean it. I promise."

"I want to go to that Mexican restaurant."

"Sure, sure, wherever. Talk to you soon. 'Bye."

Anne did not say good-bye; she softly replaced the receiver and then tore off the three pages of doodles, tossed them into the wastebasket. It had not gone as she had planned.

With that realization, the few lucid moments she had experienced earlier in the day returned with shameful insistence. Who was she fooling? She had never meant anything to him and he won't come back unless he wants sex and she'll never have him where she could hurt him because she didn't really want to hurt him, just her. And that's absurd. This whole day has been absurd—calling him, preparing what to say, pretending that he cared, that she cared. She had been a fool, and she was grateful only that she had not confronted him as she had originally planned.

Only when that bitch is in the picture do I get like this, she thought, furious with herself. It's as if I lose focus, everything gets distorted, blurred, off-balance. Like that night when I made him dinner. I went out of control and I had gotten her flowers by mistake that day. And the other evening when Janey called, I was like a raving lunatic just because she suggested that the girl might be a writer. Whenever she's around, something snaps. I've got to stop being so irrational about her. If she had any other name, it wouldn't matter. And that's a dumb reason to get so upset. It's a name, just a damn name.

Anne silently repeated this litany of logic for the rest of the afternoon, then at home that evening. She was still repeating it as she picked up the telephone and dialed 555-7315, the number that had been scribbled months ago on her note pad; the number she had never thrown out.

"Hello?"

No response.

"Hello? Who is this?"

No response.

"Hello? Hello? Who's there?"

No response. Click. Then Anne hung up, too, feeling almost as imbecilic as she had after her conversation with Arthur.

When she had come home this evening, she had tried to do a crossword puzzle, read, watch TV, in that order. She could not get Anne Fletcher from her mind, no matter how logical her interior chant. She decided that if she spoke to her, told her her name and that they both knew Arthur Dumont; had a conversation with her, then she would be able to exorcise the demon of irrationality within her. She would hear her voice, and that, combined with what Sandy had told her and what she already had pieced together, would complete the image and satisfy her curiosity.

So Anne had dialed the number. But with the first hello, she had turned mute. She suddenly realized the folly in telling this stranger that they shared a name, a man. She did not speak, and so, when she hung up, the image was still incomplete, her curiosity was not further satisfied; the demon still raged.

Anne sat in the taupe Ultra-suede chair, surrounded by the silver walls, the chocolate brown-framed cosmetic mirrors, the shuffle and slide of the hairdressers and their assistants, the ohs and nos of the clients. She glanced disinterestedly around her, wishing Jerry would schedule his appointments better. For forty dollars a haircut, she should not have to wait. Idly, she fingered the ends of her hair, contemplating leaving. But the feel was dry, split, unhealthy; she needed a trim now. She motioned to one of the hipless assistants to bring her a magazine.

Anne began flipping the pages of the current issue of *Glamour*, the preview of summer fashions assaulting her eyes with colors hot and inviting. There was an article she ignored about the morning-after pill; recipes to make chicken more exciting, which she skimmed; a page of exercises to trim the waist; an article about getting credit; a feature about six successful women under thirty-five. She began to read. The first woman was thirty and a filmstrip editor for IBM, earning a salary that afforded her the luxury of not having to cook for her attorney husband or pick up her two children from private school each day. Her picture showed her to be blonde and bland. The second was thirty-four, divorced, no children, and the owner of a public relations firm that specialized in promoting only other female-owned companies. She started the business with the money she received from her divorce settlement. Her photograph revealed a woman at least thirty pounds overweight with a smile that was falsely jolly. The third was twenty-eight years old, a free-lance writer whose first novel was soon to be published. She liked to cook, especially veal piccata; she collected porcelain boxes; she loved animals too much to keep a pet in her New York City apartment. She did not exercise regularly except for ballet classes. She loved being independent and free. Her name was Anne N. Fletcher, a name that had often appeared as the by-line for some of *Glamour*'s most popular articles.

Her name was Anne N. Fletcher.

Her name was Anne N. Fletcher.

Over and over and over again the words screamed in her brain, like a church bell ringing madly. With horrified fascination, she turned the page. There was the picture. Black and white. Sitting at a typewriter. Jaw-length hair, feathered away from her face to reveal a patrician nose, a beautiful smile, a chin that jutted too far. Anne read a line, then glanced at the picture. Read a line, glanced at the picture, and the truth of existence of this other Anne Fletcher was imprinted onto her consciousness with indisputable finality.

No, she was not a feminist, she liked men too much. Yes, she would like to get married someday if she could find a man who could be her friend as well as lover. Writing her novel and then having it accepted by a publisher were the greatest thrills she had ever known. Her favorite clothes were anything loose and unrestricting.

"Miss Fletcher?"

Her advice to anyone who wanted to be a writer was to write. Don't be afraid, just do it.

"Miss Fletcher? Jerry's ready for you now."

Reluctantly, Anne shifted her eyes from the magazine to the voice standing over her.

"What?" she whispered.

"Jerry's ready now. For your haircut?"

"Yes, yes, of course," she murmured. She hastily tore out the article and picture of Anne N. Fletcher. She patted the slickness of the paper which she kept in her lap as her hair was being washed; it was not a caress of comfort or of affection; it was the feel of ownership.

"I want to change the style, Jerry," she stated when she was seated in the chair, and Jerry, bearded, blond, inconspicuously homosexual, began to comb her hair. "A cut, not just a trim."

"But your hair is magnificent, it suits you."

"I don't care. I want it cut. Like this. Exactly like this." She showed him the picture of Anne N. Fletcher, the picture of the patrician nose, the too-long chin, the feathered hairstyle.

"Who's that?" he wanted to know.

"No one. This is the haircut I want."

"But it's all wrong for you. A cut like that will make your face too round, and it won't show up your gorgeous eyes."

"I want this haircut, Jerry. Exactly the way it is in this photograph. If you won't give it to me, I'll find someone who will." Her voice was as hard as her eyes, as tight as the set of her lips.

"But why when it's so obviously unsuitable. I really—"

Anne whipped off the towel around her neck and began to get up from the chair. Jerry's hand on her shoulder gently persuaded her to sit back down. "All right, all right," he said with a sigh. "I don't know why you want it, but you're paying so . . ." And he shrugged, replacing the towel.

"That's right," she said in a clipped tone, "*I'm* paying." Suddenly, she smiled. "You'll see," she said sweetly, "it'll be great. I'm going to look better than she does." And her painted nail jabbed emphatically at the photograph in her lap.

While her hairdresser parted and combed and cut and layered and stood back and recut, Anne felt none of the panic that usually accompanies a drastic change in hairstyle. She had not worn her hair any way but long and straight since college. That made little difference now as she watched her face take on a fuller look, as her cheekbones—never prominent—became soft and boneless under the fluttery cut. She looked pretty; not as sexy as before, but sweeter. Her eyes were like huge round green stones, and there seemed to be a youthful innocence deflected off them that had been missing under all the hair. It was a nice haircut, and she looked nice, not great. She did not care. She had made a choice, taken a step. It was a start.

She blinked and a tiny upward curve of the lips flicked across her mouth. Innocence vanished from her face as if it had been a smudge of dirt.

"You got your hair cut!" Janey exclaimed. "I think I like it. I'm not sure, turn around, let me see the back."

Anne swiveled on the barstool. "Well, what do you think?"

"It's nice, I guess. It's just so different, I wasn't expecting it. I think it'll take me a little time to get used to. What in the world made you do it? You who had to practically be drugged before submitting to so much as a trim."

"I needed a change, that's all." Anne sipped from her bloody mary. "You ought to get your hair cut."

Janey instinctively put her hand to her head, touching the reddish brown curls that sprang coillike from her scalp. "What's wrong with my haircut?" she asked, worried.

"It's dated. That afro business went out years ago. You ought to grow up, get something sophisticated, like mine." Before Janey could defend herself, Anne said, "Why did you pick this dump? You know it's always dead."

"That's not true. We've been here before when there were plenty of guys. You never told me you didn't like it."

Anne did not answer as she surveyed the room at the White Unicorn, an Upper East Side restaurant/bar with a reputation for a quiet singles scene. The two girls sat in silence for a while as the restaurant gradually filled with diners, and the empty stools around the bar became occupied.

"You hungry yet?" Jane finally asked.

Anne shook her head without lifting her eyes from the swizzle stick in the glass.

"I stopped seeing Michael," Janey said.

"You already told me that, two weeks ago when it first happened, and three times since then. I warned you he was a loser," Anne reminded her self-righteously.

"He was not!" Janey quickly came to her ex-boyfriend's defense.

"I don't know what you call a detective with three children to provide support for, but I call that a loser." Anne paused. "If he's not a loser, why did you stop seeing him?"

"I told you. He's moving to Michigan. What was I supposed to do, keep up a romance between here and Detroit?"

"It's better than nothing."

Janey looked thoughtful. "What are we going to do about New Year's? Neither of us has anybody now."

Anne turned away in disgust. "You're a child, you

know that, really a child. Who gives a shit about New Year's. That's three weeks away, and what's so important about it anyway? A lot of hyped-up hypocrisy if you ask me."

"Well . . ." Janey answered slowly, somewhat intimidated by Anne's belligerence, "it would be nice to have a date, I guess."

"It would be nice to have a date, I guess," Anne mimicked nastily, her voice whinier than the original. "When are you going to grow up, huh? Valentines and lace, that's you. 'I'll know when I fall in love.' You still believe in happy endings, Janey. That's your whole problem."

"Well, you don't, and that's your whole problem," the other girl retorted.

Anne laughed derisively. "That's where you're wrong, Janey. I do believe in happy endings, the real kind, the kind you create for yourself, not the make-believe one you have your heart set on."

"Let's not get started on this again," Jane tried, not enjoying the conversation or her friend's mood. She had needed to get out of her apartment tonight, wanted to have a few drinks and see if a spark could be ignited with someone. Anne was taking all the fun out of the evening. Janey did not want a serious conversation; she did not want to defend her idealism

"I'm not starting anything," Anne argued. "*You* started it with that business about New Year's."

"Okay, fine, can we drop it now, please?" Jane asked placatingly.

Anne hesitated, then there was a quick stretch of the lips that one had to be familiar with to recognize as a smile. "I'm sorry," she said. "I'm just being bitchy. Maybe I care more about the holidays than I like to admit."

Janey smiled, relieved that they might still have a good time tonight. "We'll find something to do."

"Oh, something isn't the problem," Anne corrected. "It's finding someone to do something with."

They laughed, and the tension drifted to the back of the room with the rest of the sounds and smoke of the bar.

"Want to see something really disgusting?" Anne soon asked. Without waiting for an answer, she reached into her purse, and tossed some paper on the bar in front of Janey. "Look at that, it's nauseating."

Janey picked up the paper, and stared at the photograph of Anne N. Fletcher. Then she looked at her friend, back at the picture, to Anne again.

"You got her hairstyle!" she declared. "You went out and had your hair cut like hers." She began to laugh. "Oh, Anne, you're really something. Just needed a change, huh?" And because she was still laughing she did not see the rage building in the emerald green eyes.

"Shut up!" Anne hissed.

"But why did you do it? Why do you want to look like her, you're much prettier," Janey pursued, undaunted.

"I said shut up, didn't I? I did not get my hair cut to look like her."

"Of course you did. It's the exact same haircut. What I don't understand is why. Your hair was gorgeous, everyone always said so."

"Maybe if you'd read the damn article instead of laughing like a jackass you'd understand," Anne said in a tone of scorching condescension.

"Okay, okay, I'll read it, just calm down."

As Jane read, Anne concentrated on the swizzle stick, turning it around and around with greater force the more she thought about the article. "Well?" she asked impatiently when it seemed that Jane was taking too long.

"I'm almost finished." Then, she gathered the pages and neatly arranged them on the bar top. "So?"

"So? That's your reaction, so?"

Janey looked puzzled. "What should I say? I told you she was a writer, didn't I?"

"And you don't think she's disgusting?"

"Disgusting? No, not at all. She seems like a very interesting girl. I don't know what you find so disgusting about her, and I still don't understand why you went and got your hair cut like hers, either."

Anne turned toward Jane's barstool, the upper half of her body hunched forward, unmasked loathing glinting off her eyes like sunlight from a mirror. "She disgusts me because she's so damned perfect. Miss Mount Holyoke, Miss Free and Independent, Miss Successful. I hate her."

"Anne, you're being totally unreasonable," Janey said quietly, startled by her friend's fierceness.

"Am I? I don't think so. I don't think so at all." She slapped at the papers on the bar. "Look at her, the bitch. She gets it all. *All!* The men, the calls, the flowers, her first novel published. I hate her." Her voice was the vicious rattle of a venomous snake.

"What are you talking about? What men?" Janey wanted to know.

Anne cut the air with a crackle of harsh laughter. "Oh, I didn't tell you, did I? Wonderful Arthur Dumont, that bastard you're always asking me about, is now seeing *her.*" This time she pushed at the papers so that they scattered over the edge of the bar and fluttered into Janey's lap.

Janey began to laugh. She tried to stop when Anne fixed her with a poisonous glare. "I'm sorry, but it *is* funny. Arthur seeing two girls with the same name. You've got to admit that's a pretty funny coincidence."

"It's disloyal and traitorous," Anne stated matter-of-factly.

At that, Janey did not try to contain her amusement. "Oh, c'mon, you're taking this too seriously. So what if she has your name and she's seeing Arthur? What in the world does that have to do with you?"

"Everything."

"That makes a lot of sense."

"Don't you see?" Anne said, her tone imploring her friend to understand, to agree. "She's taking everything away from me, my talent, my man, my career, *me*." She turned back toward her drink. "That's why I got my hair cut," she said softly. "Not to look like her but to take something from her, the way she takes everything from me. It's a little revenge—and it's only the beginning."

Jane's laughter had abruptly stopped when she heard the pride, the boast in Anne's voice. Something was terribly wrong. She did not understand what was happening, but she realized that for some bizarre reason, her friend was becoming obsessed with this other girl, someone she had never met. The concept was staggering to her, and a little frightening.

"Anne, you're working yourself up over nothing. She's—"

"It's not *nothing*, it's everything!" Anne pounced. "How dare she pretend to be all that . . . that perfect. How dare she take my name, my boyfriend . . . how dare she write a novel when I—"

Jane's voice was sharp, an order. "Stop it, Anne. Stop it right now. You have no idea how ridiculous you sound, how . . . how unbalanced." She waited for Anne to refute the accusation, for her to turn it around to make Jane seem the irrational one. When she did not, Jane felt she was being given an opportunity to restore logic to the conversation.

"This girl has taken nothing from you. So she has your name, big deal. So she goes out with Arthur. You've told me often enough that he was just another guy, so this suddenly possessive attitude makes no sense at all. You're jealous, Anne, that's really what it is."

95

"Jealous! You're crazy!" Anne hurled back.

"You know I'm right so don't try to argue. You're jealous because she's written what you want to do—done a novel. Arthur is just an excuse, it's the writing that's really gotten to you, and that's not fair." Janey paused, and when she again spoke her voice was gentler, a warm blanket of understanding for her friend to wrap herself in. "Anne, you can't blame her for your unhappiness. You can't be jealous of a total stranger, and that's what she is. You're making her into something she's not. She has absolutely nothing to do with you, with your life, with your writing. The fault is with you, not her."

"What the hell is that supposed to mean?"

"It means," Janey explained patiently, "that you take yourself too seriously." She gave a little shake of her head. "You know, you have a great sense of humor when it comes to putting someone down, but when it comes to yourself, everything is intense with importance. If it wasn't, then you'd be able to see that you're using her to make an excuse for yourself, for what you're *not* doing with your life. It's laughable to think you've had revenge on her by getting her haircut. But you believe it, you're serious about it, and that's why the fault is yours." She placed her hand on Anne's outstretched forearm. "Why can't you be satisfied with who you are?" she asked almost tenderly. "You're bright, pretty, you have a good job, plenty of men, lots of girls would be—"

Anne shook off the hand, and laughed hollowly. "Bright, pretty, a good job? Maybe that's enough for some people, for someone like you, but I want more. I deserve more. *I* deserve it, not her."

Janey stared at Anne's profile, silence finally being the only answer she had. Perhaps if she did not know her so well, if she were only an acquaintance, Janey would vow not to see her again, too appalled to want closer friendship. But Janey knew how moody Anne could be; knew she swung like a hammock in the wind with provocation as light as a summer's breeze. Her outburst tonight had been more savage than ever before, redoubtable in its single-mindedness, in its exposure of emotion. But it would pass; Jane refused to believe otherwise.

"Hey, he's not bad," Janey whispered several minutes later, elbowing Anne to look by the door where a man with a brown leather windbreaker and skintight jeans was standing.

"Hmm," Anne said with little interest. "Where's the article?"

"Right here," Janey said, handing it to her. Anne stared at the picture a moment, then carefully folded the article in four and placed it back in her purse. Janey watched her but said nothing except, "I think he's coming over here."

Anne kept her eyes on the rainbow of bottles at the back of the bar, not shifting her focus to acknowledge the presence of the man on the stool beside her. When he ordered his drink, Anne felt the breath of Janey's words on her neck: "Cute, huh?"

"Hi." Both girls turned to the male voice; Anne nodded her greeting, Janey smiled it. Then began the ritual of romance as practiced by practiced New York singles, a ritual as devoid of substance as meringue, and as tasty.

"Come here often?" the man asked Anne.

"A couple of times," Janey answered. "The food's good," she added, an excuse that never fooled anyone.

"Live around here?" he asked Anne.

"I live around the corner, and my friend lives up on East Eighty-first."

"My name's Doug."

"I'm Anne, and this is Janey."

"Jane," she corrected.

"I'm in computers," he volunteered. "Data processing actually."

"Oh, you mean like for IBM or something?" Janey asked.

"No, I work for an advertising agency in their data processing department."

Janey nodded. "I'm sort of in advertising, too. I write copy for ads in a trade journal."

The data processor did not care. "What about you, Anne, was that it? What do you do?"

Anne clasped hard onto the top of her purse that was resting in her lap. A small smile played around her mouth, and her eyes seemed to film over slightly, lessening their brightness as if with protective coloring. "I'm a writer," she answered, for the first time turning her face entirely to him. "I write articles for magazines, and I'm also a novelist."

"Anne!"

Neither Anne nor the data processor paid any attention to Janey's interruption, and so neither heard the shock in the voice.

"That's really fascinating," Doug said, pleased with himself that he had chosen the right one. He only hoped that she was not too smart; that could make things difficult.

"I like it," she agreed, her back to Jane. She laughed coyly. "I'm sure you don't read such things, but there's an article about me in this month's issue of *Glamour* magazine."

"Stop it, Anne, stop it. This isn't funny." Jane's whisper was urgent, desperate. "If this is your idea of a prank, it's sick."

Anne shot her a look of contempt that withered her into silence. She turned back to the man.

"They did an article on six successful women and I was one of them," she went on. "Not that it means anything, of course," she quickly assured him, "but it is exciting."

"I'm impressed," Doug said. "What kind of novel do you write? Something sexy, huh? I just bet you write very sexy stuff." His voice had dropped into a deep, husky insinuation of her sex appeal.

"Yes, Anne," Janey taunted from her side, "exactly what kind of novel is it? Why don't you tell us all about it?" Then, again in a whisper, "Squirm out of that one, why don't you? Now stop this, Anne, stop it!"

Anne ignored her. "Oh, I don't like to talk about my work," she said to Doug. "I'd much rather you go out and buy it."

"What's the title?" he asked.

"Well, it's not really decided yet," she said easily. "I like one title and my publishers like another. I guess we'll have to decide soon because the book is coming out early next year."

Janey sat there listening, toying with the frayed edges of the napkin underneath her glass, shredding the paper into little balls of confusion and bewilderment and disbelief . . . and fear. Why was Anne doing this? Why was she pretending, lying? What was happening to her? For a brief moment, Janey contemplated unmasking Anne, suggesting she show this man the article with its picture, but she could not bring herself to do that to her best friend. Perceptively, she realized that Anne was capable of such cruelty, if the mood were sour or hostile enough. But she would not do that; instead, she would sit mute, and listen with incredulity and wonder as Anne played this practical joke. For that's what it must be, just a joke. And at least the anger, the bitterness that had surrounded her like a hot summer fog was burning away with the pleasure of her pretense. Anne was now having a good time, and for that Janey was thankful. After all, it was only a little joke that hurt nobody.

Doug slipped his tie under the collar of his half-open shirt; he did not bother to reknot it. He got his jacket from the vanity stool where he had put it earlier.

"Great bed you got there," he remarked. "Makes it all a little sexier, know what I mean? I like it."

Anne made no comment as she put on her robe, the transparent pink batiste one. She was impatient for him to leave, and conversation might encourage him to stay.

"Sorry I can't spend the night, babe, but believe me this is no hit-and-run. We'll do it again, soon." He grinned. "Gotta have another shot at that bed."

She walked him to the front door. "Thanks, babe, it's been fun. I'll call you, huh?"

"Sure, Doug. See you."

Anne closed the door and went back to her bedroom. She thought briefly of changing the sheets, decided against it. She took out her tape recorder, turned the on switch, did not speak. She had nothing she wanted to say, not even to it. She did not want to discuss Doug, a meaningless pickup who had provided her with an hour and fifteen minutes of adequate release. And she was unwilling to relate the volatile emotions that had provoked her into tonight's masquerade.

She turned off the machine, went into the bathroom to remove her makeup. She rumpled her hair, looking into the mirror, trying to get used to this new vision of herself. She saw her reflection but there was something else in the mirror, a shadow, a shadow with a patrician nose and an inviting smile and a chin that jutted a little too far. The shadow was shaking her head, and then it began to speak. "Why? Why did you lie? Why do you hate me? Why?"

Anne leaned against the sink, staring at the shadow. And quietly she cried.

9

Arthur stepped out of the embrace and gently held Anne away from him. A crease of concern appeared between his dark brows, and the tight set of his mouth deepened the furrows around his nose.

"That was about as responsive as the prosecution when it loses a case," he said softly, without blame. "What's wrong?"

Anne shook her head silently, and slipped out of his grip. "Want a drink?" she asked.

"Sure." He went to the sofa, knowing better than to push her for an explanation. He did not think anything had happened between them, but he wasn't positive. If there was one thing he had learned about her in the months they had been seeing each other—and learned to admire—it was that in the quietest, most seemingly undemanding way, she was one of the most demanding women, no, persons he had ever met. She expected people to compete against themselves, push themselves, to see if they were capable of more, question themselves to at least insure that what they believed, they truly believed and had not simply adopted.

In the beginning, Arthur's hackles had risen the first

few times she had forced him, subtly, to explain why he did certain things. But the more it happened, the more he liked it, the more he respected her ability to do it gracefully, without hurting his pride or ego. She never tried to change him; the choice was always his, but she showed him options he had been too lazy to see. So it was not impossible that something had occurred that she wished to discuss; something about him, or them, that was disturbing her. What confused and, admittedly, worried him as he sat there watching her mix the drinks at the Spanish buffet, was that she had never before used sex to put distance between them. Either something major had occurred, or she had decided to finally use the age-old weapon in every woman's arsenal.

"Here you are," she said, bringing over the drinks. "I may have put a little too much scotch in, I wasn't concentrating."

Arthur took the glass and sipped the drink. "Strong, but good," he judged. He put down his glass, took hers and placed it on the end table, then reached for her hand. "Come sit down. You know how I hate to look up to women," he teased.

"Except from certain positions," she rejoined.

"Except from certain positions," he agreed.

She sat down, and leaned back, closing her eyes. Her skin seemed to be drawn tight against her facial bones, stretched with worry. But he thought she looked almost classically beautiful at this moment, all the breeding coldly evident. He liked her better when she was merely pretty, he decided.

She opened her eyes and smiled at him. "Caught you."

He could not wait. "What's wrong, Annie? What is it?"

She sighed, sat up, sipped from her drink, little stalling actions until finally she faced him. "It's probably nothing . . ."

Arthur shook his head. "If kissing me like a limp wad of tissues is nothing, then we're in big trouble."

"Oh, it wasn't that bad," she protested mildly.

"It wasn't too good, either," he informed her. Then: "Well?"

"You know the article in *Glamour*, the interview they did of me?"

"Of course. Even before you showed me your copy, my mother sent me·the issue with the pages clipped. I forgot to tell you about that."

"Did she really?" Anne laughed.

He nodded. "There was a cute little note attached with it. Something to the effect that it would be nice to meet Wonder Woman in person."

"You're kidding?"

Arthur grimaced. "I rarely kid about my mother. Better put, she rarely gives me something to kid about. Now, what about the article? They didn't spell your name wrong, so it can't be that."

Anne smiled weakly. "I called the writer this afternoon to thank her for the nice job she did. She's been a staffer with *Glamour* for about ten or twelve years, and I used to free-lance copyedit for her so we've known each other a while. We like each other. *Liked* each other." She looked down at her drink, then back to Arthur. "She called my a hypocritical schizophrenic, Arthur," she whispered, her voice still full of shock at the recollection.

"What the—"

"I couldn't believe it, either," Anne went on. "I should have known something was wrong when she got on the phone with this incredibly curt, 'Yes?' Usually, there's, you know, a little chitchat before we get to business. But not this time. I told her what a lovely job I thought she'd done, and I thanked her. Well, that's when she lashed out at me. Called me a liar, a phony, a bitch.

And a hypocritical schizophrenic." She tried to smile, but it was a futile effort. Even after several hours, she could find no humor in the incident, nothing to alleviate her astonishment, and hurt.

"Why?" Arthur asked. "Did you find out why she felt that way?"

"She made sure I found out, believe me. I didn't have to ask," she said ruefully. "According to her, how could I have the nerve to call her *again* and pretend everything was wonderful and fine. Did I expect that she would forget the outrageous insults I had hurled at her a few days ago."

"What are you talking about?"

"That's what I said to her. I told her she must be wrong, must be mistaken, that I had been feeling bad because I hadn't called yet to thank her. She said bullshit or something similar, then said I was a sick liar. I swore to her that this was the first time I had called, and she said that two days ago her secretary had put me on the phone and for several minutes I had told her that she was a hack, that she had made me sound like a goody-two-shoes, that my photograph could win an award for distortion." Anne's face seemed to radiate the heat of her distress. "Oh, Arthur, it was just awful. I never called her and did that. I would never do such a thing."

"Of course you wouldn't, I know that," he said reassuringly, reaching out and caressing the back of her neck.

"It's a little scary," she admitted.

"Why scary?"

Anne got up and went to one of her étagères where she began to toy nervously with a porcelain box. "Because she was so sure it was me. She was shrieking at me, convinced of my guilt and she absolutely refused to believe anything I had to say."

"Look, maybe she had a fight with her boyfriend or

her boss, or she had her period or a toothache, I don't know. She took it out on you. You were a handy scapegoat, that's all."

"Oh, Arthur, you don't really believe that, do you? This woman and I were friends. You don't talk to a friend the way she spoke to me, calling me those names, no matter how miserable you feel."

"Well, then, what do you think it was, some stranger calling and impersonating you? I mean, be reasonable."

"That's exactly what I think it was," Anne stated.

"Don't be ridiculous," Arthur said, dismissing the notion.

"I'm not. That's the only thing that makes sense."

"But why?" asked the lawyer, who dealt in logic. "Why would anyone do such a thing? What would they hope to gain?"

Slowly, Anne replaced the porcelain box on the étagère shelf and returned to the sofa. "I don't know," she said softly. "I just don't know."

Arthur was silent. Reluctantly, he believed she was right. When he had said it, in jest, hoping to minimize the entire incident, a part of him had known with certainty that that was the only possible logical explanation. But why? What would be the purpose of such an impersonation? Even as he tried to answer those questions, he was aware of his relief at being guiltless; what disturbed her had nothing to do with them. It was a strange sensation for him, this caring so much about a woman.

"What are you smiling about?" she asked. "I don't find this particularly amusing, you know," she said, hurt in her voice.

"Neither do I, Annie." He hesitated. "I was smiling," he then said, almost a whisper, "because I'm glad that . . . well, that I didn't do anything . . . that you and I are okay."

She looked at him a moment, confused, and then she understood. She took his hand and squeezed it, brought

105

it to her lips and dropped a kiss on it as light as a falling blossom.

"You know, it's probably just some jealous girl out there. Somebody who resents the hell out of your success," Arthur said. "Did the woman from *Glamour* say that yours was the only rotten call or that other women interviewed had called, too?"

"She didn't say, and I didn't think to ask. I was too upset."

"It sounds plausible, don't you think? About somebody being jealous?"

"I guess," Anne admitted. "But do you know how sick that is? I mean, my gosh, that's *sick!*"

"Jealousy is probably the most destructive emotion there is," Arthur agreed. "Who knows how some of those girls who read the interview felt—seeing six women making it when they're not, when they're living with the fantasy of someday being successful, but secretly knowing, or worse even, not willing to admit, that they're never going to do it. Try to reverse the situation. Think how you'd feel."

"But Arthur, almost everyone has *some*thing they can do."

"Sure, but it might not be what they want to do. Let's say someone is doing a terrific job as a secretary but her secret ambition is to have a showing of her watercolors. The only trouble is she's a lousy artist. Well, she's either going to be inspired by reading about a painter having a showing, or she's going to feel resentful and jealous. Do you see what I'm driving at?"

Anne's expression was questioning. "You really think that could be it? Some girl out there did this because she's jealous? It's incredible. Now I wish I had asked if there had been other calls."

"You could always phone tomorrow and find out," Arthur suggested, his smile indicating that he was not serious.

Anne punched him playfully on the thigh. "I feel better, I think," she said. "It really had me shaken up, though."

"I'm sure that's what happened. If you want, wait a week or so, then either call again or write the woman a note. By then she'll have calmed down and will be ready to listen to reason."

"That's a good idea. After all, I'd hate for her to always think of me as a hypocritical schizophrenic," she said, her grin indicating that her good humor was returning.

"Now, turnabout's fair play," Arthur announced.

"What?"

"I made you feel better, now it's your turn."

Anne was instantly concerned. "Oh, Arthur, I'm sorry. I was so wrapped up in myself that—"

He edged closer to her on the sofa, and began to nuzzle the side of her neck. "Nothing a little warmth and affection won't take care of," he mumbled across her cheek, to her mouth.

This time she was as responsive as any man would want a woman to be. "Mmm, better, much better," Arthur muttered. "A little more and I'll feel good as new." Gently, he pushed her lower on the sofa, and was about to kiss her when he saw that she was doing a poor job of stifling laughter. He abruptly sat back.

"Didn't your mother ever teach you it's rude to laugh at a man when he's excited?" he said with mock severity.

Anne's laughter bubbled forth. "I'm sorry, but I couldn't help it. Look at me."

He did, and saw nothing that would provoke laughter. "I don't get it."

"It's the couch," she explained. "One foot is dangling over the side of the couch," she said, still giggling, "my other foot is twisted at an angle that's going to give me a cramp in about one more second, and you're trying to get on top of me. It's funny, don't you see how funny it is?"

Arthur looked at her position again as she wriggled her leg out of its angle. "I guess you do look kinda funny, not to mention uncomfortable. But we could remedy that easily enough. Let's move into the bedroom." His expression was little-boy hopeful.

She shook her head and sat up. "Later, lecher. Right now, I want food. I'm absolutely starving."

Arthur groaned. "Starving?"

She nodded vigorously. "Yup."

He got up from the sofa. "You owe me," he admonished sternly.

When she rose, she insinuated herself closely against his chest, and wrapped her arms behind his neck. "I'll never forgive you," she murmured between tiny kisses, "if you don't insist on collecting." Then, with an impish grin, she lightly nipped his lower lip and stepped away from the circle of his arms. "Food. Now."

"There are names for women like you," he said as he helped her into her coat, then put on his own.

"I know, I know," she said brightly, leading him out of the apartment. "Seductress, siren, sex fiend," and with unselfconscious affection, she kissed him loudly and moistly on the cheek before turning to lock the door.

"Jesus H. Christ, it's freezing," Arthur declared when they got to the street.

Anne wrapped her arm through his. "Oh, it's not so bad. Think of it as brisk, nippy, invigorating."

His glance was heavy with disdain. "Okay," she concurred, "it's cold."

"Where do you want to eat?" he asked. "If we need a cab, you stay here and I'll—"

"Let's go close by," Anne interrupted. "One of those places over on Broadway, okay?"

"You sure that's all right? I thought you were starving."

She smiled. "They do serve food in those restaurants, don't they?"

"Yes, but—"

"Arthur, a hamburger is just what I want."

"Okay, but—" He broke off, his expression mildly embarrassed. Even after these months with her, some of his old habits still surfaced, he was thinking. In the past, with other women, it had been his custom either not to feed them at all and just get right to the bed, or wine and dine them at great credit card expense in tacit understanding of what he was to receive as compensation; and also, Anne had revealed to him, because he gave so little else of himself. Going to hamburger joints, as he called the neighborhood restaurants with huge color TVs in the bar, backgammon boards in the rear room, and sizzling burgers, was reserved for his friends, guys from the office, from his house in the Hamptons. Until Anne had pointed out, and he could still remember the silky tone of her voice when she had said it, that there were times she did not want to be paid off beforehand for going to bed with him later. It had taken hasty apologies on his part, patient explanation on hers, before he admitted his chauvinism. They still went to the better restaurants, but only when they both wanted to; most of the time, local places in either his neighborhood or hers, depending on which apartment they would spend the night, were where they ate. Occasionally, though, like before, he lapsed into old ways.

"Have you finished your Christmas shopping?" Anne asked as they started to walk.

"Not even begun. I wait until the last minute and then buy all the wrong things. But I—" He abruptly broke off at the sound of footsteps on concrete. Still walking, he turned his head to the right, glancing across the street. Nothing. He looked behind them. No one.

"What is it?"

"Huh, oh, nothing. I thought I heard someone and I like to know who's around. Can't be too safe here on the West Side," he joked. "What were we talking about?"

"Christmas shopping. You always wait until the last minute."

"Yeah, but I already got yours," he announced with a smug smile.

"You did?" she said, pleased.

"Yup, and—" Again he stopped in mid-sentence, and this time he stood in place. Anne watched him as he surveyed behind them, across the street, behind them again.

"Arthur, what is it?" she asked, disturbed.

"I don't know," he said slowly, puzzled. He took her hand. "Forget it. C'mon, let's walk faster, I'm freezing to death out here," but he inspected the street one more time. There was nothing, not even a cat. He could have sworn someone was watching them, walking when they walked, turning into the shadow of a brownstone when he looked around. That story of Anne's must be getting to you, he told himself. Hearing phantom footfalls like a typical New York paranoiac. But as they continued to walk and he heard nothing more than the sound of their own matching steps clacking off the cold cement, he felt both foolish *and* relieved.

Anne's heart thumped with nervousness while glee gurgled through her like bubbles in a bottle. She hugged herself, not to keep warm in the bitter December night but to hold the precious delight within, to be savored later. She waited against the side of the brownstone steps until she could no longer hear them walking; then she moved out onto the street, and within minutes was in a taxi heading back to the East Side.

"Sure is cold tonight. This heat burns up a lot of gas, but what else can I do, y'know what I mean?"

Anne peered through the plastic partition at a much more rotund version of Simon Greenblatt than appeared on his identification placard. "I kind of like it," she said, favoring him with a smile.

"Hey, you want I should turn the heater off?" the cabbie asked obligingly.

"No, no, I don't like it that much," and again she smiled. Usually, she loathed talkative cabdrivers; she thought it bold of them to inflict conversation on a paying passenger. People had to be kept in their proper place, and while it was unfortunate that some had to be cabdrivers, construction workers, bowling alley attendants, gas jockeys, it was a necessity of life so that there would be room for people like her. But tonight she had only generosity for this cabbie. Let him talk every minute of the ride, that would be fine with her, she thought. Tonight, everyone is wonderful.

By the time he had driven her through Central Park and over to East 74th Street, Anne had learned that Simon's wife was a blessing he didn't deserve; his two children lived in California with their families; he thought the mayor was a four and a half on a scale of one to ten, and she was a ten, different things being taken into consideration, of course, he told her, grinning. She laughed merrily and complimented him on his fine taste. At her apartment building, she tipped him well and thanked him for the ride.

"Have a good, healthy holiday," he wished her.

"You too," she said, and kept the smile on her face for the doorman, a sullen, unlikable fellow she usually ignored and undertipped at Christmas.

In her apartment, she took off her coat, turned on the heat, started water to boil for coffee. As she waited for the water, she reached for the kitchen phone. Janey will just die when I tell her, she thought as she dialed.

She let the phone ring ten times, then hung up in disgust that she wasn't home. She took her coffee cup into the living room, but she couldn't sit idle; she needed to share her pleasure. Leaving the coffee to grow cold, she went into the bedroom. As soon as she had-

111

taken out the tape recorder from the night table drawer, she was glad that Janey had not been home. She could never appreciate the beauty of tonight, Anne thought, positioning herself comfortably against the pillows, and turning on the machine.

If tonight is any indication of what's to come, then Christmas sure is the season to be jolly. I guess what they say is true, that you just can't plan because I never planned on the bonanza I got.

I want to put this down right, really make sure the emotions are exactly as they happened, because I think I'm going to be able to use this stuff, I mean, this is what I want the people in my book to feel . . . real emotions, the way they really happen.

Okay, so I'm feeling like shit tonight. It's almost Christmas and nothing, I mean, *nothing* is going right. I still don't have a date for New Year's which is no big thing I guess. But the office, it's become unbearable, making everything else seem worse than maybe it is. There's practically a work stoppage going on there just because it's holiday time. Any stupid excuse for a party and the moles come out of the office and the drones get out from behind their desks. The conference room looks like it belongs in Leonard's of Great Neck, that catering place. There're all kinds of holiday greetings up on the walls, and a permanent display of paper cups and plates and stuff on the conference table, just waiting for the next party. And the tree, jeez, that poor pathetic Christmas tree in the reception area. If it were any smaller it could be confused for a man's toupee. And of course everybody is going around very happy and friendly, and it's such a crock of crap because as soon as New Year's is over, they'll be back to their mean, boring selves.

To add to this madness, Janey has decided to go home for the holidays. Doesn't that sound too cute—home for the holidays? The first time in four years. I told her she was only doing it because she didn't have any dates lined

112

up, and she made some noises about really wanting to be with her family because Thanksgiving had been so lonely. She's been trying to convince me to go home too, but no way. I don't need to listen to my mother in person when it's so bad on the telephone. Do you know what that woman had the nerve to bring up the other day? I swear I'm gonna give up calling her if she doesn't stop, and then who'll she have to make miserable. She started talking about Tim Leland. Tim Leland, for shit's sake! That's what, nine, ten years ago. I can't believe she even remembers him. Naturally, what started her off was when she asked me about men and I told her I was going to humiliate her by never getting married. That's when she started in about Timmy, that I should have married him when I had the chance which was when he was young and didn't know better. I couldn't believe the whole conversation, it was totally unreal. She said that he was the only man that lasted more than four months and that I was too critical, that nobody was good enough for me, and the longer I waited, the more difficult it was going to be for me to find someone who would put up with my moods, and that's why I should have gotten Timmy Leland to marry me. Well, I didn't want to marry Timmy Leland, but of course that wouldn't make any difference to her. After all, he was going to become a veterinarian, and that would have made me a veterinarian's wife. Not to mention the fact that he never asked me, but I guess he might have if I'd wanted him to.

And I don't know what she's talking about other men not sticking around because I'm so critical. What does she want me to do, accept anybody just so she can say she has a son-in-law? I can't help it if I have certain standards, and if most of the creeps I've known just won't change to meet them. Besides, I've told her enough times that I don't particularly want to get married which, of course, she refuses to believe. I don't see where her marriage was such a paragon of togetherness that she should be an advocate of the institution. Didn't she ever hear of career, ambition, success? Timmy Leland, Christ.

Anne turned off the machine, and leaned back, closing her eyes against the memory of the recent conversation with her mother. It wasn't that they didn't get along because they didn't like each other, she thought; they were two very different people who had been trained to keep up the pretense of familial closeness even when there was none. She certainly didn't want anything bad to happen to her mother; she simply did not want to have much to do with her, and the point was rapidly being reached, she realized, when even the twice-monthly telephone calls were getting to be too much. She didn't need to be reminded twice a month that she was a disappointment, and not just to her mother. Because when she had to answer her mother's questions, Anne came face-to-face with negatives that were a disappointment to herself.

Abruptly, she opened her eyes and sat straighter. "Not tonight, Mom," she said aloud. "I'm not going to let you spoil tonight." She turned on the tape recorder.

Okay, now, the general picture is that I'm not feeling too terrific about things, and when you get right down to specifics, it's mainly because of that . . . that bitch. When I think of her, everything else in my life seems even more awful. Granted, the wrong numbers have just about stopped, and there hasn't even been one Christmas card delivered to me by mistake. I guess she finally decided to send out notices or something. Now, if that had been it, if it had just been a matter of a few wrong numbers and stray pieces of mail, would I care? Would I really get as upset as I do? Of course not, but it's so much more. The name, I mean, coincidence, sure, but even the spelling is the same. I could have handled that, I really could. And maybe I could have handled the fact that she's a writer, and that she's dating Arthur, but not all together, her having it all at one time. I'm sorry, but that's just not fair, it really isn't. I mean, what about me? What about my share?

114

I must admit that getting my hair cut like hers wasn't the most brilliant idea I've ever had. Not that it's bad or anything, but I've looked better. I got a real charge, though, about pretending I was her with that shmuck Doug. Of course, I felt like a shmuck myself the next morning. I don't know what gets into me when she's in the picture. I'll do things or say something and then afterwards, I'll feel terrible about it. I mean, after all, who is she? I don't know her, right? So why do I get so wound up about her?

Well, earlier tonight I was asking myself the same question, and I decided to do something about it. The last time I tried it, I chickened out and hung up, so tonight I figured I'd just check out where she lives. That's all, nothing more. Because really, even though she's a stranger, I know her, and what I know I don't like—I don't like at all. She's smug and so terribly sincere I could puke. And she's so fucking successful it makes me sick, *sick!* But I got the best of her tonight. I still have her address and phone number from back in June, so I figured I'd go over to the crummy West Side and see how Miss Mount Holyoke lives. Maybe it was a dumb idea, I don't know. I guess I really hadn't thought it out much beforehand. Where she's concerned, I seem to do things kinda on impulse, as if I can't stop myself from doing them, like a few days ago when I . . . well, that doesn't matter now. So I got into a cab and went right to her apartment building. The front door was unlocked and I went in. There was her name on the mailbox: Anne N. Fletcher, Apt. 3A. I still don't know what that middle initial stands for, and why she uses it, it's such an affectation. Anyway, the inside door was locked, of course. If it hadn't been, I think I might have . . . no, I'm *sure* I would have tried to find out which apartment was 3A. I went back down the steps and crossed the street. I must admit I was kinda excited. There was something so deliciously wrong about what I was doing. I mean, there I am checking out where she lives and she doesn't know it. It was sort of like revenge. She doesn't know what

115

she's been doing to me, does she? So why should she know what I do?

I saw only two lights on in apartments facing the street, and one of them was on the third floor. I was freezing my earlobes off by now, but I didn't want to leave yet. Maybe she'd come to the window or something, and I'd get a chance to see her, to know if that was her apartment. Well, luck, luck, beautiful luck was with me tonight. Like I said, a bonanza. I was looking up and I saw the light go out in that third floor apartment. I was really disappointed, and was about to get a cab and go home when the front door opened and there she was! She was with Arthur, all cuddly-cozy with her arm grabbing him to her, as if any other woman would even want him. I mean, what's she being so possessive about anyway?

They stood on the steps a minute or so, and I got away from the streetlight so they wouldn't see me—so Arthur wouldn't see me actually because she doesn't know who I am, of course. But I got a really good look at her, and Sandy's right, I'm prettier—much. She looks like she just got off an ironing board, all pressed and starched and proper with a dumb muffler flung around her neck and her hair blowing in the wind like somebody in a Breck commercial. She's got very high cheekbones, and a huge chin, much bigger in person than in that photograph—that must have been touched up. She was smiling up at Arthur as if he were her last chance, which he probably is. I don't know what he sees in her. She can't be better in bed than I am, so that's not it. Maybe she cooks better, who knows. When they finally started to walk, and boy, was I glad they did I was so cold, I sort of followed them. I mean, I wasn't actually following them, that's not the right word. I was walking in their direction. But Arthur, he's so cagey, the bastard heard me and kept turning around. I would have died if he had seen me, absolutely died. The second time he stopped and looked around, I moved into the shadow of a brownstone and waited until they were out of sight.

But I got much, much more than I bargained for. Now I know where she lives, even which apartment; I saw her in person and confirmed my suspicion which is that she's got about as much sex appeal as a canary, that if her chin were any longer you could tie a leash to it and walk it, that if her nose were any straighter and more snotty looking you could ask her the difference between the rarefied air she breathes and the soot the rest of us mortals take in. And, she's a clinging vine. Anybody who would hang on to Arthur—and I mean hanging on, not just wrapping her arm through his—is what I call a clinging vine. I'm sure she's the same kind of writer that she is a woman . . . a stiff. [*She laughed.*]

I'm really tired now, but it's a terrific kind of fatigue because I feel that I've accomplished something.

She shut off the machine and put it away. Self-satisfaction was mirrored in the smile, in the green spark of her eyes. Then, slowly, as she again thought about the events of the evening, a frown gradually appeared to mar the smooth surface of her expression, and the smile vanished. What did you really achieve by going over there tonight? she asked herself with disgust, the flame in her eyes doused. What big bonanza did you get? So you saw her, so you now know which apartment is hers. What did you really take from her, huh? She still has your name, she still has Arthur, she still is having a book published. So what did you accomplish with your little game on this cold December night?

Not enough, she realized. Not nearly enough.

10

By the middle of January, actually well before, by the first day of the new year, New York and its inhabitants wear a chip on their collective shoulder that does not allow a glimpse of sunshine, the dry bite of pure winter air, the eternally childish thrill at freshly falling snow, to penetrate the mufflered hearts of people and a city wearily marking time. Their energies are as buckled as the streets they ride on—how much can they withstand, after all, before surrendering? There are only three groups of people who are reluctant to see winter end: the very rich who do not spend it in New York; skiers who proselytize tediously when not asked; operators of snow removal equipment. Perhaps there are others but they are not as visible as the removers, as vocal as the skiers, as missed as the rich and their money. For the rest of the populace, for the city itself, it is a time to tolerate like the period of teenage acne: one must get through it to become beautiful.

Unlike Chicagoans, New Yorkers have no false bravado about dodging traffic in order to avoid canals of shin-deep gray mush; they do not believe it is the price they must pay for living in this terrific city of theirs;

unlike the stoics of Minnesota, Michigan, the Dakotas, New Yorkers do not feel it is a part of their pioneer heritage to freeze in line in order to see a movie, suffering the indignity of having to pay for this privilege as well. They are not hearty, brave, stolid—nor particularly tolerant. They are, in fact, both childish and provincial: they are miserable, and no one buried in a blizzard in the Midwest tundra would believe how miserable; they want relief, and they want it *now*. So, when the façade of generosity and amiability gets tossed with the wrappings of other Christmas gifts, and when the pathetic braying that passes for New Year's Eve celebration is ended, the balloon of festivity loses its air, and New Yorkers return to earth and to the mechanics of living through another winter.

For Anne N. Fletcher, the letdown was not as severe as for others. The final manuscript was at her publishers and now she waited anxiously for the printer's galleys. And she was well along on her second novel, although her agent had seen none of it yet; she was waiting until she had at least half that was more polished than rough draft. Christmas itself had been fun, with Arthur and her spending Christmas Eve in Queens, Christmas Day dinner on Long Island, and that night laughing affectionately about both sets of parents. . . .

"You know they're assuming my intentions are totally honorable," Arthur was saying. They were in Anne's living room, lying against an ottoman of pillows around the real pine Christmas tree, the only illumination in the room coming from the twinkling lights.

"Yours, too?" Anne asked, lazily running a finger over his hand on her thigh.

"Sure. It's not just the girl's family who cares about honor. With today's women, you can't be too careful," he teased.

"Mmm," Anne murmured, her eyes shut. "Well, I haven't decided yet what my intentions are." Her voice was light, breezy, but the words were not; she had thought about where she and Arthur were going, about whether she loved him, about marriage to him. She had thought about all this, but she was sure of nothing yet except how truly unhappy and empty she would feel without him. Until now, they had avoided serious conversations in the specific; love, marriage, relationships were themes to be discussed about others, and through the faceless, nameless others, their own fears and desires would be safely revealed. Anne knew how dangerous holiday times could be to a relationship. She had seen it happen once with her brother, other times with friends. The need for closeness, physical and emotional, drove people to say things they did not mean, do things they regretted once the flashing neon lights insistently demanding *happy* holidays went out. She and Arthur must not fall into the enticing trap of trumped-up feeling.

"I've waited long enough," she said abruptly, squirming out of the comfortable nest of his arms, and standing up. "I should have given it to you last night or this morning but there didn't seem to be time."

"What are you talking about?" Arthur asked, sitting up straighter.

"Your Christmas gift, of course."

"No time," Arthur said with mock indignation. "How many times did I try to give you your gift? Huh, just answer me that. I'll tell you how many times," he went on, not waiting for her to speak. "At least six since I came over here last night. But no, you wanted to wait, you wanted us to be alone with the family business behind us. And this from someone who claims she doesn't believe in ceremony."

By now, he was behind her by the Spanish buffet. He put his arms around her waist, and pressed her against him, burrowing his nose in her hair. "I have a great idea," he whispered suggestively. "Let's wait a little longer for the gifts. Let's—"

She turned around in his arms and smiled up at him. "Here," she said softly, holding out a small box that she had gotten from the buffet. "Merry Christmas."

Arthur did not immediately relinquish his embrace. He looked down at her, into the eyes that were as warm as roasting chestnuts. He took the gift. "Thank you."

"Maybe you better save that until you're sure you like it," she said, a little embarrassed.

Arthur recognized the awkwardness of the moment, the need to please and be pleased. He tried to lighten it. He shook the box. "No noise. Must be solid." He turned the box around and over in his hands. "Bigger than a tiepin, smaller than a tie."

"Arthur, come on, please open it," Anne urged.

"Gee, you take all the fun out of things," he chastised with a wide grin on his face. Then he undid the brown ribbon and the gold foil paper. When he saw the store name printed on the box, his eyebrows went up. "Alfred Dunhill," he remarked. "I'm impressed."

"I figured this way you'd know where to return it if you didn't like it," Anne explained, even more flustered than before. She had not known what to buy him, or where to get whatever it would be. The typical male gifts of a scarf or sweater or jewelry had seemed so prosaic, so easy and thoughtless. Then, just last week, she had been walking along Fifth Avenue, and had come to the window of Alfred Dunhill. The gift had practically winked at her, she remembered now, but she had hesitated before finally going in to the infamously expensive store.

Arthur lifted off the top of the box to find a sterling silver pen alongside a brushed sterling silver holder that had been engraved with his name. He took both from their cushion of puff, inserted the pen in the holder, and held it in his palm. "It's beautiful, Annie." He gave a short; self-conscious laugh. "It's so right. I've never had one before."

Anne was smiling. "You really like it?"

He nodded, and kissed her gently on the lips. "Thank you." His smile was so full of pleasure, his eyes wide and shining like brown marbles that Anne believed in his sincerity. "Now my turn," she said gaily.

"Boy, you're greedy," Arthur groused. Then he left her side for a moment to go to his coat hanging in the hall closet. He returned with a box smaller than the one that had contained his gift.

"Merry Christmas," he wished her, watching her face carefully as she slowly untied the ribbon, then threw caution aside and tore at the wrapping.

"I'm trying to be mature about this but it's not working," she confessed. "I love surprises." Then, "Oh, Arthur. Oh my gosh, it's beautiful. Oh, thank you, darling," and with the box still in her hand, she flung her arms around him and kissed him. Then she stood back, oohing and aahing over the delicate Limoges porcelain box with the hinged top and the hand-painted violets on the lid and within. Arthur had known for a while what he was going to give her, but finding the right one had not been as easy. A friend in the office whose mother collected Limoges and Sèvres had told him where to shop, and within minutes he had found it and bought it, sure of its rightness.

Anne went to place the porcelain box on one of the étagères, on a shelf that held a small mother-of-pearl and wood box from the Philippines, a gift from her brother, and two oversized photography books. There had been no other porcelain on the shelf until now, and the box stood alone against the glass like a jewel in the perfect setting. She walked back to him.

"Thank you," she said, and kissed him tenderly. His arms closed around her, his hands lowered to her buttocks, tightening their embrace; her tender kiss was encouraged to become more.

"Let's go inside," he whispered into her neck. She nodded, feeling her heartbeat accelerate with wanting him.

In the bedroom, she swiftly slipped out of her beige cashmere turtleneck and black velvet slacks. "Are you going to make love to me with your clothes on?" she asked with some surprise as she was about to remove her bra and noticed he was standing there, fully dressed.

"I just want to look at you a minute," he said almost shyly. He opened his arms, and she came into their circle. He filled his hands with the cool flesh of her back, the nylon-covered curve below.

"I love your ass," he muttered. He undid her bra. "And your breasts." He began to caress them, to kiss them. He could feel the pressure of her fingers increase on his shoulders; could hear the pleasure in her sigh. He stood up, and held her slightly away from him. "Your breasts surprised me at first," he remarked.

"Surprised you?" She began to unbutton his shirt. "Why?"

"They're bigger than they look in clothes. You tend to camouflage them. Most women built like you would show them off."

"Mmm," was all she said for she had unbuttoned his shirt completely now and was planting kisses on his chest while her hands fumbled with his belt buckle.

"Eager tonight, aren't you?" he laughed deep in his throat and pushed her hands away.

She smiled, walked to the bed. She stepped out of her panties, pulled back the cover but did not get into the bed. Arthur watched her, marveling, as he did every time he saw her naked, at how deceptive her body was. In clothes, there was a lean, almost coltish quality to her, with no appearance of flesh or roundness. She wore clothes well, and looked taller than her five foot five. But nude, there was a soft curve to her stomach, and a high, firm mound of buttocks. Her legs were solid, well-shaped. There was a definite delineation between waist and hips. But her breasts, with their ampleness, had been his real surprise, a secret gift.

"Are you going to stand there gaping all night or are you getting into this bed?" Anne now said.

"Sex fiend. Nympho," he grumbled, but quickly finished undressing.

They lay on their sides, wrapped in each other, letting the heat of their kisses slowly ignite the rest of their bodies until they began to strain toward each other, and their breath came quicker, their hands searched more selfishly.

"Don't wait, please," she urged in a whisper, her hand guiding him to get on top. "I don't want to wait."

They locked into each other, taking greedily and thereby giving so pleasurably. She clawed him further into her, her breath ragged, little puffs of sound changing in volume as her need increased. Then, finally, she fell back, her hair damp and straggly, her mouth throbbing, her body weak.

"I'm sorry," she said in a low voice as he lovingly lifted a strand of hair off her face.

"For what?" He eased off her.

"I couldn't wait. I didn't want any of the foreplay or anything. I just—"

Arthur began to chuckle. "Isn't that what the man usually says? 'I'm sorry, dear, I couldn't wait.'" He saw by how she averted her eyes that she was embarrassed. He reached out and put his hand on her chin, making her look at him. "Annie, I love it when you're like that," he said gently. "It's exciting to me. And it's tremendously flattering."

Her expression was doubtful; despite their closeness, she was still confused by the sexuality this man had helped her discover about herself.

"Really," he assured her. Then, his voice smug: "The fact that you're a hussy, a real aggressive bitch, well," he shrugged, "some men might find that threatening, but I can handle it." She punched him playfully on the arm and he grabbed her to him. She nestled her head on his chest, and softly, silently, they touched.

The rest of that Christmas evening became a preview of how they would spend New Year's Eve, quietly, together, and mainly in bed, alternating bouts of energetic lovemaking with times of deeply warm affection. And in the weeks since, Anne knew that the love she felt for Arthur, and it was that, she was sure, did not come from seasonal cause, for as patterns and routines were reestablished, tainted by the tedium of winter, her joy remained and grew each time she was with him. There was little to spoil her sense of anticipation with this new year. She never totally forgot what had happened with the writer at *Glamour*. Not even an explanatory letter and a personal note on the Christmas card she had sent had mended the rift. And Anne could try to dismiss the strange phone calls she had been getting, calls that had no voice in them, calls that waited until she answered before quietly hanging up, leaving her with the disconcerting sound of a dial tone. But the calls had not happened in a while, and even so, they were minor annoyances. In relation to what she had with Arthur, to what she had to look forward to with her writing, they were as unimportant in her life as a flea on a horse's tail.

Anne Fletcher spent Christmas Eve doing her nails in a new shade of glittering copper; trying a new granular facial that had cost $24.50 for a small tube; doing crossword puzzles. She spent Christmas Day thinking that perhaps she had made a mistake by not accepting the invitation to Linny Trotter's annual buffet for neo-New Yorkers, that being those people who did not go home to families in Minnesota and other points west. Anne had been to three of her Christmas buffets over the course of several years, and had come to hate them, filled as they usually were with sad and lonely homosexuals who prepared the food for her, and other men and women, like herself, who ate it and then waited until the next Christmas before seeing her again. Still, this year it might have been better than watching TV, having a brief and blessedly quarrel free telephone conversation with her mother, and then eating a tuna fish sandwich for dinner. She had opened her presents earlier in the week, when she had gotten them: a palette of twelve different eyeshadows and a coffee mug with her name on it from Janey; a check for twenty-five dollars from her mother; a set of three miniature cordials from Sandy, whom she had not bought a gift for this year because Sandy had not bought one for her last year.

In the days between Christmas and New Year's, Anne spent a lot of time at her health club, venting excess energy and nerves on the Nautilus equipment, on the jogging pad, in the whirlpool and sauna. She called everyone she knew who might be in town, people who might alleviate the desert stretch of time: Arthur, Doug, two girls from other publishing houses with whom she occasionally had lunch. Holiday greetings were exchanged, in Arthur's case as icily as the weather, in Doug's as remotely as a tropical sun, and there was no offer from anyone to get together. Twice she sat down at her typewriter, twice she tore out the paper, avenged her lack of inspiration by shredding the paper, then realized that she could not possibly write a good novel if she did not feel at peace with herself, which she did not.

She spent New Year's Eve going with Sandy to a series of parties that they had both heard about, open houses that they could drop in and out of. When midnight struck, Anne found herself flying higher than she ever had been on a combination of grass, scotch, and rum-soaked egg nog, passionately kissing a man she had never seen before in the apartment of a woman she had never met before. She spent the next day nursing her physical and emotional bruises until Janey got home from Illinois and called her to come over with a pizza.

"You should have gone home too, Anne." Janey was concluding her recitation of her holidays. "It was really nice. Even spending New Year's without a man was okay. It's so different when you're with your family, so much more . . ." She waved her hands in a gesture of inarticulateness, then smiled. "Just much nicer."

"Let's not go into that again, okay?" Anne said nastily. "What you've got with your family makes it nice. What I've got with my mother would have made it miserable."

"Maybe if you tried a little harder," Janey began, then immediately regretted her words when she saw the storm brewing behind Anne's eyes. "Okay, sorry. So what did you do—something exciting, a new man?"

Anne told her exactly how she had spent the holidays, and the days in-between. "That doesn't sound too terrific," Janey commented quietly. "Kinda lonely."

"It was okay, I guess," Anne said, not meeting her friend's eyes.

"Well, at least I'm glad to see you're over that silliness," Jane remarked as she went into the kitchen to get more pizza and fresh napkins.

"What silliness?"

"You know, about that other Anne Fletcher," Janey said, sitting down again at the desk that doubled as her dining table.

"I'm not over what you call 'silliness' because I was never in it," Anne said archly.

"Oh, come on, you know that's not true," Janey protested. "You really had me worried there for a while, before Christmas, I guess it was. That business at the bar and your hair and all. I mean, you were—I don't know, it was like you were obsessed with her or something."

"Don't be an idiot. It was just a little game I was playing. Besides, I still think—oh, never mind, you wouldn't understand."

What Anne was about to say was that she still thought about the other Anne Fletcher; thought about her and hated her. No, hate was not accurate, she silently amended; she would not dissipate such a powerful emotion on her. Resentment, that's what she felt; deep, flowing like a current within her, building at times for no reason, making her act on impulse, then ebbing but never really dying. She was certainly not obsessed with her; she would never allow any one person or thing to become that important to her.

"I have a great idea," Janey announced brightly, seeing the closed expression in Anne's eyes and wishing to erase it. "Let's make New Year's resolutions!"

"You're kidding," Anne groaned, her attention reluctantly brought back to her friend. "You know how many times we've tried this? Come on, it's hopeless." She laughed. "Neither of us has very much self-discipline when it comes to resolutions."

"That's not true," Janey said. "What was it, two, three years ago, I resolved to give up married men and I did it."

"Yeah, for four months, until the first new one turned up," Anne reminded her.

"Well, let's try it again. The way our luck's been running, it can't hurt."

"Okay, what should we resolve? We don't smoke, so we can't give that up. We don't eat *that* much, except I could give up Nestlé's Crunch and you could give up potato chips."

"Anne, this is a New Year's resolution, not Lent."

Anne laughed. "Let's think. You think of one for me, and I'll come up with one for you."

"Deal," Janey agreed, and the two girls fell silent, the only sound the chewing of their food.

"Anything?" Janey asked after a while.

"See if you like this," Anne said. "Your New Year's resolution is to be more realistic about men."

"What do you mean?" Janey asked, feeling a flush creep into her cheeks. "I am realistic about them. What makes you say I'm not?"

"If you really were," Anne told her eagerly, "you'd stop believing that the next one is Mr. Right and you're going to live lovingly together forever after."

"Oh, Anne, that's not fair," Janey protested softly, her eyes lowered to conceal the hurt.

"Of course it's fair," Anne said matter-of-factly. "You know what a hopeless romantic you are. I'm merely suggesting that if you resolve to be more realistic about love and men and all that crap, then you won't get hurt as much and you'll probably have a better time."

"That 'crap' as you call it," Janey said somewhat brittlely, looking at Anne now, "is the most important thing in life. And I think you've adopted this ornery, misanthropic position just to protect yourself. If you can't have what you want, then you won't have anything at all, and that's dumb. And you always want something impossible. Nobody's good enough, nothing's right enough." Janey knew she should stop, but what Anne had said had wounded, deeply, and maybe, without even realizing she was going to do it, her own resolution was to be more honest with her best friend. "That's what your resolution should be, Anne. Learn to accept a little more. Resolve to stop trying to be something you're not."

"Like what?" Anne challenged.

"Like . . . like . . ." Janey broke off, unwilling to say that Anne should stop claiming she was a writer until she wrote something; should stop thinking of herself as so gifted, as so special that ordinary people were not good enough for her. Janey could not go that far. "Oh never mind," she said. "I'm sorry. I didn't mean to get so heavy about this." She tried to laugh, but it was a forced, abortive attempt.

"No, go ahead," Anne encouraged, feeling the blood pounding in her temples, the suppressed fury making her heart reverberate like a plucked rubber band. "You've obviously been storing this up. I'd like to hear it. Really. After all, I don't hesitate to tell you when I think you're wrong."

"You certainly don't," Janey muttered, but she would not pursue the conversation. The mood was spoiled.

"Well?"

"I don't want to talk about it anymore."

"I do. I want to know what you mean about my being something I'm not. And I also want to know what in the world that has to do with love and men, which is what started this in the first place."

"Nothing, it has nothing to do with it. Let's just drop the whole thing, okay? I'm sorry I suggested it," Janey said with mounting irritation.

"Well, now you have to finish it. Come on, put your money where your mouth is."

Janey put both palms flat on the table, and fixed Anne with a burning glare. "All right, I will. You just don't know when to let something drop, do you? Okay, then, let's take men, let's just take men for a minute. You sit there making fun of me all the time because I believe in a Mr. Right. Well, let me tell you something. I don't believe in a Mr. Right, but I'm not going to make every man into a Mr. Wrong, the way you do. I keep believing, and maybe that's tougher than what you do, which is giving up beforehand."

"You're crazy."

"Oh, really? Well, let me refresh your memory a little." And for the next several minutes, she mentioned at least six men, beginning before Timmy Leland and ending with Arthur Dumont, whom Anne, for reasons ranging from what he did for a living to how he ate lobster, thought were not worthy. Anne began to laugh harshly through the middle of the diatribe. She was still laughing, and shaking her head when Janey finished.

"You know, I just realized something about you that I've never known in all these years," Anne said, pausing to make sure she had Janey's attention. "You're jealous. *You* are incredibly jealous of me. I can't believe it. I can't believe I never spotted it before. Wow, you've really got a problem there."

Janey's eyes opened wide and her mouth went slack with utter incredulity. "You're serious, aren't you?" she whispered.

"I hardly find this a laughing matter," Anne responded self-righteously. "What amazes me is my own obtuseness not to have sensed this about you before. Then, again, maybe you're just a better actress than I ever imagined."

Janey could not speak. She had never known anyone like her, anyone with that ability to turn the defensive into the offensive. One minute she's telling Anne what's wrong with her, the next, Anne is laughing at her and making *her* feel flawed and foolish. She would not even try to defend herself; she could not, for Anne was so convinced of her theory that no logical argument could possibly make her budge. Janey had seen it happen before; she knew.

"Now that I understand you better," Anne was saying, "it's obvious that jealousy motivates all your actions with me. Do you remember when we first came to New York, and we had no luck in finding jobs on a newspaper and you went off to some trade journal or something and I said I was going to become a novelist? Remember how you tried to dissuade me from that? I thought you were protecting me from the hard time I would have, but now I realize you were just tremendously jealous because you knew you didn't have the talent I have. It's the same thing. You think I'm too critical of men because you know you can't get the kind of men I can." She again shook her head. "Incredible. Just incredible," she muttered.

"Anne," Janey began quietly, her eyes on the napkin she was shredding on her plate, "if you believe what you're saying there's nothing I can do to change your mind, I know you well enough to realize that. And I'm genuinely sorry you feel that way. I can tell you you're totally wrong, but you wouldn't accept that. I wish you would try, though, because if you're convinced that what you're saying is true, then I can't see how we can remain friends."

Anne made a little clucking sound of impatience. "You're being an ass again. I'm flattered actually. Now that I know how you feel, I'll simply take more care in not hurting your feelings by talking about myself so much. Don't forget you're my best friend. I wouldn't know what to do without you so stop being so black and white about this. I understand you better, that's all, and we'll go on from there." She pushed back her chair from the table. "I better get going."

Janey nodded dumbly, then got up to get Anne's coat. She walked her to the front door.

"Happy New Year," Anne said, dazing her friend with a hug; then she left.

As soon as the door closed behind her, she shut her eyes and began to take deep, long gulps of air. "Cunt," she breathed. "Phony little cunt."

Riding down in the elevator, walking the few blocks to her apartment, getting ready for bed, Anne went over all that Janey had said, completely convinced of her falsity as a friend. There *was* something wrong with each of the men she had mentioned; maybe they were all right for girls like Janey, but for her, simply not enough. And to discover her jealousy about the writing, well, that was really something. She remembered as clearly as if it were yesterday how Janey had told her she didn't care

132

about working for a newspaper enough to go hungry until she could get a job on one, and what she wanted to try was writing ad copy. And Anne had admitted that she loved reporting, but felt that it wasn't the best way for self-expression; writing a novel would be more suitable to her talents. Janey had been the one to convince her to get a job while she wrote so that she would have an income coming in. It was Janey's fault, now that she thought about it. Janey's fault that she had not yet written her novel. If she hadn't told her to get a job, she wouldn't be stuck in that crummy office, wasting her time when she could be writing.

For one week after that evening, the two girls did not speak; it was the longest they had gone without contact since first meeting. Finally, one viciously cold and gray afternoon when the sky seemed a blanket of despair and the streets swam under their residue of watery snow, Janey called Anne, and they made plans to meet that evening for dinner. Nothing further was ever said of that night, but Anne vowed to be careful in the future. She could not ever totally trust Janey again; anybody that jealous could be dangerous.

The days slumbered by with defiant slowness, one or two of them a tease of sunlight and briskness that could never be held long enough to grow tired of. Night was long, enveloping, restricting; the hours of light were treadmills going to and from darkness. New Yorkers still tried to have their fun: by getting away, by rejoicing in the adult-high snowdrifts far away from them that they did not have to suffer through; by going indoors, to the exhibits and museums and Off-Off-Broadway shows they ignored in good weather. They still had a sense of direction, of purpose in January, even if it was rather forced. They had to keep themselves going for a while because they knew how much worse they would feel in February.

Snow as soft and plump as miniature marshmallows dropped casually to earth, encasing the morning air in a curtain of brilliant white. It was a sassy snowfall, menacingly thick and damp until it reached the ground where it magically disappeared, as if to say: "Scared you, didn't I?"

Anne N. Fletcher opened the window in her living room a crack, enough to let in the snappy air that made her skin feel chilled and tight and baby smooth. Outside, two children dressed so compactly in red snowsuits that they moved like robots, opened their mouths to lick in the crystals, and to giggle deliciously. A mailman trudged up the steps of the brownstone across the street, his gray hat covered with a fresh dusting of white, his mammoth pouch bulging with dampened deliveries. Anne breathed in the air and then turned back into the room where the heat hissed and made her wish again that her fireplace worked. It was the ideal morning for crackling logs and splintering sparks and strong, freshly brewed coffee. At least she could supply the coffee, she thought.

A few minutes later she was sitting at her dining table,

a pad and pen in front of her, a mug of coffee held in both hands. She needed to get organized; to list the various things to be done this day, and then check them off systematically so that she could leave herself plenty of time to be leisurely and relaxed before tonight. She could not motivate herself, though; she could not seem to find the energy to decide even what to wear tonight. And that was wrong, all wrong. Instead of brimming with excited anticipation, the anxiety-edged thrill over having her first publication party, Anne sat with a strange knot of uneasiness in her stomach. She found herself sighing for no reason, taking in deep gulps of air that only momentarily relieved the odd pressure against her rib cage. Then the queasiness would return, and she would feel a thickening in her throat, a buzzing in her fingertips. If this was a case of the jitters, it was unlike any she had ever had. But then, she reassured herself, tonight is unlike any party you've ever been to before.

When Matthew Holmes had told her he thought it would be a good idea to have a prepublication party for *Honorable Mention*, Anne had at first demurred, thinking it too ostentatious a gesture for a first novelist. Maybe after the book came out, but to do it before seemed to her the type of fanfare reserved for those writers whose works were awaited with eagerness by consumer if not by critic. Her agent had pointed out that a prepub party was an excellent way to generate interest, to get people expectant that something and someone special were about to be launched.

When the publishing community begins to buzz about a property, he explained, it escalates the price for a film deal, for a paperback reprint; and he cited several examples of large auctions for a book before one copy in hardcover had been sold, based solely on the prepub hype. He also pointed out that while they could wait and see if her publisher would throw a party, there was another advantage to his doing it. Holmes enjoyed a reputation as one of the best agents in the business; if *he* were hosting a party for one of his clients, people came and people listened. The hardcover publisher, not oblivious to the enthusiasm for the project, would rethink their advertising and publicity budget for the book, and their initial print run, all vital to the commercial success or failure of a title.

Anne had succumbed, without much pressure, to his arguments; if she had any holdover ideals that publishing was a profession not a business, her agent's explanations dispelled them, and she did not feel the loss. She had no literary delusions. If a shrewdly conceived and executed party would increase her novel's chance for commercial success, then she was all for it.

That party would begin at 6:30 this evening, in Holmes's Central Park West penthouse. Over one hundred invitations had been sent, and two days ago he had told her that if the weather held, she could expect to be the center of attention for all one hundred plus the extras that invariably showed up at these functions.

The lethargy, the queasiness, the constriction in her throat must all be attributable to party tension, she now decided. But it was so unlike her, and it was a different kind of anxiety. Usually when she was nervous, she got a slight stomach cramp and a burst of hyperactivity, finding busywork to keep her mind off the cause of her edginess. What she was feeling this morning; what she had, in fact, been feeling off and on for several days, was not localized, specific tension, but rather undefined fretfulness, almost a case of the creeps. The notion made her smile. "Enough of this silliness," she said aloud. With determination, she put down her coffee mug and began to write a list of things to do: Decide what to wear and make sure it's clean and pressed; check out accessories—do not leave this to the last minute! Do nails. Call Mrs. Rossmund and confirm speaking date at Holyoke. Cash a check. Change sheets. Get to hairdresser's early so maybe Philip will take you on time. *Relax*.

She replaced the top of the pen, sat back, reread her list. She was feeling better; putting her mind to work helped restore her composure. Now she had to begin to cross off each item.

Getting her phone book from her purse on top of the Spanish buffet, she went into the kitchen and put through the call to Mrs. Rossmund, dean of women at her college. Yesterday, she had received a postcard from her, asking her to call and confirm the speaking date, scheduled in three days, and to invite her to lunch. She took the postcard in with her, too.

"Hello, Dean Rossmund?" she greeted, after the dean's secretary had asked her name and put through her call.

"Hello, Anne, how are you?"

"Just fine. Actually, kind of nervous. Tonight's my publication party. Prepublication to be exact."

"How wonderful. This must be very thrilling for you."

"It is. Dean Rossmund, the reason I'm calling is to confirm our date for Friday. I received your postcard and I just wanted to let you know that unless there's a blizzard, I'll be there—and I'd love to have lunch with you."

There was no response. "Dean Rossmund? Do we have a bad connection? I was saying that—"

"Oh, we have a perfectly fine connection, Anne," the older woman cut in. "It's just that I'm rather confused."

"Confused? I don't understand. You do still want me to speak Friday, don't you?" Anne asked, frowning with puzzlement.

"Anne, dear, probably you've been so busy with your book, and I'm sure your mind's been on much more interesting things than a speaking—"

"Dean Rossmund," Anne interrupted, "what exactly are you trying to tell me?" She could feel the cramp returning to her stomach, and a ball of bile lodged itself in the back of her throat. The phone in her hands had grown slippery with moisture.

"I suppose it's perfectly understandable that you don't remember."

"Remember what, Dean Rossmund?" Anne almost snapped. "What are you saying?" Tension and frustration formed a band of pain around her forehead. She quickly shut her eyes, willing herself to be patient.

"Anne, dear," the dean explained smoothly, "you called me last Thursday, I think it was. Perhaps Wednesday."

"I did what?" she whispered hoarsely, gaping at the phone as if it were some ugly creature that had no place in her hand.

"You called. You had received my postcard and—"

"I'm sorry, Dean Rossmund," Anne again interrupted, a strain of urgency in her tone like a discordant note, "but I got your card yesterday morning. I couldn't possibly have called you before then."

"But you did, last week."

"Dean Rossmund," Anne said softly, wiping her sweaty palm on her thigh, "this is silly, I know, but what exactly did I say to you?"

"Why, you said that you had gotten the card and that you couldn't make it," the dean said, lack of understanding evident in the slow way she paced her words. "Something to do with your book, I think you said, that meant you had to stay in New York. You were very apologetic, my dear. And of course I well appreciate your position. It's not every day one has her first novel about to be published. Of course, I would have wished for a bit more notice but . . ."

The sound of the dean's voice came through to Anne, but no words. She had not received that postcard until yesterday morning. She had never called Dean Rossmund until now. Anne was suddenly reminded of the incident with the writer from *Glamour*. But the dean was a reasonable woman, she would believe her.

Anne reached within herself for a facsimile of laughter. She needed something to turn the conversation back to a reality she understood; something to ease that band of tightness pressing against her temples. "Dean Rossmund," she tried lightly, "there's been some mistake. I really didn't get any card from you until yesterday. Perhaps you mailed it last week and that's why you're a bit confused, or you dated it last week and didn't mail it until a few days ago. And you see, you don't have my new address. I moved and the mail's gotten delayed sometimes so if you want to take down my new address—" She stopped, knowing she was babbling. "It's twenty-five West Eighty-second Street," she finished frailly.

The dean's voice was gentle and tolerant. "I'll be sure to have our records changed, thank you for telling me. But Anne, I mailed the card the same day I dated it, and that was over ten days ago. The postmark and the date —did you check them?"

Anne looked at the card that had been resting on the kitchen counter top. It was dated exactly eleven days ago, not ten. Both the outside postmark and the inside date. Eleven days ago. She had not noticed. She had not thought to look. The cramp bounced like a live thing in her stomach, and her chest began to throb with pain.

When Anne did not speak, the dean took it for confirmation. "Don't be embarrassed, dear, I truly understand how preoccupied you are now. I really must be going. There's a meeting and—"

"I can still make it if you want," Anne said in a desperate rush. "I can still come up Friday and—"

"Oh, no, dear, but thank you just the same. I've made arrangements for another alumna to come. She wasn't supposed to speak until next month but she was gracious enough to—"

"What about rescheduling me, I'm sure I can arrange something."

"But Anne," the dean's laugh was a tinkle of indulgence, "you already told me you wouldn't be able to do that. Oh dear, you really don't remember, do you? I suggested setting another date, and you said that would be impossible, that I better, I think your exact words were that I better forget the whole thing and find somebody with more time on her hands."

"Oh dear Lord."

"What was that, dear?"

"Nothing, Dean Rossmund. Nothing at all."

"Well, then, I must be going. Good luck with your book, Anne, and do keep in touch."

"Yes, of course," Anne muttered numbly. "Goodbye."

Her hand trembled as she replaced the receiver. Still holding the postcard, she went back to the dining table and sat down. She sipped from the cold coffee, but she tasted nothing. She twisted a strand of hair behind her ear, and concentrated on that postcard as if it were a crystal ball containing the secrets of her future. Confusion and concern creased her forehead and dulled her eyes and set pulse points pounding in her temples, her neck. Unreasonable, unwanted fear burned behind her eyes, and she squeezed them tight to keep back the tears. The card had not come until yesterday. Had it? She did not call the dean last week. Did she?

She thrust the card face down on the table. "Stop it," she said out loud. "Stop thinking that way." She was not absentminded; she was not forgetful. And she was not losing her mind. Somebody had called Dean Rossmund, but it had not been her. Maybe the dean was getting senile, maybe that was it. After all, she was about sixty-two and always under pressure; maybe it had finally gotten to her, and *she* was confused, mixing up her speaking dates, jumbling her telephone calls. But even as she thought this, Anne knew in her heart that Dean Ross-mund was one of the sanest, most stable women she had ever known, and as far from senility as a woman half her age. Then what was going on? Who had called her? How had she known about the speaking engagement? And why? Most importantly, why was some stranger, some unknown, unseen voice calling these people and pretending to be her? For what purpose? Maybe it's not a stranger, she realized. Maybe it's somebody you know, someone you once hurt who's now trying to retaliate. But that's absurd, her common sense told her. That's sick, in fact. She knew no one who would do such a thing.

For several more long minutes, Anne sat there, willing herself to think rationally, concentrating on eradicating the fear that clung to her like a rancid miasma. She had to get busy; she had so much to do, and there was to-night. She could not let this spoil tonight for her. She forced her attention to the list. Do nails. Change sheets. Check accessories. Yes, she had to get to work.

And she did, never for one minute, for one second even losing herself to the worry that would not release her. She functioned, she performed, she pretended that all was normal and right. But it was not until 4:30 that afternoon, after she had had her hair done, cashed her check, done her nails, and was sitting with a cup of tea that she was able to bury the morning's incident and its accompanying emotions; bury them deeply so that they no longer hovered around her, ready to claim her if she let them. At 4:30 her doorbell rang and a young boy, his pimples glistening with the wetness of the still-sassy snow, delivered a box of one dozen hothouse red roses bedded in lush green ferns. The card read: *Dearest Anne, For your special night. With pride and love, Arthur.*

A smile warmed her face, her eyes; relaxed the stiffness in her neck, removed the knot in her stomach. If the formal use of her name, of an endearment that was somewhat out of character for Arthur, struck her as unusual, she did not dwell upon these anomalies; she felt good again, and safe. A gesture of love, that's all it took. He would never know how much he had done for her, she thought, lovingly removing each velvety flower and putting them in water.

Later, with a light case of pre-party jitters the only thing making her nervous, Anne took one last look in the full-length mirror behind her bedroom closet door, and decided she looked good, and would not look better if she played with another lock of hair, another darkened eyelash. She was wearing taupe-colored velvet slacks that had cost her sixty-five dollars but were worth it: they fit as though custom-made. The same color was repeated in a Calvin Klein cashmere camisole with little gold-toned beads across the straight neckline. Over this was a hip-length, two-pocketed shimmering silk charmeuse buttonless jacket in a deep, expensive wine tone. Its flowing style allowed the flattering neckline of the camisole to be noticed without revealing too much flesh. She looked chic, tasteful, and tremendously appealing, the colors just right for her pale skin, her dark hair and eyes. She wore no jewelry, and her makeup was as monochromatic as her clothing. The effect was enhancement of her natural good looks; she wore the outfit, it did not wear her.

The downstairs buzzer rang, and she went to the intercom to let Arthur in. She was waiting in the open doorway as he came up the three flights of stairs.

He lingered on the last step for a moment. "You look beautiful," he said, his voice filled with sincere admiration, and pride, and not a little surprise at how much he meant the compliment. "I love you," he added, almost to himself.

Anne heard. It was not the way or the exact setting she

might have chosen to hear those words from him for the first time, but it mattered little. They had come unsolicited, unexpected, deeply felt. "I should get dressed up more often," she said lightly.

"Undressed will do just fine," he replied, grateful for her sensitivity. When he reached the doorway, he crushed her against him. He did not kiss her, he did not look at her; he simply held her.

"Do we have time for a quick drink?" he asked, breaking away.

"Absolutely. I need it. I've been a wreck all day," she confessed, going back into the apartment. By now, she was almost convinced that her nerves were attributable to the party. Only when the conversation with Dean Rossmund pressed itself to the forefront of her mind like an obnoxious passenger on a crowded bus did she feel otherwise.

Arthur had removed his overcoat and was sitting at the dining table waiting for his drink. "No couch tonight?" Anne asked, bringing over the drinks.

"I don't want to look at you and get comfortable. That could be lethal and it could also make us very late for your party."

"I'm tempted."

"I think your agent would be most displeased."

"A point well taken," she admitted with a grin. She gave him his drink and sat down across from him. "I must say you look quite dashing yourself this evening, Mr. Dumont sir," she said gallantly.

Arthur fingered his pure silk tie and flipped up one end. "Oh, this old thing," he said feyly, secretly pleased at her compliment. He was wearing a new three-piece suit, a tweed of subtle browns in soft-as-velvet wool. He only hoped his $165 shoes would not get ruined in the still-falling wet snow.

They drank for a few moments in silence. Arthur looked around the room and noticed the vase of red roses atop the buffet. "Those flowers are beautiful," he re-marked. "Who—"

"Oh Arthur, I'm so sorry," Anne said in a breathless rush, her hand flying to her cheek in a gesture of acute embarrassment. "With everything going on and all I had to do . . . oh, I really am sorry."

With a hint of impatience, Arthur said, "What are you talking about, what are you so busy apologizing for?"

"The flowers, of course. I forgot to thank you for the flowers. They came just when I needed them. I had been feeling kind of—" She broke off, noticing the way he was staring into the amber liquid in his glass. "Arthur, what is it? You look as if you swallowed a bug or some-thing."

"I didn't send the flowers," he admitted slowly, meet-ing her eyes. "And I should have. I'm an idiot, a real clod for not thinking to do it. Instead, someone else—"

Anne interrupted with a false-sounding ripple of laughter. "Stop being silly. It doesn't lessen your macho image, you know, to admit to sending a woman flowers."

"Annie, I didn't send them," he insisted.

"But I have the card from you." She got up and re-trieved the card from where she had placed it by the vase. "Here," she said, putting it in front of him. "The evidence is irrefutable," she added with a tremulous grin as she sat down.

"That's not my handwriting."

"Of course it's not, I know the florist writes those things. But that is your name, isn't it?"

Arthur reached across the table and took her hands in his. "Annie, I didn't send the flowers. I should have. I'm an ass for not thinking of it, but that's the truth. I didn't send them. And the card, well," he shrugged, "I just don't know. Maybe there's another Arthur in your life you're not telling me about." His smile was slight.

Anne pulled her hands away. "If you didn't send them," she asked quietly, slowly, "who did?"

"I don't know."

"Neither do I." And for a few wildly uncontrolled seconds, she felt herself slip from confusion into that same unreasonable fear that had gripped her after the telephone call with the dean. There was a burning behind her eyes, tears of terror that she demanded not fall. Her stomach seemed raw, as if it had been pounded with a hammer; it ached with fright. Her hands grew cold and clammy and damp; her tongue flicked over dry lips to moisten the caked lipstick. A pulse point beat hard in her taut neck. Suddenly, she giggled.

"Annie?" Arthur said, his shoulders hunched in alarm. For those moments that had just passed, he had lost her as totally as if she were gone from the room to a place miles from him, unavailable to him. "Annie, what is it?"

She giggled again. Arthur pushed back his chair, about to go to her. The sound of wood scraping against wood pricked her conscience, and the nervous laughter died into silence. He waited until life returned to her eyes, until her lips nudged themselves into a small, but unhysterical smile. He had never seen this side of her, and he wished never to again. It reminded him, unpleasantly, of that night so many months ago in the other Anne Fletcher's bed. There was a big difference, however, he told himself. This time he cared: about the girl, about what would cause such anxiety.

"Are you all right?" he asked tentatively.

"Fine. I'm fine," she assured him, and forced herself to believe it. For now. This was no time to get unhinged, she reasoned with herself. Some sick little mind out there was playing Dennis the Menace pranks, and she was letting them get to her. They were meaningless, harmless tricks, that's all, she thought with renewed conviction, and not worth the attention she was giving them.

"I told you my nerves were shot," she said to Arthur almost boastfully. "I'll be glad when tonight is over and I can get back to normal."

"So will I," he answered with a relieved grin.

She pushed back her chair. "We better go. I don't want to be late to my own party."

"You sure you're okay?"

"I'm sure."

Arthur had just helped her on with her coat when the telephone rang. "Should I let it ring?" she asked hopefully.

"Better not. Could be your agent with some message or something."

She went into the kitchen. "Hello? Hello? . . . Who *is* this? Why don't you say something? Hello?"

Slowly, she replaced the receiver after she heard the dead tone. She glanced up; Arthur was standing in the doorway to the kitchen. "Wrong number?"

She shook her head, not trusting herself to speak. Don't panic, she told herself. Don't get upset. Don't make more of this than just another crank call.

"Annie, are you all right? You're as pale as a ghost. Who was that?"

"I don't know," she managed. "They never tell me who they are."

"What are you talking about?" Arthur snapped, exasperated.

"The phone rings, I answer, and that's it. The person on the other end never speaks." She spoke in a monotone, her eyes fixed on a point beyond Arthur's shoulder.

"This has happened before?" he asked, concerned now.

"Lots of times."

"For how long?"

She shrugged. "I don't know. A month. Two months. I don't remember."

"Why didn't you ever tell me?"

Her eyes focused on him. "What could you do about it, Arthur?" she said unkindly. "Besides, your reaction might not have been one of tremendous sympathy or understanding. I didn't have the easiest time convincing you that someone had called that writer from *Glamour* using my name. Remember? You like facts, evidence, and I wouldn't want it any other way. But please don't expect me to come crying to you when these strange things happen and I have no proof."

"Jeez, you make it sound like there's been a whole campaign," he said, shaking his head in disbelief.

Her glance was sharp. "I never thought of it that way, but maybe you're right."

"Annie, stop talking like that," he chided, "you sound almost paranoid, for pete's sake. Don't tell me you think there's some connection between that phone call to the editor, the flowers, and the heavy breather?" His expression spoke his derision more loudly than his voice.

"Who said it was a heavy breather?"

"What else could it be?" He closed the distance between them and began to button her coat. "First it's a secret admirer who sends you flowers, then some guy who gets off hearing your voice. At least I know how my competition operates," he teased in an attempt to put the two of them right again.

"That's not funny," she shot back, her eyes hot as she pushed his hands away. "The flowers were not from some admirer, and whoever's been calling me doesn't do any heavy breathing. I don't even know if it's a man or not so don't be so damned smug about who's calling and why. Believe me, I don't see any humor in this kind of harassment, and frankly, I think it's disgusting that you do." She brushed past him and into the dining foyer.

She stood by the table, a trembling hand resting on the edge for support. She faced away from Arthur; he could not see her shut her eyes against the tears that again threatened to spill; he could not see the quiver in her chin as she tried to control the turmoil within. Then, as her anger began to ebb, she regretted her outburst, and wished she could call back each word. She wanted

147

this almost as much as she wanted to tell Arthur about the phone call with the dean. But she could never do that now. She had thought she would mention it to him casually, after the party, when they would be alone. She had wanted his reaction, clear, logical as she knew it would be. But she would say nothing now; she did not dare. He knew about the speaking date, and so she would just have to lie, tell him it had been cancelled.

Briefly, her anger reerupted; she should be able to speak the truth without worrying about whether he would think her crazy. But she knew she was being unfair. Were the situation reversed; were someone to repeat to her a series of weird though unrelated incidents and try to make a connection between them, would she be any less skeptical than he had been?

She turned around. He was still standing in the doorway to the kitchen, watching her. This was as close to a quarrel as they had come since September, and the silence it brought was suffocatingly oppressive.

She walked over to him. "I'm sorry," she said, her voice cracking, eyes glassy with unshed tears.

He did nothing for a long second, then he cupped her face in his hands. "So am I. I only meant to relieve the tension and—"

"I know. I'm just a mess tonight, I guess." She leaned against him. "Hold me a little, okay?"

He did, and both felt the restorative powers of touching fill and mend them. For Arthur, too, needed emotional balm. He had been hurt, and angered as well. His flippancy had been ill-timed, but how could he have suspected that she was taking these isolated incidents seriously? Still, he should have been more sensitive; she was pulled tight tonight and with good reason, he supposed. It was the unexpected sharpness of her words that had hurt; the unreasonable reaction to his that had angered. Self-centeredly, he hoped that whoever—singular or plural—was behind the calls, the flowers, would give up his sick idea of fun. The girl he thought he knew was turning into a stranger, leaving him with the sensation of being stranded, adrift somehow without the familiar anchor he had come to expect; it was a sensation he did not at all like.

She moved against him, and he looked down at her. "I love you," she said softly.

He nodded, in reciprocity and in acceptance. "All set to be a star?" he quipped, determined to erase what had threatened to spoil.

She tried on a smile. "Absolutely greedy for the limelight," she rejoined. Then she got her purse, turned out all but one lamp, and they left. If each was a little disappointed in the other; if each was somewhat self-conscious, they cared enough to reach within themselves for understanding and tolerance. They were still new enough to each other to want to do this. By the time the cab reached Central Park West and 69th Street, anticipation for what awaited them, and two warm, unhurried embraces in the back seat, had successfully healed the frail nerves of one, the wounded ego of the other.

There is no music at a publishing party. The people do not want to be distracted from the sound of their rumors and gossip. It is, of course, a business built on words, but not primarily on those written. The boats landing at Ellis Island generations ago, with their symphony of tongues, were as a rustle compared to the buzz and hum and chirp and babble at a publishing party. Only a few exchanges are about deals, pending or accomplished, or about the book and author for whom the party is given. More often, tidbits of sexual dalliance or impending career doom, like tiny skewered hors d'oeuvres, are greedily passed around and tasted for their delicious unsavoriness. Since the industry is a small one, with but a few personalities of true gossip value, frequently the morsels are somewhat warmed over, sometimes even stale, but they still make for much fun, and even more noise.

Anne had tried to warn Arthur what the evening would be like; she had attended a few similar type evenings—enough to know what to expect, not that many that she still could not enjoy herself. But that had always been as a guest, with little at stake. Tonight was entirely different; she had known that long before the art deco-designed elevator doors whispered open onto the penthouse floor.

"Well, I can hear it's already going strong," Anne remarked.

Arthur glanced at his watch. "It's only six-thirty now. What happened to being fashionably late?"

"For free food and booze?" she laughed. "Not with this crowd."

Down the carpeted corridor a few feet they could see four portable coat racks, one and a half of them already occupied with overcoats, wool scarves, umbrellas; rubber boots, like legless soldiers, were lined up on the floor. A white-capped, white-aproned maid sat on a straight-backed chair outside the front door. A cigar box of ticket stubs was at her feet.

"Fancy," Arthur commented.

"Practical," Anne answered. "Would you want your parquet floors and antique oriental rugs to get dripped on?"

"The real thing?"

She nodded. "Wait till you see."

They gave their coats to the attendant, and pushed open the partially ajar door, slipping into a marble-tiled, mirrored vestibule glittering with the dancing lights from an overhead crystal chandelier. From there, they could see into the vast expanse beyond, a living room alive with the sounds and colors of the guests. Anne turned toward a wall that was mirror, fluffed her hair, pulled down the bottom of her cashmere camisole. With an expression eager for approbation, she asked, "Do I look all right?"

Arthur saw the roasting chestnut eyes and the aristocratic cheekbones, their color now restored; he saw the full lips, the strain gone from them; he saw the pronounced rise and fall of her breasts, the pride in her posture. "You look lovely."

Her eyes smiled her gratitude. "Then I guess this is it. Let's go."

They did not have time to stand at the arched entry to the living room and observe either guests or lush furnishings. Matthew Holmes, despite two hundred forty-odd loose pounds on a six-feet-two-inch frame, spotted Anne and glided over to her as gracefully as a sprite.

"My dear, dear Anne." He took both her hands in his and pushed his face forward for the obligatory kiss. "Look at those masses," he sighed, "and the party's not even begun. My dear child, this room is filling rapidly with the stench of your success."

Anne's laughter was unnaturally high, but Holmes seemed not to notice. "Matt, this is Arthur Dumont," she introduced. "Arthur, this is the man who's made it all possible."

They shook hands, casually sizing each other up, more out of habit than interest since both accepted the necessity of the other in Anne's life. Holmes entwined an arm through Anne's, and squeezed her ever so slightly to him. Though called "piss-elegant" by many, friends included, his sartorial excesses were in no manner designed to attract other men. Matthew Holmes liked the power of money to bring him beauty: in custom-made velvet suits, like the deep plum one he wore tonight that would look better on a slimmer-hipped body; like custom-made silk shirts, silk ties, silk underwear; hand-sewn Florentine shoes and boots; like superior wines; delectable meals, priceless and tasteful antiques and art; exquisite, accomplished women.

Money provided Matthew Holmes with freedom and the ways to enjoy it. Never married, he refused to be encumbered and bored by one woman; to be in any way responsible for someone's emotional dramas. He bought his women, therefore, as he bought the other objects of beauty in his life. At fifty-six, with too much flesh, too little dyed-brown hair, liver-spotted hands, a florid complexion and a mean, self-indulgent mouth, he had no difficulty obtaining his choice in women—such was the power of his money, such was the value of his power. Anne knew all this, only a little second-hand. Matt strutted his style of life, his reasons for it, like a thoroughbred. He never apologized for being a winner.

Anne could never have with Matthew Holmes the type of relationship enjoyed by some writers and their agents; the rapport was not natural; their bond professional symbiosis, never anything closer. So when he had squeezed her to him, she had felt her stomach pump with revulsion. It had been a meaningless liberty she wished he had not taken.

"Time to circulate, dear child," he now said. "We do have a book to sell, remember."

"I could use a drink first," she confessed.

"Would I allow you to undergo this ordeal without one?" he chided. With Arthur following, they wedged through the growing throng, Holmes, with a wave or a curt nod of his round head, dismissing those who wished to stop him en route to a small room off the living room. A full bar manned by two uniformed bartenders had been set up. Holmes took Anne's and Arthur's orders, and asked for a Perrier and lime for himself. He did not drink at his own parties, preferring to delay all his indulgences until he was alone with those select few he had invited to stay on.

"Now, Arthur, you must leave this lady in my hands," Holmes said. "It's time for business."

With a helpless shrug for Arthur, Anne walked out with her agent. From cluster to individual, Holmes presented his newest acquisition with shrewd pride. After forty-five minutes, Anne was exhilarated. Names that belonged to titans of the business—mainly from the paperback end since Matt wanted a good reprint sale—obsequiously paid homage to this potentially valuable property. If their smiles were too bright, too quick; if their eyes kept darting for a waiter with the canapé tray or for an important colleague, she did not care. This was a frothy lark, a Molière comedy of manners, and she was the dazzling ingenue. What fun, she marveled as Holmes introduced her to the vice-president of production for 20th Century-Fox films. And here comes Letitia Corwell, she saw, delighted with the effusive embrace her editor gave her.

"Darling Matt, you've created another best-seller," the physically dumpy, professionally excellent woman gushed. "Now you're going to ask for an outrageous advance on her next book."

Holmes's eyes grew sleepily innocent. "But of course, Letitia. And you'll pay it happily."

The editor gave a mock sigh of resignation. "Too true. Bound galleys are due next week, by the way," she told them.

"Great," Anne enthused. "I can still make changes in that, can't I?"

Her editor nodded. "But try to keep them to a minimum since they get expensive at this point," she advised.

"Send me ten," Matt requested.

Letitia's too bushy brows raised. "Going all out, aren't you?"

Holmes pressed his lips together, then released them; he did this three times, and Anne was reminded of Charles Laughton in *Witness for the Prosecution*. Then: "The cost of the bound galleys is a price I'm not only willing, but eager to pay."

Anne was curious. "We pay for those?"

"Darling, don't be so greedy," Letitia teasingly scolded. "Your impoverished publisher has enough problems to contend with."

"Ah, yes, Letitia," Matt said in a voice of thick syrup, "the movie sale *I'll* make will be another of those problems, won't it?"

The editor laughed. "Dear, shrewd Matt. Anne, I'll leave you now to this wonderful weasel." She kissed the air in their general direction. "Speak to you both soon," she fluttered, then turned, noticing the director of one of the major book clubs. A sale there could mean lots of money. With a wave for the acknowledged alcoholic who could make or break a book, she moved toward him.

"How're you feeling?" Matt asked.

"Fine. Terrific," Anne grinned. "It's all a little overwhelming, but I'm loving it."

"Good. There are a few more people I want you to meet—one or two I think you know," and he mentioned the names of two magazine fiction editors she had copyedited for long ago. Anne knew why they were important. If her novel could be sold for first serialization to one of those large-circulation magazines, her book's chances for commercial success were tremendously increased.

"After that," he went on, "I'm going to let you loose. Circulate for a while, then find a spot that's visible and away from the bar. People will find you, and I'll be keeping an eye out that no one stays too long," he assured her.

Her response was a tinkle of laughter, a sound of utter charm.

"You really are enjoying yourself, aren't you?"

"As long as I never for one moment take any of this seriously, I can have a wonderful time," she told him.

He appraised her for a few seconds, his lips pressing in and out again like a squeezed lemon. "If you can say that a year from now, after your book's a winner, you'll do fine," he commented skeptically. "There's Patricia Frisch, she's your sub rights director. It helps if they meet the authors they're selling. Come."

Even after another thirty minutes of greetings and smiles and thank yous to incantations of good luck, of weaving snakelike through a crowd that had spilled from the living room into the bar and vestibule, Anne felt no fatigue; she was resting on an air mattress, comfortable and high above this circus of mostly harmless falsity. Snatches of acerbic wit at the expense of an absentee colleague could occasionally be heard, as could the death knell for a rival's book; and voices seemed to grow louder, more shrill as the time and liquor flowed. But there was an intensity and energy among these people that she found exhilarating; and, undeniably, a glamour that set them apart from people in other businesses, even if, as she suspected, it was self-proclaimed and somewhat dated.

There was little evidence here, she had noticed, of fashion. The men, with one or two exceptions, had on rumpled jackets and dulled shoes; the women, many of them young and overweight, wore their hems too high, or their slacks fit artlessly as if to deny body, sexuality; their blouses and sweaters seemed seasons old, creased, nubby, another denial. Even granting that they had not had time to go home from the office to change, there was a stylelessness about them that Anne believed belonged to any occasion and which she found almost endearing. Only the older women seemed to have taken pains with their grooming, and they to an extreme, trumpeting a call for attention.

Matt had introduced Anne to a dowager agent, a one-time queen bee now retired who was nevertheless invited to every party and usually came, her reputation still impressive, her opinions still valuable. A large woman in her late sixties, her snow-white hair was piled in thick waves around her head, a coiffure reminiscent of the forties. A floor-length brocade caftan shot through with gold threads did little to hide her bulk as the evident powder and rouge did little to camouflage the cob-webs of age in her face. There were others like her, women who, Anne thought, remembered publishing parties of another era when the variety of deals and the amounts of money were not as important as the image of the publisher; when the editor was as much a star, if not more, than the author.

As Matt had once told her, and as she had even begun to see for herself, the business today was filled with young upstarts, he had called them; boys and girls whose self-image was as a combination Max Perkins-Richard Zanuck. Creative wheeler-dealers who wanted to make a splash, quickly, and moved from publishing house to publishing house to film company, with the book and an author only vehicles for their own upward mobility. He had said this without rancor, and only a little regret for the simplicity of earlier days. In a way, he had confided, it was better now. Playing at business was a luxury no one could afford, and if those running the companies today were less meticulous, perhaps even less able than their predecessors, they were also, ironically, more successful, and with that he had no complaint.

During her tour of the room, Anne had tried to keep a discreet eye out for Arthur. She knew how clannish the people at these parties could be, and she hoped he was managing. The few times she had spotted him, he had seemed fine: circulating or speaking with someone. Once they had caught each other's eyes, when he had been nodding in either agreement or sleepy boredom—Anne would have to ask him which later—to the words of a rather obvious homosexual who was wearing a yellow suede western scarf over a crepey neck; he had a dyed red toupee and a waxed graying moustache, and emphasized his statements by periodically reaching out and touching Arthur on the arm. Anne had sent a small smile Arthur's way and he returned an almost imperceptible roll of his eyes. She looked for him again now as Matt led her to the woman he wanted her to meet. She saw him near the doorway to the bar. He was leaning against the wall, alone, observing; she longed to go to him, to touch base with reality, but there was no time.

Arthur was content to stand alone for a while and be an audience to the scenes played before him. He was enjoying himself, which was not often possible at functions he attended that were primarily filled with competitive attorneys. His identity for the people he had met this evening was as an adjunct to the star, and while it was not a position he wished to find himself in permanently, it was serving as an opportunity for him to relax. If Annie was the person he believed her to be, she would not be taking this any more seriously than he was, and later, privately, they would share what they had seen and heard, and laugh at the innocuousness of it all.

He glanced down at his empty glass, and decided to have one more drink. It would be his last. He knew the party would go on for quite some time, and Annie had to stay. He did not. By prearrangement, they had agreed that if it got too much for him, he should leave and she would meet him back at her apartment later. Arthur had at first objected strenuously and gallantly to this generous suggestion of Anne's, then more faintly when she convinced him that she would be too busy to spend even snatched seconds with him. By now, he had seen enough to know she was right. He held little interest for these satellites orbiting the current star; once his identity was established and shown to serve little purpose for them, their eyes dulled with politeness, their drinks suddenly needed refilling, a cigarette urgently had to be found. And they fascinated him only slightly more. He turned into the bar, his mind made up to have the drink and leave.

In the entryway to the living room, calmly surveying the crowd for the two faces of interest to her, stood Anne Fletcher. One face she was pleased to see had left the immediate area of the living room. She did not want Arthur to know she was here, not if it could be avoided.

She had only now decided this, when she had spotted him standing against the wall. Until this moment, she had had every intention of making sure he saw what he had been missing.

Her boss had offered her his invitation, with a cryptic remark about life being full of coincidences. Anne had not understood but readily accepted, glad for the chance to attend a publishing party. When she read the invitation, she understood too well the meaning behind his comment. Resentment flared, then died as she realized what a gift had been handed to her. It was a little frightening, having it all right there before you, almost frightening enough to avoid—the reality could not possibly be as delicious as the fantasy. But, in the final analysis, it was too precious an opportunity to pass up.

She had planned a two-fronted assault, and one was certainly for Arthur since she was sure he would be here. She had dressed with him in mind as much as *her*. An hour was spent on makeup alone, and she knew her eyes had never looked so enormous and bright, her face never more compelling with the shimmering little specks of gold dust she had powdered on. She was wearing a new, blueberry-colored silk tunic, cut to a deep vee in front, that moved against her body in clinging detail, and gray satin pants so tight that eating would be a physical impossibility. She knew she had never looked better, had planned it exactly this way.

But it would not be for Arthur after all. Seeing him smugly standing there, so superior, so self-confident, she suddenly had no desire to risk spoiling her evening. And he could spoil it if he wanted to. He might not be as pleased to see her as she imagined, might even try to get her to leave. He would not provoke a scene, of that she was sure, but he might make it difficult, impossible if he chose, for her to get near the real reason for being at the party. It was not worth the self-satisfaction she would feel watching her physical impact on him.

She walked into the living room, aware of the eyes appreciatively, and curiously, upon her; glad for once that she knew so few people in this stratum of the industry that her path to her target was relatively direct. Anne waited patiently, studying, observing, until the woman talking with her sauntered off; then she moved in.

"You're Anne Fletcher, aren't you?"

Annie smiled with practiced ease, and nodded.

"So am I."

"I beg your pardon?"

"Anne Fletcher. That's my name."

Annie stared at the girl before her, long enough for it to register that she was exceptionally attractive, that she was probably the girl Arthur had told her about, and that she herself was flustered and tremendously interested. She grinned. "Well, hello."

"I gather from the way you said that that Arthur's told you about me," Anne remarked.

"Then you are *that* Anne Fletcher?" Annie asked, slightly uncomfortable with this unexpected situation.

"If you mean the one Arthur dated, yes."

Annie laughed a bit self-consciously. "This is so amazing. I've never met anyone with my name before. Not that it means anything, of course, but it is unusual."

"Mmm."

"Look, let me find Arthur. He's here and I'm sure he'd like to see you."

"Oh no, don't. He might not appreciate the past and the present meeting up like this," Anne hastily pointed out.

Annie considered that. He might not appreciate it, but she certainly did. It was not often that a current girlfriend got the chance to see other examples of her man's taste. If this girl was typical, Arthur certainly had let a good thing go.

"You're right," she said brightly. "It'll be my little secret."

They spoke then about publishing, about Anne's job, about how infrequently she got to go to parties like this.

"It must be so exciting for you," she commented, making a sweeping gesture with her body and her hands and her eyes to encompass the room, using the time to see if Arthur was anywhere in sight. "When is your book due to come out?" she asked.

"In around six weeks or so, I think. Arthur mentioned that you're interested in writing."

"Did he?"

"Perhaps you'd like Matt to take a look at what you've done. He—"

"I don't have anything ready to show him yet," Anne said curtly. She hesitated, then: "Actually, if you wouldn't mind, I think I'd rather you look at it first."

"Me?" Annie smiled self-deprecatingly. "I wouldn't dare judge another's work. I'm not exactly qualified."

"Oh, but you are. You're being published, aren't you?"

"Yes, but—"

Anne's smile was beguilingly imploring. "Please? I'd feel so much better knowing a professional like yourself took the time with it."

"Well, I suppose," Annie replied slowly. "But I really think—"

"Thanks so much. I'll call you soon and we'll get together for lunch, okay? Maybe by then I'll have something to show you. If not, we can always discover what more we have in common." She laughed, drawing the other girl to join her.

"It is ironic, isn't it?"

"Mmm," Anne agreed. "Well, I'll let you get back to

161

the others. I just wanted to introduce myself, and congratulate you on your book. I wish you lots of luck with it."

"Thank you. Maybe the next time we're both at one of these things it'll be for you."

"Maybe."

At ten o'clock, Annie knocked on the door to her apartment, having given her keys to Arthur. When he opened the door, she came in, wordlessly tossed purse and coat on a dining room chair, kicked off her shoes, and plopped onto the couch.

"I'm pooped," she said when he sat down next to her. "How long have you been here?"

He glanced at the glass on the table. "About two and a half brandies longer than you."

"I didn't even see you leave. I'm sorry, sweetheart, it was so hectic and—"

"Hey, it was *your* party, remember. Besides, we agreed I'd come here if it got too much."

"That's true, still . . ."

"I tried to signal you I was going but Matt had his arm around you and some hideously fat woman and I couldn't catch your eye."

"Fat woman? Oh, I know. She's an editor at a rival publisher who pays more than mine does."

Arthur poured a brandy for her, and they chatted about the party, he mostly listening as she chirped gaily about this editor, that movie person. Exhausted, she leaned back against the couch, eyes shut.

"Arthur?" she said after a while.

"Hmm?"

She opened her eyes. "Tell me about Anne Fletcher."

"What!"

"Tell me about Anne Fletcher," she repeated, grinning as she sat back up. "The one before me."

"I know which one you meant, dammit," he said irritably.

"Well, tell me."

"Annie, what the hell brought this on?"

Incredible green eyes. "I don't know. Just curious, I guess."

"Just curious, huh? One minute we're talking about the party, the next you want to know about some girl I used to make it with. There's a logical connection there, I'm sure, but it escapes me."

Annie smiled. "Come on, don't be so defensive. Is she pretty?"

He shrugged. "Yeah, I guess," he muttered.

"You guess?" she pressed, knowing exactly how pretty.

"Yeah, she was pretty, okay? Shit, what *is* this?"

"Every woman is curious about this kind of thing, Arthur. Humor me, okay?" He looked at her skeptically and nodded. "Smart?"

He hesitated. "I suppose, I don't really know. We never had any what you might call serious conversations."

"Oh, more the pillow talk type of thing, huh?"

"Annie, jeez, come on!" Arthur said, acutely embarrassed.

She reached out and put a hand on his arm. "I'm sorry," but her smile, amused, knowing, told him she was not.

"If now you ask me if you're better in the sack than she, I swear I'll—"

"Nope," she shook her head. "In fact, I'm tired of talking about her."

"Good."

"Except for one thing."

"Now what?" he asked wearily.

She waited a beat. "Is she nice? A nice person?"

"Annie—"

"Please, Arthur. Just answer me that."

"I don't know if she's nice or not," he said with exasperation. "I told you what it was like with her."

"I know, but still, you must have drawn some conclusion."

"Is this the end of it?"

"I promise," she assured him.

Arthur pondered the question seriously, remembering the fathomless eyes, the thin unyielding lips as much as he recalled the occasional laughs, the sexual release. "No, I don't think she's really a nice person," he finally said quietly.

Annie said nothing. She would not tell him, not that she had met her, not that she might help her, not that she would have lunch with her. It would be, as she had said, her little secret, and she felt no dishonesty about not sharing it with Arthur. Besides, she reasoned to herself, he would only get annoyed if he knew so why bother him with something basically insignificant and unimportant?

She put down her glass, took his away, and snuggled closer to him. "Let's," she kissed him, "go," another kiss, "to," kiss, "bed."

I am very proud of myself, and will remember tonight for a long time as an occasion of great self-control. What a consummate actress I am. [*Laughter.*] Congratulating her and wishing her luck. It's a good thing the bitch didn't know what kind of luck! Bad, evil, the worst kind, that's what. Standing there, the center of attention, all those people paying homage to her as if she really was somebody. She's nothing. Nothing at all. If her clever agent hadn't had a party *before* publication, he wouldn't have gotten such a great turnout. I'd bet anything her book is commercial tripe and doesn't sell worth a damn. Then all this hooplah will make her and her smartass agent look the fools they really are.

I must admit she's prettier than I remember from that night I saw her outside her apartment. There's something patrician about her that's sort of appealing if you like the type. I certainly can't see anything special about her, though. I mean, she doesn't look or sound particularly bright. It should have been me those people were coming to wish well. Me instead of her who was having a book published. I'm smarter, prettier, and I know I'm more talented. But she's tough. I've got to give her that. She seemed cool, unruffled, untouched by what's . . . Dammit! I hate her so much I can feel it like a boil of pus. [*Laughter.*] That's good, Anne, that is so very, very good. And you're going to have to lance the boil, instead of just squeezing gently.

She turned off the tape recorder, put it away, and remained lying in her darkened bedroom, staring at visions on the ceiling only she could see. And then, a tightening constricted her chest, and her fingers gripped the edge of the comforter. "You fool. You silly idiot," she hissed out loud. "What do you really hope to accomplish?" Four seconds passed on the digital clock before she knew. Everything you deserve. That was the answer, and it was silent.

13

For the next several weeks, it was almost possible for both girls, in their own separate ways, to forget, perhaps only repress, the troubles that had gnawed at them earlier in the new year. If Anne N. Fletcher's stomach contracted in sickening dread whenever the telephone rang, she was learning to live with it. Every week, she received at least one, sometimes two of those calls, the kind of voiceless horror that left her shaking afterwards with disgust that some person out there needed to do this to her.

Her hardened, imperturbable friend Karen decided it was a rejected lover. Arthur was convinced it was a sickie, someone who did not know her, but had picked her number at random from a configuration of digits he had stumbled upon, and when he got bored he would push other buttons on his phone until he found a new victim to harass. Her brother thought she should get her number changed; Matt said that would be foolish, people needed to reach her *easily*.

Anne did not change her number; she did not stop answering her telephone; she did not get an answering service or machine, all possibilities that would have eliminated the quick shutting of her eyes, the sudden dryness in her throat, the punch in her gut when the telephone rang; the trembling that secured her after she hung up. She wished it would end, but until it did, she was coping with it.

She never did find out who sent her the dozen roses or who had called Dean Rossmund, and she had stopped caring. Occasionally, before she would fall asleep some nights, or sitting at her typewriter, having difficulty with a particular passage in her new novel, or at a boring movie, she would find her mind drifting back to those incidents, to the strange call with the editor at *Glamour*. She would wonder who and why, and a little shudder would run over her heart. But it was past, and she found nothing to be achieved by dwelling on yesterday's incidents. Besides, there was no need since only the strange, voiceless telephone calls interrupted the melody of her days.

Anne Fletcher, too, seemed to have quietly regained control of herself. The girl who had thrown her so off-balance no longer stalked her mind as constantly or insistently; her tape diary recorded disgruntlement with the office, unpleasantness with her mother, disappointing encounters with men, hope for the imminent start of her novel, annoyance with the weather, Janey, the cost of living. Nothing had changed in her life; she had simply resumed living it.

About a month after Matt Holmes's party, on a dull steel-colored Sunday morning that begged living creatures to remain indoors, Anne Fletcher stretched contentedly in bed. She was unwilling to begin the day, enjoying lying lazily in the warmth, remembering the pleasures she had experienced last night, and the previous Wednesday night at the skilled hands of Richard Keever, a brawny, concrete hulk of incredible sexual prowess. She had met him at the juice bar in her health club. The short sleeves of his gray, sweat-stained T-shirt tightly emphasized bulging biceps; pectorals seemed molded by a master of anatomy; thighs encased their muscularity in machine-hardened flesh. He was a fascinating physical specimen: no excess, yet not sinewbound.

They had started chatting, both agreeing that they preferred to use the facilities of the health club in the evening, almost near the nine o'clock closing time when there was less noise, few people. They each changed into bathing suits for a swim, which consisted of Anne swimming three horizontal laps in the thirty-foot pool, then watching Richard do twenty vertical laps and climb out unwinded and glistening. From there dinner at an expensive steakhouse; Richard was an architectural engineer and had earned the right to eat well, he told her. From dinner, without hesitation, to his apartment on East 28th Street. She had invited him to her place, instinctively feeling that at long last the platform bed would be properly employed. But he had two rules, and saw no reason to break them with her: his apartment only, and no sleeping over. Anne did not care that much, not enough to give up the opportunity.

She had come into the office Thursday morning so unmistakably happy that Sandy had been compelled to remark upon it, and Anne needed no prompting to reveal the cause of her good spirits. He had called Thursday afternoon to make a date for Saturday, and last night had been even better. Lying in bed this Sunday morning allowed Anne the luxury of anticipating future nights with him; she sincerely hoped that he would not quickly prove disappointing, as so many other men did once they were taken out of the bedroom. She would not concern herself with that now, however; not even inevitable reality could spoil her mood this morning.

She tossed back the comforter, dawdled a moment more with her legs dangling over the side of the bed, then got up. She put on her robe on the way to the front door. Home delivery of the Sunday *New York Times* was an indulgence she permitted herself. During the week she bought the paper on her way to work; on Saturdays, regardless of the weather, she bought it at the card/candy/stationery store three blocks away run by two Korean émigrées. But Sundays the paper came to her like a reward.

She picked up the bulk, deposited it on the table in front of her couch, then went into the kitchen to prepare a pot of fresh coffee. When it had brewed, she took the Melitta pot and her Salton hot tray into the living room, plugged in the tray, and got comfortable.

Anne had a system to reading the Sunday *Times*. The employment section came first although she knew jobs of her caliber were never listed; it was more a way of checking on how little other people were being paid. Then came arts and leisure, with a studious ten minutes spent on the week's TV listings. The magazine section was next with a cursory scanning of the articles, more attention to the fashions, food, and design features. She would turn back the magazine to the crossword puzzle, then lay it aside until she had finished the rest of the paper.

She did not, of course, cover every part of the massive Sunday paper. Sports, business and finance, real estate were rarely glanced at. Travel usually appealed to her only in the dead of winter. She liked to read the front section to see if anybody she knew was engaged or had gotten married; to check whether the stores were having sales. She read the book review because she felt she should; she was in publishing after all. She did not like the book review; she felt it was pretentious snobbery disguised as intellect. She had no patience for the ecstasy wasted on books that few of the buying public would ever read, and she had only contempt for the claptrap on the best-seller lists.

She was on her third cup of coffee when she picked up the book review. The cover article was about Edgar Allan Poe, and two new biographies of him. She flipped the pages, scanning the ads, stopping to skim a first paragraph and last if the review was short enough.

She certainly had not been looking for it. She might even have passed over it if she had not just read the review of a new novel by a woman writer she enjoyed. So her eyes went down the columns naturally, and when the name leaped out at her, it was with the impact of a physical assault. Anne Fletcher. It was as if someone had taken the remaining hot coffee in the Melitta and splashed it on her face. She stung, all over. Her skin felt prickly, hot, red. She was facing a wall of fire and she did not know how to get to the other side. Flames of pain danced about her, licking back into life wounds that she thought had healed. She began to read, words, fragments of sentences, petals of praise, sharp shards of criticism.

> "*Honorable Mention* . . . first novel by the not-unknown magazine writer Anne N. Fletcher . . . enthusiastic if not totally laudable first effort . . . strong characterization of the rich, young, morally lazy ladies indigenous to Manhattan . . . men lack the dimension of the women . . . a wit in her wisdom that is refreshing, surprising . . . somewhat predictable and weak in plot . . . purposelessness of the people reflected in author not knowing where to take them and end the story. . . . Still, highly readable . . . strong pacing . . . natural flow . . . would translate well into film with its visual style of story-telling . . . look forward to more from this talented if yet unfocused new writer. . . ."

She reread it, wishing to carefully select, like a berry picker, the words and phrases of criticism, and feed on them. She wanted *something* to ease the ache. She placed the review section on the coffee table, and leaned over it, the upper half of her body rocking back and forth, back and forth, as the black and white newsprint blurred before eyes turned to glass. There was nothing for her to take out and embrace; nothing for her to hold close as vicious; nothing for her to project as painful upon the other girl. It was the kind of review she dreamed of for herself: to be called talented, to be called readable, commercial but not a hack. A *good* writer who would sell. And it was all happening to the wrong girl.

She stopped rocking, sat back against the pillow of her couch. She sipped from her mug of coffee. She looked out into her living room, eyes closed in upon herself, the two white spots appearing around her mouth, bracketing in the torment. Her scalp seemed itchy, as if each hair had been ripped out and the root exposed. Her neck hurt; she could not support the deadened weight her head had suddenly become. There was no feeling in her fingertips, her thighs. She could not move; numbness controlled her, and somewhere in her mind that struck her as peculiar. Numbness is passive, it does nothing, yet it was active now, dominating her will. Then, she shut her eyes, folded her hands together in her robe-clad lap. If one were to come upon her now, observe her posture, her immobility, the image would be of a girl at prayer, silently, deeply invoking sustenance. And perhaps she was doing exactly that for when she again opened her eyes, their opacity had vanished; they were clear, bright, seeing eyes; her mouth relaxed, her hands came apart, her shoulders lost their rigidity. There was movement and feeling and thought once again.

A vague, secretive, almost sexual smile hovered around her lips like a bumblebee around a flower. Conviction strengthened her; pleasure mobilized her. She got up and went into the kitchen. Once there, she stood for seconds only in front of her utility drawer, that catch-all container in almost every kitchen where useless papers and stunted, eraserless pencils, where twine and scissors and loose spools of thread and rusty needles, where forgotten recipes, reminders, telephone numbers —where the discards of daily life are tossed, as dead as if they had been cremated in an incinerator except that no one is willing to admit their demise. She pulled open the drawer, and began to rummage through the refuse when the telephone rang. The sound startled her; for a quick moment, she did not recognize it, and she turned to stare at the unfamiliar instrument. The third ring delivered her, and she answered.

"Hello?" Her voice was soft, querulous, distant.

"Hi, it's me."

"Janey?"

"Who else? I called to find out how last night went," she bubbled.

"Last night?"

"Uh-oh, that forgettable, huh?"

Anne did not answer immediately, and Janey mistook her silence. "Hey, I'm sorry. You want to talk about it?"

"No, no, it was great," Anne quickly assured her. She glanced at the open drawer, and the smile twitched about her mouth. "My mind was elsewhere, that's all," she added.

"So tell me," Janey urged, "how was he?"

Anne laughed. "He was great and so was the evening. I like him."

"When are you going to see him again?"

"I don't know," Anne answered with some irritation. "When he calls and asks me, I suppose."

"Didn't he say anything definite? Didn't he make another date or something?" Janey pressed, believing that there was no security to be had from a man who finished one evening without commitment for another.

"No, he didn't say anything definite," Anne replied with more impatience. "Boy, sometimes I can't believe you're really almost twenty-nine years old."

"What does my age have to do with this?" Janey retorted.

"You'd think you would have learned something by now. What guarantee are words?"

"True, but at least they're something."

"Bullshit."

"But you had a good time?" Janey asked, refusing to be drawn into an argument.

"Yes, he's really nice. You should listen to me and join the health club. All kinds of guys there."

"Yeah, well, but—"

"Just answer me one thing. Have you met as many men in your pottery, yoga, and modern dance classes as I have at the health club?"

"No, but—"

"End of argument," Anne said with finality.

"Hey, I almost forgot. Did you look at the *Times* yet?"

"Some of it."

Janey's voice held the glee of one-upmanship. "See the book review?"

"Some of it," Anne repeated, stealing another quick look at the open utility drawer.

"Did you get to the review of your 'archenemy' Anne Fletcher's book? Pretty funny typo," she gloated.

"What typo?" Anne asked, caution creeping into her voice.

"The way they dropped her middle initial. In the review itself, they got it right, Anne N. Fletcher, but didn't you see at the top, they left it out."

"Why is that funny?"

"Because if you didn't know better, people could think it was you. Of course that's—"

Only a breath-long pause before: "But it is me." Softly, with total conviction; the foreman and the jury's verdict.

Janey was instantly appalled. "Anne, come on now!"

"What? What's wrong?"

There was a nervous giggle from the other end. "You can't be serious. You don't really—"

"Janey," Anne said with forced patience, "please stop babbling. I thought the review was pretty good actually," she went on conversationally. "I especially liked the part about my being talented. I told you I was good, didn't I? Now maybe you'll believe me. By the way I'll get you—"

"Anne, stop it!"

". . . an autographed copy, if you want. Maybe your mother would like one, too. You know, I really think this is a selling review. Now I'll be able to quit the job and concentrate full-time on the writing. You have no idea how difficult it's been—"

"Stop it, please, stop it!" It was a shrieking plea for order, sense, real life; a voice on the edge of hysterical incredulity.

The silence crackled in Janey's ears. "Anne?" she whispered tentatively. "Anne, are you there?"

"Yes."

"Say something," she urged.

Anne sighed audibly. "You just told me to shut up and now you want me to talk. You're getting me very confused."

"I want you to tell me you're joking."

"Joking? About what?" she asked innocently.

"Oh, shit," Janey muttered. Then, louder, "Please quit this, Anne. It's not funny."

"I'm not trying to be funny," Anne calmly insisted. "What's wrong with you this morning? You're not making any sense."

Janey's laugh was again high-pitched, nervous, a cackle. "*I'm* not making sense! We ought to have instant replay of what you've been sounding like. An autographed copy, for pete's sake!"

"Well, if you don't want one, fine. I thought you might like it, but obviously I was wrong." She took a breath, and when she again spoke, her voice held sadness and regret. "I guess I should have known you would react this way. I forgot how jealous you are of me. I had kind of been hoping that you could share all this, but I see it's not possible. You know, Janey, I'm sure that there's something you're good at, too, you just have to put your mind to it and—"

"SHUT UP!"

Silence, as Anne contemplated hanging up on her best friend, decided against it. Another time, another Anne would have done so instantly, but she no longer had to vent anger and frustration in such a final way. She understood what Janey was going through; how well she could empathize with the outrage and injustice and yes, admit it, the jealousy of someone else's success. But she was finished with all those hostile, self-destructive, counterproductive emotions now. She knew exactly what she had to do, and the sense of purpose gave her a certain peace and tolerance of which she had never believed herself capable.

How easy it was now to reach out and help Janey through what must be this devastating period of self-evaluation. The poor girl must be feeling absolutely worthless, but a lot of the fault was her own. Janey had never wanted anything as much as she had wanted to write, to be published, to be called talented. She had never stood by helplessly as another stole what should have been hers; as another flourished with *her* bounty. But all that was over with now, and she could afford to be generous and forgiving.

For her part, Janey had also been considering hanging up on her best friend. There was such rage in her that her fingers had begun to cramp where they held the receiver. The heated feeling did not come from the accusations and the patronizing; that stung quickly like a stray chip off a lit match head; she could brush it away and the pain with it. Far more lasting in its infuriating effect upon her was the utter conviction, the sureness, the boldness with which Anne was lying. And mixed with the anger, though she was unwilling to define it as such, was fear; fear that Anne was not lying, that she was telling the truth as she believed it.

"I'm sorry," Janey now said quietly.

"That's all right, I understand how you feel."

"Do you? Do you really?"

"Of course. You're upset and I don't blame you. It can't be easy to sit by and watch your best friend get reviewed in *The New York Times*, and know that soon she's going to be famous and people will be—"

Janey cut in, this time gently. "You're doing it again. That's what I've been talking about. You sound as if you wrote *Honorable Mention*, as if you were reviewed, as if the other girl's future, oh, I don't know how to explain it," she faltered, confused. "I guess what I mean is that you're talking as if you're that other Anne Fletcher, and you believe that what she's done you've done."

Anne's laugh was breezy, slight. "Now *you're* doing it again. You keep insisting that I didn't write this book when I really did. I don't know why you won't believe me."

Janey opted for reason. "Is your name Anne N. Fletcher?"

"Of course not. You know that."

"Then why does it appear that way in the body of the review?"

"Because the printer obviously made a typographical error. It's correct in the heading," she explained reasonably.

"It's incorrect there and right in the review!" Janey cried.

"I can't deal with this anymore," Anne said curtly.

"You can't deal with it! *You* can't! How the hell do you think I feel?" Janey's fear and anger had melded into trembling indignation. Thoughts churned in her brain faster than she could utter them. "Look, let's be sensible about this," she tried. "You and I both know that you did not write any book, that this other girl whom you seem to be absolutely obsessed with—"

"That's not true!" This was the first time Anne lost her self-control, her voice coming across shrill and defensive.

". . . obsessed with wrote it, and why you're pretending otherwise is beyond my comprehension." The slow, rational, steady stream of words was being made with an effort, but Janey was determined that logic would prevail, that Anne would admit her game, that normalcy would be restored. And once it was, once this fraud was exposed, she would say good-bye—permanently. She could no longer support this friendship; she no longer had the inclination or the stamina to ignore and excuse. Even if Anne were to somehow pass this off as a joke, which Janey believed she might attempt, too much irreparable damage had already been done, too much ugliness exchanged. She did not understand Anne anymore; she had become a personality so removed from what she had grown used to that she almost felt as if she had never known her. The depths and their secrets were of a stranger, and one she did not care to cultivate as a friend. She would walk away, but she had to try one final time to get Anne back, the Anne she thought she knew.

"You did this once before," she now said, "with that guy Dave or Doug or something at that bar. It was after you got your hair cut like hers and you pretended you had done a novel, and that you had been written up in *Glamour*. I thought that was terrible but—"

"That was a prank, I told you, nothing but a joke," Anne interjected.

"That's right, that's what you said, and I believed you." Janey's voice was breathless, as if the weight of what she was feeling was taking its toll on her. "I don't know why I did," she added softly, "I guess because I needed to."

"What is that supposed to mean?"

"It means that I needed to believe that my best friend was someone I knew, someone who wasn't . . . that she wasn't—"

"Wasn't what?" Anne urged impatiently. "Come on, say it. Wasn't crazy?" She laughed suddenly, a quick dismissal of the notion. "You have no sense of humor," she accused as an afterthought.

"Is that what you call that night at my apartment when you said I was jealous of you—a joke?" Janey said, her voice stronger, her need to protect weakened. "Is that what you call this hideous charade you're playing now —a joke? If so, you're the one with no sense of humor. No, no, that's not true. You have a sense of humor, all right, but it's the sickest thing I've ever seen."

"Poor, poor Janey," Anne said with a sigh. "It's really so sad, you know that? I never realized before what a pathetic little creature you are. I really feel sorry—"

"Stop it, Anne."

". . . for you. You just can't accept my success gracefully. It's eating away at you something awful. But—"

"Anne, I'm begging you, please drop this. You don't know what you're saying. You don't know how horrible—"

"Oh, Janey, it's okay, honestly it is. I understand what you're going through, the inadequacy, the frustration. Before I wrote this book I felt exactly the same way."

"You did not write that book," Janey said evenly.

Anne laughed. "Of course I wrote it. Why is it so difficult for you to accept that?"

"You did not write that book," Janey repeated. "I'm not sure why you won't admit the truth, but it's sick, Anne, sick and very dangerous. You're going to get into an awful lot of trouble if you don't stop."

"Trouble? Don't be ridiculous."

Janey had run out of words. Fear and disgust gripped her into silence. There was just one thing she wanted to know, but she doubted she would get the truth.

"Why, Anne? Why are you doing this?" she asked quietly.

Anne did not reply immediately. Her eyes again darted to the open drawer, rested there a second, and then she spoke, a whisper, so low, so thick with pain that the words were barely audible. "Because I have to." And gently, she hung up the telephone.

She did not move. She took a deep breath; a breath of fatigue and remorse and ending, for she knew she and Janey were no longer friends. It did not really hurt; what she had to do, she had to do alone, and she had, in truth, outgrown her friend. There was no room in her future for an unimaginative, ordinary, jealous girl like Janey. Sad, yes, it was sad, she decided, and also necessary. And so the ten-year-old slate of a friendship was wiped clean.

She went over to the utility drawer, and finished what she had begun before the telephone call. She got out the scissors, not the old, loose-hinged manicure scissors but the sharp pair she had borrowed from the office one weekend and never returned. She took them into the living room.

The coffee pot was still on the Salton hot tray, and she could smell the bitter, burnt brew. She did not unplug the cord, nor remove the pot. That would have to wait.

The book review section was as she had left it: turned back to the page on which *Honorable Mention* appeared. Without hesitation, she methodically began to cut it from the page, carefully snipping off any ragged edges, getting it neat and even. With the pen she had brought earlier for the crossword puzzle, she marked on the bottom margin the name of the publication and the date. Then she rose, went into her bedroom for a sheet of plain white typing paper, an envelope, a stamp. Back in the living room, she penned a quick note to her mother. It was not a boastful letter; she mentioned only that her writing a book had been a surprise she had been saving for her; that she would send a copy once it became available; that the use of the initial N. in the body of the review was a typographical error; and that she would be in touch again soon. Then she took the *New York Times* review, put it over the letter, folded both, and placed them in the envelope.

She sat back, the earlier sense of purpose now joined by a feeling of accomplishment. Everything that had happened before had been merely a prelude; a tease as compared to what now would occur. Gone was all doubt; gone was any relic of conscience; gone was confusion, hesitation, self-examination that perhaps she would not gain this way; that perhaps she was striving toward something unachievable; that perhaps she could not be what she wished to be. Anne was convinced, as an audience is by the art of illusion.

She got up and went into the bedroom. There was much she needed to say, to remember, to use again someday. She took out the tape recorder, and sat on the edge of her bed. Her posture was rigid, every muscle, tendon tight with tension. There was a lusterlessness to her eyes; they were hiding her from the outside, shielding her from reality; the white spots flickered like amber caution lights, and her lips formed a thin line of self-involvement. She turned on the machine.

You, dear tape diary, have been a part of this from the beginning, so it is only fitting that you know that it will end, and soon. I'm going to see to that.

You know how patient I've been all these years. You know I've tried to write and you know how difficult it's been. The same can be said of men. I've tried so to find decent men with whom I could enjoy a good, interesting relationship, but it's wrong to compromise yourself, and that's why I haven't really succeeded in either area.

This summer I knew I was coming close; it was just a matter of time before that special novel I know I have in me would have been written, and Arthur and I were developing into something special. Really, we were. I don't know when it all began to change, I guess in the fall, around September or October. That's when I started to feel out of control, no, it was even worse than that, I began to see myself slipping away, and everything I wanted, everything I am was mirrored in her, in that other Anne Fletcher.

I tried to dismiss her letters and phone calls as mere nuisances, and even when I found out about her and Arthur, I could have lived with that. But it's become one thing after another, and I've got to do something about her now. You understand, don't you? Janey doesn't. I could tell from the call this morning, and other times we've spoken about her. Well, I shouldn't be so disappointed in her for not seeing that I have to do this.

I have to destroy this other girl. It's really the only way I can get *me* back. She's the one to blame for what's been going wrong in my life. If it weren't for her, I'd have Arthur now, and my novel would be written and published, and I would be what I deserve to be. It's so unfair. She has everything I've ever wanted. If I don't stop her, there'll be nothing left of me.

So I've made a decision. Believe me, I don't like what I have to do, but I have no choice. I have to show her that she can't keep hurting me this way. I am going to destroy her, the way she's been destroying me. Eliminate her, the way she's been eliminating me. I don't exactly know how, but I'm going to do it. You understand, don't you?

I think that having made this decision, I'll be able to write. She's been an awful block to my concentration and energies, you know. I wish Janey could see things my way, but she's so unimaginative. She simply cannot fathom my needs, and how this girl is hindering me. It's sad that Janey is the way she is, jealous and insecure. I'm going to miss her, I think. At least she was someone to go to the bars with. But then, I probably won't need to do

181

that anymore because I'm going to get Arthur back. Yes, I'll get him back.

The hidden side of a human nature. I don't know what made me think of that now. I guess because I believe that you can push a person only so far before the darkness shines. You understand, don't you?

The tape continued to wind although she was no longer speaking. There were some thoughts she could not share even with her machine.

The first time he read the letter, a pulse of shock began to throb in his throat. The second time, his hands trembled with hurt and rage. He reread it now for the third time:

> Dear Arthur,
>
> It is with great difficulty and much thought that I write you this letter. There is no easy way to do this except to be straightforward. I have decided that it would be better if we did not see each other anymore. I like you, and I will always think of you with the greatest fondness, but I feel my future is about to take wings, and I do not want the responsibility of caring for another's feelings during this fragile period of my life.
>
> Please don't think too poorly of me. Perhaps when you have a chance to read this letter dispassionately, and consider what I am saying, you will realize that I really have no choice. I must be free now, and not feel guilt if I am not there for you when you want me.
>
> Remember me with love if you can, but at least try to remember me.
>
> With deepest affection,
> Anne

In his spacious living room, Arthur sat back against a pillow of his gold-colored velveteen modular seating

unit, his hands resting lifelessly on his lap, the letter a
limp napkin. He still could not believe it, and if he were
to read the letter a thousand times, he would never be
able to believe it. What had happened? How could he
have been so *wrong* about someone? Four days ago, they
had been like two little kids prancing and dancing
around her apartment, reading aloud from *The New York
Times* review. Four days ago! Now this. It didn't make
any sense.

He had been nothing but supportive of her writing
from the beginning; she knew how proud he was of her,
how understanding when she told him she was working
on her new book and couldn't see him on a particular
evening. And what was this shit about responsibility for
his feelings—she had assumed that long before the book
review came out, for christ's sake; that's what a relationship was all about. Well, fuck it! Maybe she can kiss off
the other assholes she's known like this, but she's not
going to have such an easy time of it with him. A *letter*,
for shit's sake. A fucking Dear John letter as if he were
some fucking GI!

Bristling with injured pride, he stormed into his bedroom, letter still in his hand. He got as far as dialing
the first three digits of her telephone number, then slammed down the phone. No, dammit! he told himself. I'm
going over there and we're having this out in person.
And if she isn't there, I'll wait if it takes all fucking
night!

Twenty minutes later, Arthur was standing on the
street in front of Anne's brownstone. The early March
night bit into him, but he felt only the heat of his anger.
He climbed the stoop steps, pressed the intercom to her
apartment.

"Yes?" came her voice.

"It's me. Let me in," he ordered in a clipped voice,
caressing the letter that was in his overcoat pocket.

"Arthur! I wasn't expecting you."

184

"Are you or are you not going to let me in?"

"Of course I am."

The buzzer rang, and he went in. A splinter of light cut through onto the landing when he reached the third floor, and he saw it was coming from her door which she had left slightly ajar.

"Anne?" he called out, going in and closing the door behind him.

"Be right there," she answered from a distance.

He unbuttoned his coat, flung open the cashmere muffler that had been wound around his neck. His heart hit hard against his chest, and in his ears, it sounded like the *spiing* of a racquetball against the far wall. He who had worked so long, with such effort, to be a master of self-control; he who had learned the value of it professionally, personally, was shattered with self-disgust at this moment for the only control he was exercising was not to charge into the bedroom or bathroom or wherever the hell she was hiding from him, and shake loose an explanation. Instead, he sat on the edge of the sofa.

And then she was standing in front of him, and for a quick moment, he was nonplussed. There was no mistaking the red-rimmed eyes, pinky with recently shed tears. Her mouth quivered into a weak smile of welcome. Well, good, dammit, he thought. She should be nervous and upset after what she's done to me!

"Hi," she said quietly. "I wasn't expecting you."

"You said that already."

"Don't you want to take off your coat?" she asked, tilting her head slightly with surprise at his harsh tone of voice.

"Am I staying that long?"

"What do you mean? You can stay as long as you want."

"Really? Well, it's nice to know I'm good for a last fuck. I guess that's something."

"Arthur," she said, frowning, backing away from his atypical crudeness. "What are you talking about? What's wrong?"

"What's wrong?" he repeated, removing the letter from his pocket as he got up. "What's wrong? What the hell do you think is wrong when I get a letter like this?" He flung it out at her. She did not reach for it, and he saw her face shrink and pale as if he were dangling an oozing, slimy, life-draining creature by its squiggly tail. She backed further away, her shoulders hunched, until she was standing by a dining chair, eyes darting confusedly from the letter to his pinched face.

"What is that?" she whispered.

"Oh, cut the crap, will you?" he said gruffly, tossing the letter onto the coffee table. "You know damn well what that is, you wrote it."

Her frown deepened, and he began to wonder what exactly was going on. Of course she wrote it. Well, there was no signature, the whole thing had been typed, but so what? What does a lousy signature mean on a Dear John letter, not a helluva lot. He realized he was trying to convince himself; suddenly, somehow, the situation had become confusing, like seeing out of a pair of glasses with one broken lens.

He picked up the letter and went to her. "Did you or did you not write me this letter?"

Slowly, she took it from him, and standing at the dining table, she read it. He watched her face closely, saw her eyes widen, lips compress, eyebrows crease. He turned to remove his coat, put it down on the sofa. When he again faced her, she was sitting in the dining chair, staring at him, the letter facedown on her lap.

"I never wrote this letter," she said in a dead voice.

"Anne—"

"I swear to you, Arthur, I did not write this letter. There's been some horrible mistake. It's like the day with the flowers you didn't send. You've got to believe me. I love you, Arthur. I would never send a letter like that."

He continued to study her, and though his heart still played a hard rhythm, it was not with anger and damaged ego, but with almost frightening doubt and bewilderment. If she had not sent the letter, and now he knew she had not, then who had—and why?

"I believe you, sweetheart," he said gently, "I believe you." He reached out and began to stroke the top of her head as a father might do to a child, a pure gesture with no demands.

"Who sent it? Who would do such a sick thing?"

Arthur shrugged. "I don't know."

"There aren't that many people who know about us, Arthur. It's got to be one of them. Someone so jealous they want to spoil what we have." She was trying not to cry, and so the tears lodged in her throat, making her voice thick, the words indistinct.

"Annie, it could be anyone. Someone we met casually at a party. Someone who heard about us from another person." He shook his head. "It would be impossible to try to figure out who's behind this."

"I'm scared," she admitted in a small whisper.

He laughed off the idea. "A stiff drink will cure that." He went over to the Spanish buffet and prepared two brandies. "Go sit on the couch and get comfortable," he told her over his shoulder.

"Drink this. It's the Dumont remedy for all that ails," he announced with a bravado that he knew sounded false.

She sipped obediently, then she looked at him, eyes round with worry. "Arthur, what's going on?" she asked. "Why is this happening to me?"

"I don't know, Annie, but don't get all upset. I'm sure it's nothing that—"

"You call that letter nothing?" she flared. "You call what happened today nothing?"

187

He was immediately interested. "Something *else* happened?"

She brushed back her hair and avoided his eyes. "Anne, what was it? Was that why you were crying when I came in?"

She lowered her head in silent affirmation. "Tell me what happened."

"It's so strange," she finally mumbled. "I mean, it doesn't make any sense."

"You let me be the judge of that."

She looked at him, and attempted a smile. "You sound just like a lawyer."

"You're stalling."

"Okay, I'll tell you, but it won't make sense to you, either. I came home this afternoon around four, four-thirty, I guess it was. Louis was in the first floor hallway as I was about to go up the stairs."

"Who's Louis?"

"The superintendent. He's very nice. He really cares about the building."

"Okay, so you met Louis in the hallway. Then what?" he prompted.

"Well, whenever we see each other we always have a little conversation—you know, about the weather or how expensive everything is, that kind of thing. Today, we did that, just as we always do, and then he said the strangest thing." She sipped from her drink, remembering the conversation, the innocence with which he had told her.

"What? What was so strange?"

Still she hesitated. Then: "He said I had a lovely cousin and he hoped I didn't mind but she said it would be okay to let her into my apartment to rest before she took the train home."

"Why is that strange?"

"I don't have any cousins, Arthur," she said tonelessly.

"No cousins? Come on, everybody has cousins."

"I didn't mean that. Of course I have cousins. Four male cousins, two live in Los Angeles, one in Maine, and the other is currently in South America."

Arthur digested that news with the difficulty of swallowing putrid cheese. "Four cousins, all male?" he repeated doubtfully.

She nodded. "And don't ask me if maybe there's some female cousin out there I never heard of or met because I already called my parents and asked them the same thing. There is none."

"Did you ask Louis what she looked like?"

"No. I didn't think to," she admitted.

"Would he remember if we asked him now?"

"I doubt it. He would probably just say she's lovely again or something like that."

"Is this guy Louis usually so willing to give people access to your apartment? That seems like quite a liberty he's taking," Arthur stated.

"Don't be ridiculous," Anne said. "He's never done anything like it before, and probably the only reason he did it today was because her story was so plausible and she looked respectable." She took a breath. "Louis isn't important; the fact that some stranger got into this apartment is. Arthur, someone was walking around here, touching my things, my clothes, sitting in that couch, maybe lying on my bed. Who knows what she was doing?" Her voice was rising shrilly. "Why, Arthur? Why?"

He could sense how close she was to breaking down, and in a way he could not blame her. A cousin she did not have, a letter she did not send; more than enough to put a person on edge.

"All right, let's try to figure this out," he urged. "Is anything missing?"

"I don't think so. I don't have anything that valuable. A TV, the stereo, some books and records, the porcelain boxes. Combined they're not worth that much. No, Arthur," she said, shaking her head, "whoever came here didn't come to steal. Not anything tangible, at least," she added in a murmur.

"What do you mean, nothing tangible?"

"I feel . . . I feel as if someone came here to learn more about me, to find out how I live, what I'm like . . . oh, I don't know, it sounds ridiculous when I say it." She sighed, looked away, but she could feel his eyes on her, sense the disbelief.

She glanced up at him. "You think I'm crazy, don't you?" she said hoarsely.

"Of course not," he assured her. "I'm trying to think, that's all, to make sense of what's been happening. Why in hell would someone go to all the trouble of getting in here and then not take anything?"

"I told you," she whispered, as if to say it louder would be to make it more true, "someone wants to be part of my life."

"Hey, enough of that kind of talk!" Arthur said sharply. "Granted, this is pretty weird, but let's not get melodramatic."

"Melodramatic!" Anne cried, sitting forward, her face twisted with hurt. "How dare you accuse me of being melodramatic! I wasn't even going to tell you what happened if you hadn't come storming in here like a marine sergeant. How dare you sit there and put labels on what I'm feeling. Why don't you try to be a little more understanding, Mr. Self-Control? How would *you* be feeling if someone had been in *your* apartment, some stranger? Huh?" She slumped back, exhausted, ashamed, and over it all like hardened icing, fear.

Arthur moved closer to her and took one of her hands in his. "I'm sorry," he said contritely. "You're right. It's just that I find this so damn hard to believe, to make sense of."

She squeezed his hand. "I know. Look what it's doing

to us. We're yelling at each other and getting angry over some . . . some creep."

"Annie, I wish there was something I could say, suggest some course of action to find out who's behind this, but I can't," he admitted helplessly. "I just don't know what to do."

She said nothing in the face of such impotence, blaming neither him nor herself for it. To continue to dwell on the incidents would accomplish nothing. She pressed her lips together in a gesture of determination, and a hint of life returned to her eyes. "Let's burn that awful letter," she declared with a new lilt to her voice.

He understood the effort she was making, and felt a small shiver of relief. "In a minute," he said. "You said something before that really bothered me and I want to clear it up."

"Arthur," Anne said with a small laugh, "anything I say tonight should not be held against me."

"I'm serious. You said you weren't going to tell me about what happened here today." He shook his head. "You can't do that, Annie. You can't keep those kinds of things from me. You mean too much to me, and shutting me out like that, well, you're not that selfish. How would it have been if I had gotten that letter and just kept it to myself, never confronting you about it? We'd be in some sorry state now, right? Well, it's no different with what happened to you. So it's weird, so it sounds pretty nutty when you tell it, but still, it happened to you and that makes it important to me. Okay, Annie? No more secrets?"

"*No* secrets?" she teased, hinting at hidden sexual escapades.

"Well, if you mean you and Louis the super . . ." he said, joining the game.

She laughed and leaned in for a kiss. "No secrets, I promise," she whispered against his cheek. "Now, you burn the letter and I'll get the champagne, and would you please take off your shoes and get comfortable because I'm not letting you go home tonight," she stated matter-of-factly.

"Champagne, hoo-hah," he commented, slipping out of his shoes.

"It was such a nice surprise," she told him, going into the kitchen. "It came from Gil Bassett with a lovely note. Did I ever mention Gil to you?"

"No," Arthur called back. "Another discard from your scandalous past?"

"Quite gay, I'm afraid," she said, returning with the champagne in an ice bucket, and two crystal flute-glasses. "What a gorgeous man and what a waste of it," she said with regret. "He sent the champagne because of the book, which is what surprised me. He's been in Norway filming for the past six months or so. He's a cameraman. I didn't think he even knew about the book. I certainly didn't tell him."

"Well, you know how those things get around."

"I suppose." She grinned mischievously. "Unless, of course, some stranger sent them with his name."

"Annie, come on, don't—"

"I'm only joking." She lifted her glass. "To no more secrets," she said lovingly.

Anne silently debated with herself whether to tell Arthur about the phone call she had gotten this afternoon, and decided against it. Having lunch with Anne Fletcher was not really a secret, not the kind he meant. After all, neither of them detailed their every movement for the other. She knew, however, that she was rationalizing. Well, maybe she would tell him *after* the lunch. He'd be a little angry, but by then it would be over, and she'd have no reason to see the girl again.

CHAPTER 15

"That's fine, Matt."

"Hey, what's wrong? I just finish telling you that we might go high five figures, maybe even hit six in the reprint deal, and all you can say is 'that's fine' with about as much enthusiasm as a condemned man. A little more feeling, please."

"I'm sorry," Anne apologized. "I've had a lot on my mind lately. It *is* terrific news and of course I'm excited. A little incredulous, actually, but I'm not complaining."

"This'll seem like peanuts if the movie deal I'm working on goes through," he told her. "As a matter of fact, that's one of the reasons I called. I'm leaving for the Coast day after tomorrow, and I'll be there for at least ten days. If you need me, for the first five days I'll be at the Beverly Hills Hotel, after that at La Costa. I like to go there and work off some of this excess lard. It's a great excuse to overeat when I come back home."

Anne laughed. "I love you just the way you are."

"Of course you do, dear child," he agreed. "I'll take the new outline and—what is it . . ." Anne could hear the leafing of pages over the phone. "Fifty pages. Hmm.

Quite a lot. Well, I'll take all of it and see if we can get a movie nibble."

"What outline, Matt?" she asked slowly.

"Of your new novel, of course, as yet untitled it says here."

Her laugh was quick, nervous as if someone were tickling the soles of her feet. "I don't know what—"

"I must say I was rather surprised by this material," he went on. "Different style from *Honorable Mention*. Not necessarily bad, but different."

"How?" she asked in a whisper, feeling the fist in her gut pushing her breath out in hot little gasps. No, no, no! she silently screamed, and she wrapped her free arm around her middle, as if to hold in her center, protect her core.

"How? Let's see," Matt was saying. "Rather journalistic, I would call it. Very tight sentence structure—simplistic, actually. Almost no description. I'd like it more, I think, if this were a mystery or suspense novel, but in a love story," he clucked, "I'm not sure. We'll see. Your ego isn't shattered by what I've said, is it, dear child?"

"No, of course not," Anne quickly assured him. Her vision was blurring as if someone had put a strip of gauze around her eyes, and she felt dizzy, light-headed so that she had to lean against the kitchen wall or risk slipping down to the floor. The effort of support weighed on her, a heavy cargo that might topple from her grip any second.

"Matt, be a dear and send me back all that material," she said, filled with wonder that her voice worked normally, that he could not hear the nerve-defying scratch it made on the air, like a fingernail against slate.

"Oh, come now, it's not that bad. I told you, just different."

"You're being very sweet, and very kind, but I really want it back. I must have been drunk or something when I sent it to you. I never meant you to see it yet, I was just toying with it," she said in a rush. "Please, Matt, send it back," she repeated, sure that he could catch the crack in her voice.

He did not answer. "Matt, it was a mistake," she said, "and I'll really be upset if you show it to anyone. I'm upset that even you saw it. Please return it."

"You're quite sure?" he finally said.

"Yes."

She could hear his sigh—of relief? resignation? "All right, then, it'll be in the mail today. I suppose you know what you're doing."

"Thank you," she said, and was able to stand up straighter. She wanted to get off the phone. "Have a good trip."

"I'll see you when I get back, with wonderful news I expect. 'Bye, dear."

"Good-bye."

Quickly she was in the bedroom she had turned into an office. She went to her desk; everything was exactly as it had been yesterday morning, the last time she had been working. The outline for *Tenderly*, fifteen typewritten pages, margins filled with the hieroglyphics of changes and ideas, was face up beside the typewriter. Page 97 of the first draft was in the machine, no more than twenty lines written. The other ninety-six pages were in a neat pile, face down on the other side of the typewriter.

Exhausted with the enervating fatigue of mental turmoil, she sat down at her desk, held the pages of the first draft in her hands like a fragile gift. She had sent nothing of her new novel to Matthew Holmes. *Nothing*. It was all here. She had not lost her mind; she was not committing acts of which she had no recall. But that was small measure of comfort. She was holding on to sanity with a strip of weak twine; it was stretching and straining, and she did not know if she would be able to pull herself back up before it snapped and she plummeted.

Her whole body, from her scalp down to her calf muscles, seemed to be quivering. She put down the pages, wrapped her arms around herself, but the trembling only increased, as if each nerve were being vibrated. She did not need to look into any mirror; she could feel the color draining from her cheeks, taste the rawness on the inside of her lower lip where her teeth pinched and nibbled with hungry fear. She knew there was moisture on her forehead, cold sweat like the slow drops from a melting ice cube. Where her stomach used to be now existed a burning hole, the acid of anguish having eaten away at it until that part of her body hurt no less intensely than if it were in actual flames. There was pain all over, acupuncture needles pricking at her flesh relentlessly, little scavengers of her senses. Never before in her life or in her imagination had she known such utter and complete terror. *Terror.* To feel yourself dying is to know fear, she always believed. This was worse. To feel yourself dying in your mind—no, no, being murdered in your mind was . . . terrifying.

She put her hands on top of the desk and pushed herself up. She did not move, though; she did not know where to go, whom to confess to. How much could she burden Arthur before he would leave her, disgusted not with her but with whoever, whatever was dragging him into this mess, the cause more than the effect. And the point would have to come when *she* would disgust him, when he would think unwillingly of madness, as she herself was tempted to do. She could not speak with anyone about the fear; they would find excuses and explanations no matter how illogical and farfetched, for it was far safer to do that than to believe there was someone trying to harm her.

She knew, though. She had been reluctant to accept it before, but now she knew that nothing was coincidence; that each event as far back as the telephone call with the magazine editor had been executed with forethought and deliberation. There was nothing accidental and random about the voiceless calls; nothing unplanned about the letter to Arthur, the call to the dean, her roses. And now her professional life. Fiendish and clever, she thought. To know so much about her, to know her boyfriend, her agent, where she lived; what power in that knowledge, what a weapon. And she was as helpless as a baby in swaddling clothes, unable to move and protect herself against the next assault.

Standing there, leaning against the edge of the desk, she began to cry. Not sobs, not weeping, not hysteria, but hot, stinging tears that came without warning, as the terror in her blood had crept up on her unexpectedly. She felt claustrophobic; trapped in a state of powerlessness. She did not know what to do except to go on with her life and pray that this vicious plucking at her mind would end; that whatever motivated that person out there to stalk her sanity would diminish in importance and need for satisfaction; that whoever that person was would tire of the hunt. If not, she did not know how it would end except in the collapse of the strip of twine. She could only be so strong . . . hold on only so long.

Stiffly, sniffling back further tears, she left her office, and went into the bedroom. It was nearly twelve o'clock, and she had that appointment at twelve-thirty. She had no appetite, and no desire to listen to Anne Fletcher talk about writing, or anything at all. And she certainly was in no frame of mind to give professional advice. But she knew she could not sit in her apartment, playing victim, waiting for the next strike. She would go out and meet Anne Fletcher for what she hoped would be a quick lunch, then she would go shopping and concentrate on spending money instead of losing her mind.

Twenty minutes later she was showered and dressed in brown tweed slacks, white silk blouse, and a brown velvet boxy blazer. Over this she would wear her raincoat since there was still a damp chill to the air, but she would let it swing open to pretend that spring was almost here. She had suggested they meet at Swiss House, a midtown eatery where many publishing people lunched, and had made the reservation for them. If she could find a cab quickly, she would not be too late.

Anne had no difficulty getting a taxi, but traffic was heavy, and it took them almost twenty minutes to get to the restaurant. She knew the reservation would be honored for at least a half hour, and she assumed the other girl would have the sense to wait as long.

"I'm Miss Fletcher. I have a reservation for two at twelve-thirty," she said to the maître d' when she was inside the restaurant.

He nodded and turned to the book kept on a small table near the bar. A clock was also on the table, indicating the time as 12:45, but he made no mention of the lateness. He ran his hand down the list of reservations, twice, before he came to hers.

"I'm afraid that reservation's been canceled, madam," he said after seeing the bold line crossed through her name.

"Canceled?"

"You don't remember?"

"If I remembered I wouldn't—" She stopped herself from completing the uncharacteristic snideness. "No, I'm sorry but I don't," she said with a make-believe smile.

"You called not more than ten minutes ago and said you would have to cancel. I didn't remember until I was checking for your name," he explained. "You told me you wouldn't have time to reach the other party and would I please apologize to her when she arrives." His eyes darted to two newcomers. "Your guest hasn't shown up yet, but do you now want a table or are you still canceling? I'm rather confused, madam."

"You are saying that ten minutes ago *I* called and canceled?"

"Yes," the maître d' said, losing interest. "Do you want a table?"

"But that's impossible," Anne said, stunned by this information. "I was in a cab ten minutes ago, I couldn't have called you."

"Madam," he said with thin patience, "you called, you said you were Miss Anne Fletcher and that you would have to cancel your lunch plans. Now you're here. Does that mean you'll be eating lunch?"

"No, I guess not," she muttered, and turned around, leaving him to the waiting party.

She stood outside the restaurant a few seconds, still somewhat dazed by the bizarre turn of events. Thinking about it, she realized that of course the maître d' had gotten her confused with the other Anne Fletcher, that was the only logical explanation. But why hadn't she called to tell her? She must have known earlier that she wouldn't be able to make it. Probably, on any normal day, Anne would not give the incident a second thought except to be somewhat put out and irritated. But today, after the call with Matt, it seemed like one more way to disorient and unnerve her. What was so peculiar was that Anne Fletcher had seemed so pleased when they made the lunch date, so eager. It must have been something important to have made her break the appointment on such short notice.

A few blocks away was Saks Fifth Avenue, and she walked over, strolling past the windows filled with spring and summer clothes, trying to get up the enthusiasm to go in and shop. But she couldn't do it; she would go home and see if she could work. If the jumble of doubts and questions and worries filling her brain would not let her do that, she would escape into sleep for a while.

She walked west to Broadway for the subway. The platform was only moderately crowded at this hour, the people staring straight ahead as if the avoidance of eye contact would be protection against danger. Anne sought out appearances that conformed to her image of harmless, and then stood near a Puerto Rican woman and her baby, and a well-dressed woman of about forty carrying an attaché case. She never felt safe in the subways; she took them when they were expedient or when she thought the hour was less open to the risks of mugging, pickpocketing, and sexual insult.

After five minutes of waiting she could see the others moving closer to the edge of the platform for the arrival of the incoming train. She too moved up as she heard the shrill scratchings of the wheels down the tracks. The first car was clanking loudly into sight when she felt her heartbeat accelerate and pound brutally with disbelieving terror. Her legs were suddenly liquid, her fingertips tingled numbly. Her eyes and mouth rounded simultaneously into fear-stricken circles as she felt the hands on her back, the fingers spread wide on the poplin of her coat; felt the momentum she was unable to stop pushing her forward, forward, closer to the edge of the platform, to the rush of the subway train. Instinctively, her hands flew out in front of her, holding on to air. Her mouth was still wide open, screaming for help in a silent howl.

And then it was not air her hands held onto but the solid metal of the subway car, stationary, protective. The doors slid open, passengers jostled off, on, and still she leaned against the side of the car, blind to the stares of those who noticed her immobile form, deaf to the languages and noises, numb to everything but the finest, most total, almost an exquisite terror, so perfectly did it control her. To decide to move was to think, and her mind was no more able to function than were her watery legs. Suddenly, she felt contact against her shoulder and she bolted upright, such naked fear deforming her face that the man, a Japanese businessman who seemed to be asking if she needed help, began to apologize and move cautiously, hastily away from her, looking over at her, mumbling, until he was far down the platform. She stood motionless, seconds only, as her skin hummed back to life, the blood coursing down from her head to her fingertips, to her thighs and calves and toes, giving her the ability to go on.

She did not run up the subway steps; she did not have the breath for that. She gulped air as if she were being suffocated, short, hasty inhalations that were life-sustaining, barely. When she hit the street, she moved midway down the block, away from the subway entry, forever now a place of obscene fear. She was weak, like a sick person, an old person, a baby, her muscles seemingly unaccustomed to functioning with adult vigor. People walked past, none of them stopped; she recognized the expression on their faces: curiosity, not interest. She waited until her heart stopped hurting; she had never realized until now how painful a heartbeat could be. Soon she hailed a taxi. She gave him her address and sat back, staring out at a city that might have been a deserted western mining town for all she saw of its people. She tried, during the ride as her body regained its normal patterns, to liken the terror she had experienced to something she knew, something familiar. If she could say to herself that this was like . . . that it reminded her of the time when . . . perhaps it would not be so awful. But there was nothing similar in her past. The fear of surprise at a horror movie; the fear of wood creaking at home when her parents were out at night; the fear of an "almost" auto accident—nothing could compare to the pure terror of feeling yourself on the brink of death as someone tried to kill you.

She knew that was what had happened. She was as convinced of it as if she had planned it herself. The timing had been so perfect, so exact. Too perfect, she realized with a start. Whoever had pushed her had not meant to kill her, but to scare her, perhaps warn her how deadly an enemy she had. The lucid, logical, sensible part of her rejected the concept as absurd, alarmist, utterly mad. The memory of her body slamming hard against the wall of the train, the palms of her hands stinging with the impact—she could not risk being logical any longer. And she could not face whatever was out there alone anymore.

She paid the cabbie, walked up to her apartment and bolted herself in. She went straight for the kitchen phone to call Arthur, not bothering to remove her raincoat. Then she remembered that he was out of town and would not be back for a few days. Her father. Her father would know what to do.

She was reaching for the receiver when suddenly the still of the room was shattered. She pulled her hand away as if it had come into contact with a poisonous snake, and she stared at the phone, ring after ring. Tears started streaming uncontrollably down her face and she began to mutter to herself, incoherent pleas for help. She was petrified; her chest again began to heave with the effort of breathing. Someone knew she had just come home; someone was watching her—the timing, again exact, perfect. No, coincidence, an accident. Deliberate, planned. Her mind warred relentlessly, driving her further into herself, into a state of devastating confusion teetering on collapse. Trembling, her entire body a nerve swollen and raw and exposed, she answered the phone.

"Hello?" came her tear-heavy rasp.

"Anne, hi. What happened to you?"

"Who is this?" she whispered weakly.

"Anne Fletcher. What happened to you at lunch? I waited and waited, finally I decided to leave."

"You've been at the restaurant?" she asked incredulously.

A surprised laugh. "Of course. We did have a lunch date, didn't we?"

Anne felt as if the walls of the kitchen had shrunk, and

she was slowly, inexorably being pressed into a small ball of madness. "Didn't you cancel the lunch date?" she asked.

"Cancel? No, of course not, why would I do that?" Again her small laugh. "I waited an hour, even more. I got there around twenty-five after twelve. Swiss House on West Fiftieth Street, right?"

"I was there," she said. "I was late but . . ." She swallowed, trying to remove that lump in her throat that made breathing so difficult. She undid the tie to her silk blouse. She felt as if she were choking; she could not seem to get enough air down into her lungs, and she was hot, she was sweating she was so hot.

"Well, I don't know what happened," Anne was saying. "I finally figured something held you up and you couldn't get to a phone."

"The maître d' said you called and canceled and that you couldn't reach me and he should give me that message," Anne reported in a monotone.

"He said *I* called?"

"Well, not exactly," Anne admitted, recalling the conversation. "I gave him my name and he told me I had called. I assumed it had to be you because I knew I never phoned him."

"But that's ridiculous," the other girl said. "I never called, believe me. I was looking forward to this lunch with you."

"But then why would he say that? Why did he say Anne Fletcher had called if neither of us had?" She could feel herself panicking, that light-headed dizziness engulfing her as if she were treading deep water and could barely keep her head in the air.

"Look, those guys get mixed up all the time. I wouldn't worry about it."

"Yes, of course, that must be what happened. Uh, Anne, do you mind? I'm not feeling too well. I think I better go now."

"Oh. Nothing serious, I hope."

"I'll be okay. Some rest will help."

"Well, can we make another date? I really want to get together with you.",

"Okay, but—"

"I have a great idea. Instead of lunch, why don't you be my guest at my health club? It's a terrific place with a swimming pool, indoor tennis, sauna, whirlpool, the whole works. It'll be fun."

"Well, I don't—"

"Come on, it'll be good for you. You must be under tremendous tension now with the book and all, and a little relaxation would do wonders. Then we can have dinner after and really talk. What do you say?"

Anne was not sure if the image of relaxing as the other girl enthusiastically painted it, or her own mental fatigue finally made her agree. "Okay," she said, "sounds like fun."

"Fabulous. When would you like to do it—tonight, tomorrow?"

"No, I don't think so."

"I know how busy you are so why don't you tell me when's good for you?" The icy nip of sarcasm in the voice was barely perceptible.

"Next week sometime, I guess," Anne said listlessly.

"When next week? Tuesday, Wednesday, when?"

"Thursday." She picked the day mindlessly, not trying to recall whether she had another date scheduled. She picked it because it was a long time away and she would not have to deal with it for a while. A long time away, and she might not even be alive then. The unbidden thought sent a convulsive shudder through her, and she quickly blinked her eyes to erase the picture.

"You sure?" Anne pressed.

"Next Thursday's fine."

"Okay, take down the address. It's one forty-four East

Seventy-eighth Street. Meet me in the lobby at say, oh, seven-thirty."

"In the morning?" Anne asked, aghast.

"No, no," the other girl laughed. "At night."

"Isn't that kind of late?"

"It's better then. We're practically guaranteed court time and it's less crowded all around. By the way, you do play tennis, don't you?"

"Not well, but I play."

"Great. Then I guess I'll see you next week. And don't cancel out on me again."

"I didn't cancel this time," Anne said quickly, sharply.

"Just kidding. 'Bye."

"Good-bye."

She no sooner hung up than she regretted agreeing to see Anne, at her health club of all places, and with dinner afterward. At least lunch provided a time limit; dinner offered no excuse to get back to an office or leave for another appointment. Arthur will be furious, she thought. Oh, well, one date with the girl wouldn't kill her.

She stepped out of the kitchen and took off her raincoat. She was not so hot now; she had stopped sweating and in fact felt chilled. She knew the temperature in the apartment had nothing to do with it. She was cold from fear, from the dark shadows preying upon her mind. Someone *had* sent Matthew Holmes material under her name; someone *had* called the Swiss House and used her name to cancel the reservation; someone *had* tried to push her against the subway. She had not imagined any of this; she was not making it up; she was not going crazy. Who? Why?

"Oh, dear Lord, help me. Please. Help me," she cried out loud as a bolt of pain shot from the nape of her neck up the back of her head to grip her at either temple in a vise of anguish.

16

"Shit, piss, fuck!"

Anne tore the paper from the typewriter and squeezed it into a ball which she tossed across the living room. It missed the pile of similar white balls which had accumulated on the couch, dropping to the rug where a few other strays had fallen.

She inserted another piece of paper into the machine, and typed: Page 1, Chapter One. She pressed the automatic carriage return and let six spaces fill the page; she was ready to begin. Again. She leaned over the machine, elbows on the dining table, hands supporting her head. She sat back in the chair, hands in her lap. She sat rigid, hands poised over the keys.

"Dammit, dammit to all hell!" Out came the paper to be squeezed and tossed.

She got up and began to walk around the living room. It was inexcusable and unexplainable, she was thinking, disturbed enough for the white spots to shade her thinly pressed lips. She should not be having this much trouble getting her own novel started. She was more at peace than she could remember ever having been before: her mother was on a three-week vacation in Mexico, leaving her blessedly free of strife; the job was the job, but she wasn't letting it get to her; and there was Richard who, admittedly, was wearing thin but still provided some tremendous sexual release. It was too bad he was so unintellectual, only reading trade journals and history. But, for the most part, she felt good with herself and her life; she could sense her future, golden with importance. Then why was she still having this damn-awful difficulty writing good stuff, the real thing. With crap, the type-writer had clacked cheerily along as if with a will of its own. With what she would be proud to put her name to, nothing—blank pages, a silent machine. She knew how talented she was; why, then, couldn't she write some-thing truly worthwhile? The desire was so strong, so vital; she could not reconcile that with the inability to execute.

She told herself not to give in to the creative frustra-tion. Soon, so soon, it would be gone, and then nothing would stop her. She knew it.

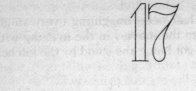

Anne N. Fletcher never called her father, or anyone else. She could confide in no one; she could not burden those who cared about her with unwarranted worry, and it might be unwarranted, for harassment was not truly dangerous, and the push against the subway had not been lethal, merely malicious. She tried these arguments of rationality on herself like new clothes, but nothing fit correctly except what her instincts told her; what they said was so horrendous, so bizarre, so utterly implausible that she could not repeat them.

Her parents came in for dinner one night, and commented on how pale she looked, tired, and advised that she was working too hard. She agreed with them, and promised to get some rest. She could barely concentrate on their conversation. She was sure, positive really, that someone had watched her leave her apartment and had followed her to the restaurant six blocks away. She could feel the eyes behind her; had not imagined the start-stop of footsteps as if they belonged to a mechanical windup toy whose movements she determined. She was even more convinced when she got home three hours later and the phone rang the instant she entered the apartment, the deadly dial tone being the caller.

Then, one day, one entire night nothing happened, and it was as if she had been imagining every single thing. She had gone to the movies in the evening with Karen, and when she got home she stood by the kitchen with her coat on for a solid five minutes, timed by her wristwatch, waiting for the phone to ring. She doubted the continued silence; it struck her as wish fulfillment, not reality. Then, a sensation of relief washed over her, strong and unexpected, and she found her knees buckling as if with fear. She permitted herself the luxury of wondering whether it was all behind her, whether this nightmare was ended. At 7:30 the next morning the phone rang, the voiceless haunting began again, paralyzing her. She could not work; she was afraid to venture out of the apartment. She did take one positive action, however; she called the telephone company and arranged to have her phone number changed and made unlisted; they would do it the following week. For a few hours, that made her feel better. She imagined that once her telephone number was changed, there would be no access to her, but then she knew how false that thinking was. Whoever was out there still knew where she lived, and she could not move with the ease and speed of changing a telephone number. Whoever was out there could still follow her and push her, and send strange letters and make damaging calls. Those horrors she could not stop.

She slept poorly; not restlessly from bad dreams but lightly from a sense of expectancy, as if to give herself over to deep sleep would leave her unguarded for too long.

Arthur called twice from San Diego, and it was like having a conversation with a stranger. She could not chirp and chatter when fear pressed upon her and so a distance entered her voice, and her responses became monosyllabic and uninviting. He repeatedly asked if anything was wrong, and she repeatedly lied, saying she was tired. She knew that was a mistake, for if she decided to tell him everything that had occurred, which she wavered about doing, he would doubt her now. If she were really as frightened as she claimed to be, he would reason, why pretend that nothing was wrong? why hold out on him? She was losing the case for herself, she knew, but how could she relate the terror she felt like a constant headache over a telephone to someone thousands of miles away preoccupied with his own business? He could do nothing for her from San Diego except worry about her . . . or worse, wonder about her and her sanity. If she decided to tell him anything, it would have to be when they were together again.

One evening the phone rang on four different occasions and she did not answer at any time. She sat on her sofa, listened to the ringing, praying each time for it to stop. Then, finally, she took both phones off their hooks. She could not bear the sound, nor the way her heart jumped high into her throat then sunk low as if she were on a roller coaster. It took her too long to recover each time the ringing ended. While she sat there, as if listening for the phone was her occupation, and waiting for the fear was her duty, she thought. She thought of people she knew, well and not so well, who might hate her enough to torment her this way. People and incidents, long since relegated beyond memory to formless shadows that needed insistent prompting for even vague recollection, were sought with eager purpose. It was this lack of knowledge that was hurting her so, as the possession of knowledge was aiding the adversary. But she could come up with no person who would want to drive her mad. She had hurt people in her life, unwittingly and otherwise, but enough to warrant her destruction? She did not know; she did not want to believe it possible. Victimizing her was the work of a stranger, a deviously clever stranger; it had to be.

Then Arthur returned, and she was going to cook dinner for them. She had decided to do this in order to concentrate on something besides herself; cooking was a pleasant therapy, and maybe an evening home with Arthur would give her the courage to trust him completely with her fears.

She spent over two hours at the grocery stores, stopping in several to get the right ingredients, to make sure the vegetables were fresh, the condiments exact. Each hand held a heavy shopping bag by the time she got home that Saturday afternoon, and she had put both down in front of her door to get her key when the phone began to ring from within her apartment. In a flurry, she had the door open, dragged the two bundles into the foyer, and was in the kitchen. If Arthur gets stuck at the office, I swear I'll kill him, she thought as she reached for the receiver.

"Arthur, don't you dare tell me you can't make it," she said without preamble. "You've given more than enough Saturdays to that firm of yours." When there was no response, she said, more quietly, tentatively, "Arthur?"

And then she realized it was happening. Her head dropped back on a stiffened neck, a small gesture of giant despair. For a few hours she had forgotten, but that was not to be. There would be no relief, no respite, and in a way she understood that. She had become an obsession for this person, and as such, she occupied all his thoughts. There was no relief for whoever needed to do this, and so there would be no relief for her. She understood this in the space of two breaths, and then she brought her head forward. Perhaps because she had been momentarily freed; perhaps because she knew how helpless her situation was; perhaps because she genuinely felt it for the first time, Anne got angry. Her eyes turned darker, flinty, and her jaw hardened into place with an almost painful clenching of her back teeth. She looked at the receiver as if it were a filthy maggot.

"You sick pervert," she hissed, each word delivered like a gunshot. She thought she heard a quick, shocked intake of breath at the other end. Good, good! "You sick, disgusting animal. I've had enough, all I'm going to take. You don't scare me so you better start getting your kicks from some other victim. All you do is sicken me. If you think you're hurting me, or frightening me, think again. And soon you won't even be able to do that, you sick, sick pig you!" She ran out of epithets and courage at the same time. A small tic had begun in her left eye, and she touched it gently with her free hand, watched, with detached curiosity, her fingers trembling. She still had the receiver against her ear, and now she heard the hum of the dial tone. "How dare you hang up on me!" she screamed. "How can you do this to me, pig, pervert, animal!" And she shouted into a dead telephone until the tears came. In a blind, jerky motion she slipped the receiver back onto the hook. Then, with a start, she wiped at her eyes and ran to the living room windows. She knew there was a telephone booth at one end of the block. She could not see far enough in either direction. She ran into the bedroom, closer west, but it was still too far away to see.

The explosion over the phone, the effort of trying to see the person depleted what little strength she had left. She felt defeated, a netted butterfly helplessly pinned for prodding and poking by a wily captor. Listlessly, she walked back to the foyer for the groceries, and like an automaton, began to put them away. There was no joy, no anticipation in her actions or her mind. The resentment that had spurred the anger had come too late, and had proven ineffective. And the fear that she had been living with like a twin sister reasserted itself in an insidiously evil manner: she did not tremble with it nor sigh with it; her fingers did not go numb, her thighs weak; her head was not gripped in its vise nor her chest pounded by its beat. No, now she breathed with it, as a soldier breathes with the fear of the enemy sniper hidden in the trees.

For the rest of the afternoon and into the early evening, she woodenly performed her functions of preparing the food and table and herself. She was going through the motions and she knew it; just as she knew that it was only a matter of time before she would sit huddled in a corner, wrapped by fear, as the mad sit huddled, wrapped and insulated against life by insanity.

As soon as Anne opened the door for him, Arthur grabbed her to him, crushing her hard against him, inhaling the scent of her, absorbing the sensation of feeling her again.

"I've missed you so damn much," he said into her hair. "I could hold you like this forever." He moved her only far enough away so that he could kiss her, lingeringly, tenderly. "I love you, Annie, I really do love you." He gave a short laugh. "I sound surprised and I shouldn't be. I guess it's how much I love you that surprises me a little." He pressed her into him again, listening to their heartbeats, embarrassed for his emotion. She stirred in his arms, and he stepped back, leading her by the hand into the living room. She had not spoken a word.

Arthur let go of her long enough to remove his beige pigskin blazer, fold it over the arm of the sofa; he sat down, tugged at her hand to join him. "Sit down and let's neck a while," he said, only partly joking.

She did not smile as she pulled her hand away. "I'll fix drinks."

"Drinks can wait."

"No. I want one." She left him in the throbbing silence of her unfriendliness. When she returned a few moments later with drinks and the sausage rolls and miniature quiches she had prepared as appetizers, he was holding the copy of her book that had been on the coffee table.

He hefted the book, ran his fingers over the cover. "Feels good, doesn't it?" he said with a smile, wanting to chase away whatever was separating her from him. When she did not respond, he put down the book and rose halfway. "Here, let me help you with that. Mmm, they smell delicious." After she sat down, he offered his glass in a toast. "To us."

She met his glass, but not his eyes, and she did not speak. "Okay, what's wrong?" he asked, not hiding his irritation.

"Nothing," she said curtly.

"Oh sure. You greet me like I'm a smelly rag you want to stick in the laundry, you won't sit down next to me, you won't even toast to us. Sure, nothing's wrong, that's your normal lovable self. Christ, give me a break."

"I'm tired."

"Then say that. Don't act like I've got a disease."

"I'm saying it, I'm tired."

"Maybe I should go and let you get some sleep then." He could feel, as he uttered the words, the rush of adrenaline, the dire need for her to insist that he stay.

All she did was shrug, apathetically.

He put down his drink, twisted on the sofa and grabbed her by both shoulders so that she had to face him. "What the hell is going on?" He held on to her and he looked at her, not with the prejudiced eyes of a lover, but objectively, clinically. And so, for the first time that evening, he saw the little gray pouches under the unexpectedly dull sable eyes. Two lines led from her nose to her mouth. She was sickly pale underneath the makeup, and he could see that the application of blusher was thicker than usual. She even felt different, he realized, bonier, unyielding.

214

"Annie?" He said her name tremulously, concerned. "What is it, honey? What's wrong?"

She shook her head, unable to speak.

"This is more than tired, honey. Something's happened. Tell me, you've got to tell me. Remember, no secrets." He was trying to keep his voice light, coaxing, as if speaking to a wayward child, but within him was deep worry. What was happening to her that frightened her so dreadfully? And he knew she was frightened: the slightest touch of his hand on her made her start and recoil; the stoniness of her body was as if in preparation for attack.

"Anne . . ." he prompted.

She gazed at him, brows creasing, lips feeding on themselves as she struggled to decide. Silently, she got up from the sofa and went into her office. When she returned, she had a pile of typewritten pages which she gave to Arthur. Puzzled, he began to read; after about four pages, he looked up.

"Is this your new novel? It's so different from the first one I can hardly believe you wrote it." He grinned. "You're more talented than I gave you credit for being, able to write in different styles like that. I must—"

"I didn't write it."

"What?"

"I said I didn't write it. I did not write any of that." She sat down again, her eyes riveted to the pages in his lap.

"I don't understand. Why did you give them to me to read?"

Anne did not answer immediately. She closed her eyes, quickly, silently praying for him to believe her. When she looked at him, she saw that he was frowning and that he had not taken his eyes from hers.

"Matt sent those pages to me," she finally said. "He got them in the mail. I didn't even know about it, but he called me a few days ago to tell me he was going to

California and he'd bring the chapters and outline of my new book with him." She stopped speaking for a minute, seeing if perhaps he would grasp what had occurred without her having to detail it, but his look of confusion was still evident.

"Arthur," she said, leaning toward him, "I never sent him these pages. I never wrote them. The work I've done on my second novel is inside, it's very rough, even the outline is still rough. I'm not ready to show it to Matt yet. Don't you understand?" she said imploringly. "That person, that horrible sick person who's been calling me and who sent you that letter, that sick mind sent those pages to Matt using *my* name!"

Arthur glanced down at the typewritten pages, over at Anne. "That's ridiculous," he decreed.

"I knew you wouldn't believe me," she said, almost a groan. "Arthur, I didn't send Matt those pages. I didn't write them. Don't you see, don't you realize what's happening?"

"No, and I think you're getting really—"

She sat back, her head against the sofa pillow, her eyes on a fixed spot on the other side of the room. "I knew you wouldn't believe me," she repeated dully, "I knew it."

"It doesn't make any sense," Arthur tried to defend himself. "Why would anybody go to all the trouble of writing an outline and chapters of a novel and then use somebody else's name?"

She looked at him, her expression beseeching him not to doubt her. "Why would anybody go to the trouble of sending you a letter in my name, or sending me flowers, or getting into my apartment and not taking anything? Of course it doesn't make sense, but it's happening. You've got to admit it's happening."

Arthur shook his head. "Okay, these things may have happened, but it's crazy to think one person is responsible for them all." He was beginning to feel strangely uncomfortable, awkward, as if in the presence of a handicapped person with whom he wanted to behave normally, not patronizingly, but could not. He loved this woman, and he respected her. She was intelligent and stable and sensible. Yet the things she was saying, the associations she was making . . .

"Annie, you're tired. I can see it in your face. You're working too hard and your imagination is running away with itself."

She glared at him, then jumped to her feet and walked to the window, away from him. "Sure I'm tired. I haven't been sleeping well because every damn time the phone rings I don't know if it's that voiceless horror or not. And I'm tired because I lie awake at night thinking if he tried it once, he's going to try it again, and the next time might be for real."

"What the hell are you talking about?" Arthur demanded, getting up and going over to her.

"Forget it," she snapped, "you wouldn't believe me."

"Dammit, tell me what the hell's been going on."

"Okay, you want to know, I'll tell you," she practically screamed. "Someone tried to kill me earlier this week." She saw his eyes widen, saw him reach for her, but she turned from him. She could feel the tears stinging and she breathed deeply for self-control. Her back was to him as she spoke. "I had just come from this crazy mix-up at Swiss House where I was supposed to meet Anne Fletcher for lunch, except—"

He brusquely grabbed her shoulders and turned her to him. "What did you just say?"

"Lunch, except she didn't show up."

"*You* were supposed to have lunch with Anne Fletcher? When did this cozy little friendship begin?" he asked harshly, dropping his hands and taking a step away from her.

"Oh, Arthur, I was going to tell you about it," she said wearily. "I met her at my party."

"She was there?" he asked, aghast.

Anne nodded.

"And you didn't tell me." It was a statement, flat with disappointment.

"I would have, really. I just thought it was kind of—oh, who knows, cute, interesting, call it what you want, for two of the women in your life to meet. I wasn't being sneaky or anything, maybe just a little more female than usual. Anyway, it doesn't matter."

"It does to me," he muttered. "Have you met her for lunch before?"

"No, this was to have been the first time."

"I can just imagine the conversation you two were going to have. Me. For appetizer, entrée and dessert." He shook his head, disgusted.

"That's not true," Anne protested. "We were supposed to discuss her writing. She wanted me to look at some stuff she had done. Then there was a strange mix-up with the reservations or something—I still don't understand it—and she never showed up. This was the same day Matt called about . . . about that other novel, so I was really in a daze when I left the restaurant. That's when I went to take the subway home."

He said nothing, glaring at her, wishing he did not suddenly wonder what other subterfuges she might have practiced on him, if there were *men* she saw when he was not around. Just as suddenly, he knew how ridiculous he was being, accusing her when she had done nothing so terrible, projecting acts of which she simply was not capable.

"Tell me about it," he said calmly.

Her voice cracked with strain as she spoke. "I was standing on the platform. It wasn't very crowded. I was upset about all that had been happening, I was thinking about it when the train started to pull in. It hadn't come to a complete stop when I felt hands on my back." Her eyes rounded with remembered fear. "All of a sudden these hands were pushing me. Arthur, they pushed me into the train! I fell against the side of the car. Oh, it was so horrible, so horrible!" She could no longer hold in the tears, and she buried her face in her hands until Arthur stepped closer and took her in his arms.

He held her, feeling her shoulders heave, hearing the misery in her sobs. He could not remember being so inadequate or confused. He wanted desperately to believe her; this was the woman he loved more than he thought he could ever love someone; this was the woman whose intelligent, sensible, logical approach to people and relationships and emotions had altered his own attitudes. What had first attracted him to her, what he had come to admire so much was her common sense. But that was not in evidence now, and all his training held him in doubt of her. She talks of someone trying to kill her, he thought, of voiceless telephone calls, of a cousin she does not have, a letter she says she did not send, pages of a novel she claims not to have written. But how did he know she was telling the truth, *how did he really know?* And the treacherous thoughts disgusted him for even entering his conscience. He could not help himself, though. He had no proof that she was telling the truth; no actual proof that she was not making everything up out of an exhausted imagination. Perhaps loving her was enough reason to believe her, but he needed more. He needed something tangible so that he could help her. All he had now was her conclusion that one person was behind all the incidents, and that this person wanted to kill her. He had as much difficulty accepting that as he did the suspicion that she was losing her mind.

She stepped back from him, but he held her by the shoulders. The tears had stopped; she was glassy-eyed, the lines from her nose to her mouth etched deeper, the sallowness of her skin more evident. He met her stare.

"You don't believe anything I've said," she whispered, seeing what she had dreaded to see in his eyes. "You think I'm crazy, don't you?"

"Annie, of course I believe you," he said halfheartedly, dropping his hands. "It's just that—I don't know —it's just that I think you're making associations where none belong. I mean, it's possible that a lot of coincidence is behind all that's been happening."

"Coincidence!" She gave a short, humorless laugh, and walked back to the sofa but did not sit down. "No, Arthur, it's not coincidence. For a while, a long while, I thought it was, but I realized this week that every single thing that's taken place, every unexplained letter and call has been diabolically deliberate. Someone out there has been trying to drive me mad, and by pushing me against the subway train, that person was warning me that if one way isn't successful, he's willing to try another."

"Oh for pete's sake, make sense, will you?"

"Somebody tried to kill me. Why won't you believe that?" she cried.

"Someone accidentally bumped against you and put your equilibrium off. That's all it was, and you're making it some big-deal threat. Nobody tried to kill you and nobody's been trying to make you crazy. You're doing that just fine by yourself."

She stared at him and began to nod her head. She slumped down in the sofa, watching the shame darken his eyes and tighten the muscles in his jaw, his neck. He came quickly over to her, sat down, reached for her hand, stopped himself. "I'm sorry," he said softly, "I didn't mean that."

"Yes you did. I knew you'd feel this way." Her voice, her eyes, her body—all of her was numb and tired, utterly exhausted.

"You've got to try to understand how I feel," Arthur said. "I mean, if I were talking the way you've been, wouldn't you think I was a little paranoid or something?

I mean, come on, it's only natural to question what you're saying," he defended himself again.

"No, I wouldn't think you're paranoid," she told him. "I would wonder about it a little, yes, but only a little, and then my trust in you, and my belief in you would erase all doubt. If you felt something strongly enough, no matter how improbable it might seem to me, I would believe you."

"Annie, I—" He stopped, not really knowing what to say. He was miserable, his conflict devastating him. He loved her and at the same time he suspected her of wild, senseless imaginings. He sympathized with the agony of her harassment, yet he could not conceive of an association between the incidents or of a deliberate motive linking them. He wanted to believe her, wanted to see with her eyes, but he could not; he simply could not let go of years of training and practice in logic, evidence, proof. Oh, he worked on instinct, he thought; many times that was the key, but then came the proof, the tangible that made it real. Instinct, gut-level reactions proved nothing, and neither did Anne's suspicions.

He would try again. "It's not impossible that you *are* overwrought, is it?" he asked gently.

"Arthur, please, let's not discuss this anymore. You've told me how you feel, and I can't fight that. I just don't have the energy to try to convince you anymore."

"Please, just listen to me a minute, okay? Now, you've been working hard on the new book. You've been doing some interviews on the first one, seeing me, seeing your friends—all this takes its toll. It's not just physical energy, it's the mental, and that can be even more exhausting. So isn't it possible that you really are done in, mentally wiped out? I bet if you went away for a few days, did nothing but rest and relax, you'd come back and laugh at the silly scenario your mind's created."

He watched her carefully, waiting to see signs of self-doubt, and the subsequent acceptance of his words, waiting to see a nod, a glimmer of a smile, some signal that would tell him yes, you're right. But there was no expression on her face except distance, as if she had been lightly dusted with a makeup that removed her from his reality.

"I think you'd better go now," she stated.

"Annie, please. Would you just please listen to me?"

"I have listened to you, Arthur, and I don't care to anymore. You've said what you had to say, what I knew you would say." She shook her head, and her smile was sad. "So much for no secrets."

"Dammit, Annie, stop this! I love you, I want to help you, but you're making it impossible!"

"No, Arthur," she said quietly so that the loudness of his voice seemed to echo through the room, "you're making it impossible because you refuse to believe me. Until you do, you can't help me. It's that simple, and that complicated."

"I can't deal with this," he said, getting up. "I don't know what you want from me. I told you what I think but because I don't agree with you, you want me to leave. That's as crazy as everything else you've been saying." He began to storm around the apartment. "Dammit, why won't you try to look at it my way?"

"I have, and it doesn't work."

"It doesn't work!" he shouted. "Oh, and I suppose linking some weird accidents to the devious plot of some mastermind out there—some single person who wants to kill you, no less—I suppose that works! Yeah, sure, that works all right. For a paranoid, for a sick neurotic, it works just fine!" He did not mean to explode, to call her names, to say what he had been thinking, but he was frustrated in his inability to reach her, and in his helplessness to stop her hurt. "Oh, Annie," he murmured wearily. He retrieved his jacket, and walked to the front door. "Annie—"

"Go, Arthur, just go."

In the ride down in the elevator, in the street, walking aimlessly for several blocks; later, back in his apartment, with the tuna sandwich uneaten on the plate, and the newspaper unread in front of him, Arthur's mind see-sawed. Up with anger—at himself and at her; down with regret for the cruelty of his words. And regardless of which way his emotions swung, always present, steady and solid in his gut, was the awful fear that he had lost her forever, but that he would be loving her for a long time after that.

The food she had spent hours preparing spoiled, wilted, soured. The candles dripped to death. She did not move from the sofa for several hours. The sound of the door closing behind Arthur reverberated in her mind; she heard it over and over again, the finality deafening. She sat there thinking, almost with admiration, how clever her tormentor was. She had little left of importance; almost every facet of her life that mattered had been tainted: her school, her job, her writing, her apartment, the man she loved. And her life itself. Control had slipped from her like silk through fingers. She would continue to function, to get through the hours and days performing her duties, making the motions of an existence. But always she would be waiting . . . waiting for the next voiceless telephone call, the next shove over a platform, the next violation. Arthur was wrong: she was not losing her mind, she was not crazy. She only wished she were. The mad had learned to deal with terror, she had not.

Arthur spent Sunday morosely pretending to read the papers, even more fraudulently doing some work he had brought home from the office. Several times during the course of the day he had gone into his bedroom, reached for the telephone, walked away. He did not know what more to say to her; the next move, the gesture to rejoin had to come from her. As harsh as his words had been, he could not take them back, even if he did not believe in their rightness, which he still did. He had twisted and convoluted her arguments, her convictions into every possible reasonable structure, but they remained illogical to him. He simply could not accept what she so determinedly clung to as truth: that there was one single person victimizing Anne N. Fletcher. She was a victim, most certainly, of a few coincidences, of a crank caller, but more, of an overactive imagination and overworked nerves. He wondered if all writers, by necessity, saw and felt and sensed what mere mortals could not, their creativity giving them both the gift and the curse of too vivid perception.

At about seven o'clock that evening, the telephone

rang. He raced into the bedroom, grabbing up the receiver before the second ring.

"Hello?" His voice was breathless with hope.

"Hello, Arthur, how are you?"

"Who is this?" His stomach dropped, and his heart felt as if someone had punctured it, letting out all the wishful yearning that had kept it pumping.

"It's Anne. Anne Fletcher. I haven't spoken to you in a while, and I just thought it would be nice to say hi."

"Oh, sure, hi, how've you been?"

"Fine. What about you, still traveling a lot?"

"Off and on," he replied disinterestedly.

"Still with your girlfriend? She's getting pretty famous now, I bet."

"Look, Anne, I've gotta go. I'll speak to you soon."

"What? Oh, okay, Arthur, soon then. 'Bye."

After he hung up, he stared a moment at the receiver recalling something from the other night. It made no sense that his Annie and this other one should meet. Sure, he could see Annie helping her out, but hadn't the request struck her as peculiar? Didn't she find it odd, if not just awkward, to become friends of sorts with someone he had once dated? And Anne Fletcher herself—she had never seemed to him the type of girl to ask anyone for guidance, least of all with something she viewed as intensely as her writing.

Where the hell were his brains the night of the party, with all those questions out of the blue about Anne Fletcher? He should have suspected then, but he had had just enough brandies not to care very much. Amazing that he hadn't seen her at the party—no, not so amazing really. The place had been packed and he hadn't thought he'd see any familiar faces so he hadn't looked for one. Strange that she hadn't found him, she was never the shy kind; then again, he left pretty early and she might have gotten there afterward, he carefully reasoned. The unexpectedness of her call, coming soon after Annie had let slip about her, well, the timing was weird but he was making too much of it. Forget it, that's all, just forget it, he told himself.

With that, the true disappointment over the call not being from Annie settled in. Moroseness congealed into depression; he felt alone, stranded, unsure, a target in a shooting gallery, pockmarked with self-doubt. Maybe Annie was right, about several things. Maybe loving her was reason enough to believe her, no matter how implausible her conclusions. And perhaps one person *was* responsible for it all, including, most especially including the shove against the incoming subway train. If so, if indeed one of unbalanced mind had conceived and executed these terrible acts, then what in hell's name was he doing sitting here, feeling sorry for himself instead of protecting her? But how to protect against an unknown? There were no clues, no significant quirks to reveal personality, motive. He had absolutely nothing to go on except what she had told him. And dammit, that was not enough!

And so the depression gave way to guilt that he was being selfish, pompous, unloving, stubborn, a real bastard. Any other man in the same situation would help, and ask questions later. But no, he had to be the attorney at all times, looking for the damned real, provable, actual. She could be in danger at this very second while he was regretting who he was and that he was incapable of change, incapable of allowing the seed of doubt in his opinions to grow into complete belief in hers.

He was so busy in the office Monday that he had no time to think what had occurred between them, but by Monday evening, alone in his living room, the television blasting, every lamp lighted and doing nothing to lift his gloom, anger began to insinuate itself into his thoughts. Outrage at her for placing him in this position, for confusing him, for becoming different so that he no longer knew her but loved her still, and so loved a stranger. The more he reviewed her behavior, the angrier he got until he needed to do something that would hurt her, something selfishly gratifying. But what? He could call and tell her they were through, but that was a little like convicting the murderer after he had been electrocuted. He could write her a letter . . . saying what? proving what?

Another woman. That was it, he eventually decided. He would see another woman, have sex with another woman. And how would that hurt her? he argued to himself. How would she know about it? That didn't matter; *he* would know what he had done, and that would have to be satisfaction enough.

He began to think of women he could call who would be a sure bet, welcoming him into their bed with no argument and no need for an explanation about his long absence. He had been out of circulation for so many months that he could come up with no one. He had, in the top drawer of his dresser, a brown Moroccan leather telephone book, several loose bits of paper, back flaps of envelopes, matchbook covers, cocktail napkins. He had not gone to this directory since shortly after meeting Anne; he went to it now. Many of the names remained just that for him: he had never called them and had no recollection of the girl. A few he remembered with indistinct pleasure or distinct disfavor. He thumbed through the leather telephone book, once, twice, the second time more slowly, less selectively. Soon he bent the spine back on the F's and grinned. Of course. He should have thought of her immediately. Anne Fletcher, perfect. No hassle, no stern lecture on where he'd been keeping himself because she *knew!* And she was a sure thing, always had been. Hadn't she just called him, as if to let him know she was still available? As if she had an idea he would need her now. She was weird at times, and the sex was not the greatest, but hell, this was a one-shot. And her name, he enjoyed the irony of her name; there was something so sweetly just about getting back at Annie with this other Anne Fletcher.

It was past ten o'clock; that did not make him hesitate. She picked up on the third ring.

"Hello?"

"Anne, hi. This is Arthur Dumont."

"Arthur, well, what a surprise, you calling me."

"Yeah, well, I was a little out of it the other night, sorry about that. Listen, Anne, I was wondering. It's been a long time since I've seen you. How about getting together?"

"That would be nice, but what about your girlfriend? Won't she be jealous?"

"I'll worry about her," he said sharply. Shit, I hate this game. Oh, Annie, why are you making me do this? "So, what about it? Want to recapture old times?" His laugh was hollow, uninviting.

"Sure, I'd love it. I always did have a good time with you." The purr in her voice elicited a grimace at his end. But he needed what she could provide.

"How about tonight?"

"Tonight? I couldn't possibly. It's almost ten-thirty."

"So what? That still gives us the whole night."

"No, I don't think so. I'm already undressed for bed."

"Better yet. That'll save precious time."

He heard her giggle, and felt a wave of disgust. "What do you say? I can be over in ten minutes."

"No, Arthur, I really don't want to. How about tomorrow night?"

He fleetingly wondered if he would still be interested tomorrow night; if his crust of anger would live that long. If not, he could always cancel out at the last minute. "If that's the best I can do, I'll have to take it."

"Terrific. Say seven, seven-thirty?"

Too early. He had no intention of springing for dinner, not even on expense account. "Nope, it'll have to be late. I've got a dinner meeting with a prospective client," he lied.

"Oh," and he heard her disappointment. "When then?"

"Not before nine-thirty, probably more like ten."

"Well, okay, but that's awfully late."

"Just wait up for me."

She giggled again. "See you tomorrow, Arthur."

He hung up without replying. He contemplated calling someone else, but it was late, and he did not feel like going through the verbal gymnastics again with some other bimbo. No, he would wait until tomorrow night, and if his desire as well as his self-righteous indignation abandoned him by then, well, he would find some other way to prove that he did not need her.

By Tuesday evening, his desire—physical and emotional—had diminished not one bit. In fact, there was such hostility in him toward all women that he had been driven throughout the day by the image of himself pummeling Anne Fletcher to her mattress, fucking her and fucking her until she lay limp, until every man she had after him would be as an unending quest to repeat the ecstasy he brought her. With such thoughts motivating him, he was at her apartment by nine-fifteen, curtly instructing the doorman to announce him.

"Your name, sir?"

Arthur vaguely remembered this doorman as the one who had been so supercilious the evening Anne had prepared dinner for him. He gave the now obsequiously smiling man his name.

The doorman, with no jolt of familiarity with the name or face, announced Arthur to Anne when her intercom clicked on. "She says go right up, Eleven D."

She was standing in the doorway of her apartment waiting for him, and suddenly, that evening together flashed before him: the diaphanous dress, the musky perfume, the candles, the venomous words, the passivity in bed, the peculiar way she had closed herself off. His stomach tightened and he considered turning around and leaving. His stride kept taking him forward.

As he drew closer, saw her more clearly, his brow furrowed into a frown, and he had the odd sensation of his face being drained of blood, of getting pasty and white. Her long, auburn-hued hair was gone. Instead of brushing her shoulders, it was now cut in a feathery, layered style *exactly the way Annie wore her hair*. Coincidence, that's all, he told himself, but that did not stop his stomach from again seeming to ball up into a hard knot, this time with inexplicable dread.

She was smiling broadly when he reached her. She moved aside to let him in, then took both his hands in hers. "I'm glad you could come earlier," she said. "You look wonderful."

"So do you," he said dutifully, then saw that it was true. She was wearing beige gabardine slacks and a Kelly green sweater that made her skin glow. The haircut, the color of the sweater set off those remarkable eyes that shone almost hypnotically in an indisputably pretty face. "So do you," he repeated with more feeling.

"Well, come in, sit down. What are you drinking these days?" she asked, shutting and locking the door.

"Scotch on the rocks will be fine," he told her, going into the living room. He did not sit down immediately, but stood there, eyes alighting on objects that were dearly familiar to him, disconcertingly out of place in this apartment. As he saw first one incontestable piece of evidence after another, he tried to calm himself, to tell himself, no, what was he thinking was absurd, too unbelievable. He was tired; the pressure and aggravation were getting to him. It could be just that. It could be, but he knew, with sudden, uncanny clarity, that it was not. The similarity of the haircut had been one small thing, easy to dismiss as coincidence. But now, in front of him, here was an apartmentful of proof, and like a house of cards, all doubt, confusion, questions, any need to be convinced—toppled, gone as if they never existed. If this was not proof he could take into a court of law, it was all the proof *he* needed. *He knew.* If only Annie had told him earlier about her, he thought rapidly; if only he had been given some indication sooner, things might never have reached this point. The connection had been there the whole damn time, but Annie had to go and get female on him! Be fair, he told himself. Even if she had told you, would you *really* have made the association, or would you still have been stubbornly resistant? Oh Annie, he cried, I'm sorry, I'm so sorry!

"Here we go," he heard Anne say, and he sat down on the couch, sure that his plaster face of pretense would crack, and she would guess his newfound knowledge.

"It's been a long time, Arthur," she was saying. "Too long. How have you been?"

"Fine, overworked but fine." He must control everything about himself tonight: his expression, his voice, his eyes, every gesture. Any performance he put on before a judge was amateur compared to now. "And you?"

"Well, very well," she told him. "I've sort of settled down, I guess, learned to take one thing at a time and not be so impatient." She smiled self-consciously. "I used to get furious if things didn't go exactly as I wanted them to, when I wanted them to. Now I'm more tolerant, calmer. I like myself better this way," she added with a small laugh.

"It certainly seems to agree with you," he said. "What prompted the change?"

She shrugged. "Maturity? No, that's too glib. I think before I expected everything as my due. I still do," she laughed again, "but I'm willing to work for it now, work hard. Do you understand what I'm saying? It sounds awfully confusing even to me."

"Sure, I understand, but what do you mean before? Before what?" Before you went crazy? Before you decided to destroy my Annie?

"Oh." She paused, and he saw her eyes get an almost sleepy look of secret knowledge in them. "Just before."

"Well, to the new you," he toasted, lifting his glass.

The green eyes pierced him with a stare of such intensity that he felt he would never be able to look away. From a distance, he seemed to hear the sound of her glass tapping his, and he was released.

They drank in silence for a few minutes, and Arthur knew that despite the revulsion he was feeling for her, for the obvious proof before him, he would stay with this girl, as long as he could to discover what else existed in her deviant reality. He would sit with her, and drink with her, and listen to her lies for as long as it took to trap her, because that's what he had to do to save Annie. He was as sure of this as he was of Anne Fletcher's guilt. And if it wasn't tonight, then it would be tomorrow or the next day. But he would trap her, and stop her, of that he was certain.

He got up, walked over to a corner by the window where he fingered the leaves of a dried silver dollar plant that was in a vase on a small wicker table. He had never seen a silver dollar plant until he met Annie, and never one that had been left to dry and then painted. He had been fascinated by it; a living plant at one time and Annie had created what was almost a work of art. It was the only plant this Anne Fletcher had in her apartment, and he did not have to ask where she saw it for the first time. Annie's superintendent was a witness, if it came to that. Cousin, some cousin! He had doubted her even about that. He felt as if he would gag and retch on his own self-loathing. But it was not enough just to see the evidence; he wanted to watch her squirm in a corner like a suckered fish.

"You like them?"

He turned. She was reclining against the back of the couch, one arm across the top, straining the sweater across her breasts. The low lighting from the table lamp washed her in a soft golden hue, and he thought he had never seen a woman look so ethereally erotic or erotically ethereal, he was not sure which, but it was as disturbing as it was exciting. He wanted to reach out to see if she were indeed there; wanted to slam his mouth hard against hers, wipe out the secret smile, the self-possession that had never been there before. He wanted to hurt her.

"Nice," he commented. "Unusual. You didn't have them before, did you?"

"No, they're new. I got the idea of letting them dry out and then spray-painting them silver."

"From where?"

"From where what?"

"Where'd you get the idea to do this? I'd like to tell my mother about it," he improvised.

"Oh, who remembers."

"Try," he pressed.

She stared at him a moment, then laughed lightly. "Well, if it's that important to you, in the Village someplace, I think. They were part of the display in a boutique window and I liked the way they looked so I went in and asked how it was done." She lifted his drink from where he had left it on the coffee table. "Your ice is melting down. I'll freshen it, okay?"

He nodded, waited until she was in the kitchen before moving away from the plant.

"Hungry?" he heard her call out. "I've got some cheese and crackers if that dinner you had wasn't enough?"

"Sure, fine," he answered. He had eaten, if two semithawed tacos and a can of beer could be called food. He had been ravenous when he first got to the apartment, and hoped she would give him something. Now he had no appetite, just a raw, seared feeling in his gut from anger.

He walked over to the glass and chrome étagère that had not been here before, that was exactly like those in Annie's apartment. He noticed the small stereo unit on the top shelf; he looked around for the speakers, found one on the floor near the dining table, one on the far side of the TV stand.

"Fresh drink and food," she announced, coming back into the living room and sitting down.

"New?" he asked, pointing to the étagère.

"Mmm. I really need another one. I keep my books in the closets, and it would be nice to get a few of them out. Every wall would have to be lined with shelves to hold them all, though."

"Stereo's new too, isn't it?" She nodded. "You ought to lift the speakers. You'd get better sound if they were off the floor."

"Really? I didn't know that."

"You could get hooks and put them on the wall. They're small enough to hold." If he didn't know better, this almost seemed normal, he thought.

She shrugged. "I don't listen to it all that much. It's more for people I have over. Do you want to hear some music? I don't have many records as you can see."

His eyes followed her pointing finger to the bottom shelf. He dropped to his knees, scanning the few record jackets: *Rhapsody in Blue* and *An American in Paris* conducted by Leonard Berstein—Annie's favorite; two Peter Nero albums; the Beatles' *Abbey Road* which Annie played endlessly; the score from *A Chorus Line*, another Annie favorite; a Barry Manilow album, a double record disco set by Donna Summer. How much more had she seen and taken as her own? he wondered with deep revulsion.

"Very varied taste," he remarked, getting to his feet.

"Like I said, it's not for me. Anything there you want to hear?"

He shook his head. "Your job must have improved or at least you must have gotten a raise. These things cost."

"The job's pretty much the same, but I did get a raise. I would have made these changes anyway, though."

"Oh? Why?"

She smiled disarmingly. "Part of the new me."

"Is writing part of the new you?" He asked the question as idly as he picked up a small box from a middle shelf. He was curious how she would handle the answer; how much she believed her own mythology.

But she did not reply, and he turned his attention to her. She was leaning forward on the sofa, her eyes going through him, beyond him. He was reminded of that night when she had lain in bed with the same locked-in expression. He thought he saw her lips tighten, saw the shadow of two white spots graze either side of her mouth.

"Anne?"

She lifted her mouth into a smile, and her eyes came back to him. "Sorry, I was just thinking of something." She sipped from her drink. "How's your girlfriend's book selling?"

"Okay," he replied curtly. He was aware that she had not answered his question; aware, too, that it had been deliberate. But he would get around to it again, in time. He looked down at the object in his hand, at the two others on the shelf. Three small porcelain boxes. He had spotted them before, but touching them, here in this apartment, it was as if he was somehow violating Annie's cherished treasures. His hand was unsteady as he replaced the box on the shelf.

"These new, too?"

"Yes, my new hobby. Like them?"

"Very pretty. Unusual kind of hobby, though, isn't it?"

His mouth had gone dry, it tasted rancid to his tongue. There was a weakness under his heart, as if he had been sparring gently in the ring when his partner had suddenly hit him with a solid punch. It was getting so difficult to breathe, to speak normally.

"Not really."

"Where'd you get the notion to collect them?"

There was a hard, quick flare from her eyes, then she smiled into her glass. "Oh, from a friend."

Bitch! You sick perverted lying bitch! "When?" he managed. "When did you start?"

"You and your questions," she answered lightly. "I don't know, a few months ago. Why the big interest in porcelain boxes—would your mother like them, too?"

"Curious, that's all. Anne Fletcher also collects them."

He did not take his eyes from her face, waiting to see a flicker of fear, just one small indication that he had gotten to her, that her impervious disregard for reality was no longer a secret.

"That's nice," she said indifferently. "Why don't you sit down and have your drink? I'm getting tired of watching the ice melt and ruin them."

He stared at her, feeling the perspiration dampen the underarms of his pale blue Italian cotton shirt, feeling the grit in his mouth, a cobwebby disorientation in his mind. But he sat down next to her and picked up his glass.

"I'm glad you decided to call me again," she said after a few moments. "We always had a nice time together."

"Well, you know how it is," he faltered, making an effort to smile.

She cocked her head and grinned at him coyly. He forced himself not to look away. "I saw you not so long ago. At your girlfriend's publishing party."

"You were there? I didn't see you." The surprise he tried to put in his voice sounded hollow, obviously fake to him.

"I deliberately avoided you. I decided you might not want your current girl to see what her competition was like. Would put you in kind of an awkward position. I met *her*, though. Didn't she tell you about it?"

"Uh, no. I guess she felt the same way you did, that I wouldn't like it too much." He paused, then casually: "What were you doing there? I thought you didn't get to go to many of those things."

"Oh, I don't, but that one was special. I wouldn't have missed it for the life of me. Meeting your girlfriend was the best—"

"I wish you'd stop calling her my girlfriend," Arthur burst out, loathing the almost obscene insinuation she placed on the word. "She's a friend, okay? Just a friend."

Anne's eyes widened in surprise. "That sounds sort of final." She smiled. "I suppose that's why you called me. It doesn't matter, not really. I knew you'd call again. It was just a question of time."

"What do you mean?"

"We had good times together, Arthur, something special going for us. There might be some side trips along the way, but I knew you'd get back to me." She put a hand on his knee, pressed slightly, significantly.

Arthur squirmed, his smile a plastic decal he sloppily pasted on so that it came out crooked and weak. Good times? Something special? Am I part of the fable, too?

"We were supposed to have lunch together last week, your *friend* and me," she resumed, "but she canceled out at the last minute. I don't know what happened, I guess something came up that couldn't wait. We're getting together later this week."

"You are?" Arthur's mind was racing. Annie had said there was a mix-up with the reservations, not that she had canceled. Another lie from this sick bitch, another subtle way to drive Annie mad. And why hadn't she told him they'd made another date? Because you never gave her a chance to. His hatred, his disgust for Anne Fletcher was so strong at this moment that he dared not look at her for fear that she see it all in his eyes.

"She's going to be my guest at the health club on Thursday," Anne told him. "Then we're having dinner. Speaking of which, you haven't been around the club much lately."

"Why the health club?"

"I thought it would be fun, and besides, it's relaxing, good for—"

He lifted his eyes to her face. "Why?"

"Why what?"

"Why do you want to get together with her?"

"Refill?" she asked, ignoring his question.

"How come you want to see her, Anne? It's kind of unusual, isn't it?"

"Unusual? No, I don't think so. I admire her, I like her work, and I think she could help me with my own writing. Besides, we might even become friends." She leaned in closer to him. "After all," she smiled, "we do have a lot in common."

He heard everything she said, heard the sincere, casual, *sane* way she spoke, but still he had no trouble believing the pit of madness this girl had dug for herself. Perhaps he should be feeling pity, he was not sure, for it was sad that disillusionment could rule one's life so completely. Pity, though, he usually reserved for someone who could not help himself, for someone caught in a condition not of his own making. Anne Fletcher did not deserve any emotion but utter contempt, any treatment but the cruelest.

He made his expression bland, guileless. "I was asking you before, Anne, but we got sidetracked. What about your writing? You've talked about it so many times, but I've never seen anything you've done."

"Oh, I don't like to show it around, it's kind of embarrassing."

"I'd really like to see some of it. I don't get many

238

chances to read a work in progress," he said with what he hoped was his most appealingly boyish grin.

"Doesn't *she* show you what she's working on?"

"Who, Annie? No, she—"

"Is that what you call her, Annie?"

His silence was affirmation, and he was furious at his slip. "Well, do you have anything I can read?" he asked again, more harshly.

"Oh, I don't know, Arthur..." She hesitated. He waited, studied her obliquely, how the eyes shut him out, how the pulse beat in her temple and the vein in her neck tightened into visibility. He sought her hands; they were on her thighs, positioned like small claws. Was he making her nervous, finally?

"I'd really like it if you'd let me," he cajoled. "I know how personal writing is, and—" He stopped, the clear gaze from her eyes back on him. His heart stepped up its beat in excited anticipation as he realized she was going to give in.

She got to her feet. "I'll be right back."

Arthur was able to spread one cracker with cheese by the time she returned; he put it on the plate uneaten as she handed him several pages. He took them, a sense of *déjà vu* creeping over him like a vine.

"I'm sorry it's just a carbon," she said. "The original is buried under some books." She smiled at him as she sat down. "I hope you like it."

He lowered his eyes to the first page. He kept pretending to read, turning the sheets of paper long after he had stopped absorbing the words. He was not mistaken: he had read these exact same words only a few days ago. They had been meaningless to him then except to precipitate what had become such a wrenching argument. Now, reading them for the second time, he shuddered not at what they said but at what they told him, at their horrific implications.

He raised his eyes; she was watching him carefully.

Flames of fiery anger licked at him; only by hurting her would he ease his own pain, and that he could not do yet.

"I'm impressed," he said, revolting himself. "You're good. You're very good."

The green eyes glittered, a flush swept her cheeks, and he was repulsed by her beauty. "I'm so glad you think so," she gushed. "You're the first person I've shown these pages to. I was going to give them to Anne and I've been so nervous about what she'd think. You've made me feel much more confident."

He did not know what effort of will permitted him to sit there talking to her, stopped him from banging her against a wall and throttling a confession from her. But he knew he had to bide his time; knew he had to accumulate as much information as possible, and then use that information against her.

"What are you planning to do with your novel when you're finished?" he asked.

"Give it to an agent. Matthew Holmes if he'll take me."

"I'm sure Anne can help you there."

She nodded. "I hope so." She reached for the pages. "Here, let me put that away."

Arthur did not relinquish the sheets, an idea coming to him. "Anne, why don't you let me keep this a while? I've met a few people in publishing recently, and maybe I can do something for you." Proof. Tangible proof to take away with him. But was this proof of telephone calls that haunted, and letters that denounced love; was this proof of mysterious flowers and nonexistent cousins and threatening shoves against moving trains? Yes. It was proof of a madness capable of anything.

"You?" she said. "Oh, I don't know, Arthur. I wouldn't want to put you to any trouble."

"Hey, no trouble. A couple of calls, some stamps, nothing to it."

"Well . . ." She still hesitated. "It's my only copy."

"I thought you said you have the original."

"Yes, of course, the original."

"Look, if it'll make you feel better I'll get this Xeroxed in the office and bring the carbon back to you. Unless you want to give me the original to Xerox," he suggested, sure of what she would say.

"No, that's okay. I'll hold on to the original."

"Then it's settled."

She nodded happily. "Now you have to let me do something for you." And she leaned forward so that her breasts brushed against his arm, and one hand came to rest high up on his thigh. He shivered involuntarily, and she increased the pressure on his leg, mistaking his reaction for desire. He was incapable of going to bed with her, he realized; he would not be able to do it, not if she stroked and caressed and sucked and licked all over his body, all through the night. There was simply no way he would be able to perform.

"How about another drink now?" he asked, drawing away.

She rubbed his thigh, pouted. "Only if we have it in the bedroom."

He nodded, and they got up, she going into the kitchen, he into the bedroom. The two night table lights were on low, pink bulbs casting a sensual rose over the white frame of the platform bed. He would have to stall, he was thinking; either keep them both drinking until she no longer wanted sex, or until it was so late that he could claim exhaustion and be believed. He could always say he was sick—a sudden stomachache or something. He would think of a way out, any way out before he would climb into bed with her.

He did not want to sit on the bed and get comfortable so he wandered over to her vanity table, filled with jars and pots, loose hairs from her comb, used tissues dabbed with colors, a dozen cotton swabs scattered around and under. The vanity stool held several fashion magazines and two crossword puzzle books. Annie would never allow this kind of clutter, he thought. She kept her bathroom sparkling, her makeup in a little plastic purse on a shelf, a clear Lucite wastebasket under the sink. No table strewn with cosmetics in her bedroom, suffocating him with cloying femininity. Annie. Dear, sweet Annie. I'm going to help you. I promise.

With no place to sit but the bed, he went over to it. A hardcover book was on the built-in night table. The dust jacket had been removed and the back was facing spine to the wall. He picked it up, turned it over. *Honorable Mention* in gold stamped letters. He smiled, pleased, proud. He wondered if she had bought a first edition. He flipped through the front matter, getting to the title page before the copyright page. He glanced desultorily at it, looked again, frowned. Something was wrong with the type, he realized. It didn't look the same as his copy. He turned the page, saw Anne had gotten herself a first edition, went back to the title page, troubled by a difference he could not determine. *Honorable Mention*. Anne Fletcher. The publisher's logo. Nothing wrong with that.

And then a beach ball bounced in his stomach, and he could feel the shock travel down to his groin; his testicles seemed to shrivel. His eyes stared and stared until the letters blurred before him. The back of his neck prickled; his armpits were soaked; even his crotch seemed suddenly damp with sweat. He kept his finger in the book, turned it over so that he could read the spine. *Honorable Mention*. Anne Fletcher. His skin began to itch, and he wondered if he would break out in hives the way he had as a child when nervous. He could not believe what he was seeing, what it meant. Again he looked at the spine. Again at the title page. His eyes had not deceived him, of course they had not. He saw exactly what was there: Anne Fletcher.

She had blacked out the initial N. with magic marker. She had obliterated the N. so that it seemed as if she had written the book.

Gently, he replaced the book as he had found it, spine to the wall.

He was numb, emotionally voided.

"One fresh scotch on the rocks as requested."

He jumped up at the sound of her voice. Had she been standing there watching? Had she seen him discover the book? It didn't matter. He had seen enough, heard enough, tolerated enough.

She offered the drink to him, but he ignored her out-stretched hand. She shrugged, put the drinks on her vanity, sidled up to him, arms slowly snaking up his chest, around his neck. He did not move, staring down into those sick green eyes with ill-concealed revulsion. She took a step back.

"What is it?" she whispered. He could not trust himself to speak. "Arthur, what? What's happened? Don't look at me like that, *please.*" She took another step away, menaced by the ferocity of emotion in his face.

"Why did you do it?" His voice was a low-pitched growl, a watchdog protecting the valuables within.

She laughed uneasily, and a hand came up to brush away hair that had not fallen. "Do what? Arthur, what are you talking about? You're acting so peculiar. Come on, let's go to bed."

"I asked you a simple question. Why did you do it?"

"I don't know what you're talking about." The words came out with a layer of thin, nervous anger.

Arthur pointed to the book on the night table. She followed his finger, and after a moment's pause, she gave a peal of light laughter. "Is *that* what's gotten you like this? Oh Arthur, how silly." Again, a sound of de-lighted laughter, delighted and relieved. "I did that as a lark, a little private joke, that's all. I wanted to see what it would look like, you know, to have my name in print. That's all it means." She began to walk toward him.

"A lark," he repeated woodenly.

"That's right. Now, come on, let's not waste any more time." She shook her head as she neared him. "You really had me going there for a moment," she admitted with a grin. "You seemed so—I don't know—so *dangerous*. Actually, it was kind of exciting."

Arthur moistened dried lips with a bile-thickened tongue. "I better go, Anne," he managed. "I don't feel too well."

"Go?"

He nodded and brushed past her, out of the bedroom. She followed him to the front door. "What's wrong? Can I get you anything?"

"No. I'll take care of it at home."

She shrugged helplessly. "Well, if you really have to. But call me soon, okay?" He nodded wordlessly. "Oh, wait a minute," she said. "You almost forgot the pages of my novel."

She went into the living room to get them. "Here. Let me know what happens."

"Oh I will," he assured her.

"Well, feel better." She unbolted the locks and let him out. She stood in the doorway, smiling as he walked toward the elevator. He never turned, and still smiling, she locked herself back in.

"What the hell do you mean that number's been changed? I want that telephone number!"

"I'm sorry, sir, but it is now unlisted," the operator advised.

"Listen, this is an emergency. Are you going to give me that number or will I have to go to your supervisor?" he threatened.

"Sir, it is the rule of the telephone company. We cannot give out unlisted telephone numbers. That is why they are unlisted. Of course, for a real emergency—"

"Oh, fuck off," he muttered and slammed down the phone so hard that it gave a delayed ring.

Arthur refused to accept that Annie had changed her number so that he would be unable to reach her. If he was of a mind, he would camp out on her doorstep until he spoke to her, and she knew he was capable of that. No, she probably did it to get rid of the voiceless caller, and *I've been so busy in the office I've barely glanced at my messages to see if she's phoned.* He looked at his wristwatch. It was almost midnight; he was tempted to go over to her place right then, but decided against it. She needed her sleep, and he needed to think.

He went into the living room, sat down heavily on a modular unit. *Why? Why?* What could drive a person to such an obsession that she would need to emulate, then destroy? What had Annie ever done to this girl? They were strangers; they never met until that night at Holmes's party. Was her success as a writer the cause? Could *he* be the reason? He did not know. So unanswerable what can push the human mind—no, the human emotions over the edge to uncivilized actions. He did not doubt that Anne Fletcher had gone over the brink; if she were not certifiably mad, she was pathologically disturbed; she functioned in a reality self-created, self-determined.

Abruptly, he got up and went over to the bar he had had fashioned from an antique floor radio. He poured himself a large brandy, liked the way the thick warmth soothed his stomach, washed away the sourness in his mouth. He considered, then dismissed the idea of going to the police. They would need more proof than a few pages of a novel, more even than an apartment filled with similarities, more than a book insanely altered. He could not directly accuse Anne Fletcher either, as he had almost slipped and done; denial came too easily and would still leave Annie exposed and vulnerable. No, Anne Fletcher had to be trapped, lured in and snared until she flailed feebly for release, which would come only after a complete confession. He wanted her helpless and hurting; he wanted her to feel her skin crawl with breathless fear. If she wanted to be Anne N. Fletcher so desperately, then she would have to know what Annie knew: stark terror.

CHAPTER

19

At six-thirty the next evening, Arthur was pressing the intercom to Annie's apartment. Only an unusually frenetic day at the office had prevented him from being there earlier; the pace had not, however, stopped him from worrying about her or altered his decision about what had to be done.

"Yes?"

"Annie, it's me, Arthur. Let me in." She buzzed him in without saying anything.

When he reached the landing, she was standing in the doorway to her apartment, as Anne Fletcher had been the night before. There the similarity ended. Although it had been only a few days since he had last seen her, the ravages of her ordeal were more visible than before. She had looked poorly on Saturday evening, but nothing like this. The loss of weight was achingly evident. Her face seemed longer, her chin jutting, cheekbones almost pointed with the sinking of the flesh on her face. Gray hollows framed eyes glassy and haunted like a petrified animal's. Her hand trembled visibly as she pushed a strand of hair behind her ear, a gesture so familiar to him that he thought his heart would splinter for her pain. As he stared at her, he loathed himself with a fury for having doubted her, for having walked away from her, for having suspected her of creating her own madness. How alone she must be feeling, how vulnerable and helpless.

"Annie—" he began, then stopped when he saw she was shaking her head.

"Not a word about it," she urged. "I'm just so glad to see you, Arthur. I was afraid I had ruined everything and I didn't know what to do. I couldn't bear thinking about it."

He closed the door for her and walked into the living room. Now that he was with her again, he did not know what to say. He had considered only what they had to do, and now he realized he had to tell her what had prompted his reevaluation, that it had been because he had been with Anne Fletcher, had intended to take her to bed. How much more hurt could he inflict upon her, could she tolerate? But it was the only way, and she would have to forgive his weakness.

"Can I get you a drink, coffee or anything?" she asked.

"No, come sit down, I want to talk to you."

They sat on the couch, silence an unwelcome guest. Neither was comfortable, neither knew how to eradicate the bitter words exchanged between them. They avoided each other's eyes, avoided physical contact until Arthur could no longer stand it. He turned his head and looked at her, and his stomach balled up at the sight of her tears.

"Oh Annie," he groaned, and brought her tight against his chest. The frailty of her set his heart thumping with renewed disgust at himself, and a deep anger for Anne Fletcher.

"I'm sorry," she faltered, pulling away. "I didn't mean to do that."

"Shh, it's okay, everything's going to be okay."

Her eyes rounded with a glimmer of hope, then dulled over again. She shook her head, pulled further away.

"Trust me, Annie, everything's going to be all right," he said more emphatically.

She glanced at him, desire to trust and believe straining the muscles of her face; memory of the other night dueling with that desire.

"You don't look so terrific," he remarked, trying to keep his voice light. He was not yet ready to admit what he had done; he needed more time to bridge the distance he had put between them.

"I don't feel so terrific," she said, not quite matching his tone. "I don't sleep much, and food doesn't agree with me."

"All that's going to change. And speaking of change, were you ever going to get around to giving me your new number? I was pretty rude to a telephone operator last night because of you."

"Of course I was going to give it to you, it's just that I've been so preoccupied and we did have a fight and all."

"I know, I'm teasing." He paused, then: "Anything more since I saw you?"

"A few calls until yesterday, that's when the number was changed. There might have been more, but I've been too afraid to leave the apartment." She gave a short laugh, a humorless, tear-thick sound. "I'm in a fine state when I don't dare go outside. I guess that means he's won."

"It's not a he." He had to tell her; had to stop thinking of himself, of the consequences to *them*. She was all that counted now. "I've been a pigheaded fool, Annie," he rushed on. "I didn't believe you and if it hadn't been for last night, I still might not believe you. But now I know how wrong I was, what a mistake I've made."

"What are you talking about?" Annie said. "What happened last night, and why are you so sure it's not a he? You're not making any sense, Arthur."

"Try to understand what I'm about to tell you, why I did it."

"The way you've understood me?" she shot back.

"Annie—"

249

"Okay, I'm sorry. What is it? What made you change your mind?"

He studied his lap as he spoke. "Last night I was with Anne Fletcher." His voice was barely a whisper, but she heard.

"Anne Fletcher? Why? I thought you didn't like her."

He glanced at her, away again. "I was hurt and angry and I needed to get back at you, retaliate in some way for what you were putting me through."

"For what *I* was putting *you* through! That's—"

"I know, I know, don't say it. But that's how I was feeling so I called her. I liked the irony of your names. I thought there was some kind of justice in, uh, well, let's just leave it at that."

He looked at her again, and saw she was shaking her head, but the smile, though small, was sincere with understanding.

"It wouldn't have meant anything," he said feebly.

"Wouldn't have? That sounds as if nothing happened?"

"Nothing did, at least not that way."

"Oh?" Her eyebrows went up. "A new position that didn't work, is that it?"

"Annie, I never—" He heard her laugh, a genuine sound of humor this time, not the smothered cry for help it had resembled before. "I went over there last night and nothing happened because . . . because . . ." Christ, he did not know how to get the words out. He had it all figured, how he was going to burst in here with the great news that he knew who was behind everything and how they were going to stop her, but now, now he felt as tongue-tied as an adolescent asking a girl to dance at his first coed party.

"Arthur . . ." Her voice pressed him into speaking, and he began to tell her what he had observed, finishing by unclasping the manila envelope he had been holding and pulling out the carbon of the novel.

"It's extraordinary," she managed after reading only one page.

"It's sick."

She gave him back the pages. "What you've said still doesn't prove that she's been behind the other things, the push against the subway, the calls, any of it."

"No, it doesn't prove everything but it certainly points some pretty strong suspicion in her direction," he argued. "If only you had told me about her before."

"Would it really have made any difference?" she asked quietly.

His answer was to press his lips together and look away from the deep hurt in her eyes.

"She said you canceled that lunch date with her," he continued.

"That's not true!" Annie cried out. "I got there late, but I was there. I told you, that was the day Matt called about those pages. I didn't want to have lunch with her, I was so upset, but I went anyway. When I got there, the maître d' told me I had called to cancel the reservation. I knew I hadn't so I assumed it had been she and that he hadn't gotten confused because of the names. When I got home, she called, said she had been waiting at the restaurant and why had I broken the date. But I never did break it, Arthur, and if she says otherwise, she's lying." Her distress and outrage were reflected in the scratchy indignance of her voice.

"Didn't it strike you as peculiar that she would accuse you of canceling?" he asked.

She shrugged. "I suppose it should have, but I had other things on my mind . . . like who had pushed me against a subway train!"

"I'm sorry," he murmured. "I'm only trying to show you what she's capable of, how possible it is for her to be involved."

Uncertainty kept her silent a few seconds, then she slowly nodded her understanding. "Why, Arthur? Why would she need to do this? That's what bothers me the most, I think. I mean, I believed that whoever was responsible was some kind of sickie, a real psychopath, but Anne Fletcher, well, she's a regular person, you've gone out with her, spent time with her. I met her at my party, spoke with her on the phone. She's a perfectly normal human being."

"Obviously not," Arthur remarked dryly.

"I'm supposed to see her tomorrow evening. At her health club."

"I know."

"She told you?" Anne said, surprised.

He nodded. "And you're going to keep that date."

"Of course I am. Why shouldn't I?"

"Because she could be dangerous."

"Arthur, stop talking like that, you're frightening me."

"Good. That's what I want to do. If you meet her tomorrow unprepared, thinking her an innocent, then you'll be frightening me." He saw the questioning in her expression, in the tilt of her head. "Annie, listen to me. That girl is capable of anything, do you hear me, *anything!* If you meet her tomorrow trusting her, you could be in serious danger."

"I don't want to listen to any more of this," she snapped, getting up and going over to stand near the Spanish buffet, away from him and his ominous words.

Undaunted, he rose and followed her. He put his hands on her shoulders, twisted her around. "What if it *was* her? What if she was the one who pushed you against the subway train?" His voice was soft, calm. "If she tried it once, she could try it again, or even something worse. Do you dare risk that? Do you?"

"What reason would she have?" Annie asked. "Because of our names, because of you? Those aren't reasons to kill someone."

He dropped his hands and leaned against the buffet. "Remember when this first began, back with that call to the editor at *Glamour*, and I said that whoever had called her had been very jealous of you?"

"I remember, but what you're implying is more than jealousy, Arthur, it's madness."

"That's right. I'm telling you that what I saw in that apartment, especially her passing your book off as hers, well, that's jealousy carried to an extreme, a *mad* extreme." He stopped to let the meaning of his words sink in. "Don't you see?" he went on more urgently. "She's got fantasy and reality all mixed up in her mind. She wants so to be what you are that she's trying to make herself into you. And I think she would do anything to accomplish that. Right and wrong as we know them don't exist for her any longer. The only wrong is what stops her from getting what she wants; the only right is what will help her."

Annie did not answer at once. "What if you're wrong?" she finally muttered. "What if she's guilty of jealousy but not of the rest? Then what?"

He sighed ponderously. "I guess then we start over. But I don't think I'm wrong."

Silence as she studied his face, seeking sure and solid answers there that would necessitate no further action on her part. She was so tired; it would be easy to give in, give up, let her tormentor have his way. Her way. What if it *was* her way?

"What do you want me to do?"

Arthur's smile was jubilant with relief. "We're going to trap her at her own game."

They returned to the couch and he explained what he wanted of her. He said the police could do nothing for them at this point, they were on their own. The way to stop her was to frighten her, terrorize her with knowledge, the way she had been doing.

"But I don't know anything," Annie pointed out.

"Yes you do. You know everything that's been done to you and everything I've told you about her apartment."

253

"How will that trap her?"

"It's your show of strength that will do it. If she believes you suspect her, she'll give herself away."

"By doing what? I still don't see what you hope to accomplish," Annie said with exasperation.

"Just listen to me a minute. If she's convinced you're on to her—and more importantly, that she can't frighten you anymore—she's lost the psychological edge. You'll have her on the defensive, wondering what *you're* going to do with this newfound knowledge—go to the police, turn it around and use it on her, whatever. It's a form of blackmail, psychological blackmail. She'll be the one who's afraid now, and she'll show it."

"You think that'll make her stop?" Anne asked dubiously.

"No." Arthur hesitated. "I think that will get her to make one desperate move."

Anne's eyes rounded as the menace in those words became clear. "You're saying that—"

"I'm saying that I think she's too far gone, too lost in her own warped, confused vision of herself to tolerate being a victim. I'm saying that I think she's going to take the threat of the push against the train and carry it to the next step."

He watched her carefully, concerned that he had scared her anew, that the burden he had charged her with was too heavy. But it was the only way. He had thought about it and thought about it; tried to find other means to put a stop to Anne Fletcher, but all other ways required waiting, passively sitting by and letting the next move come from her. That would leave them unaware of when she would strike again; when, and how lethally. They had to confront her, that was the only solution. Confront her, terrify her, get her to act so that they could act. And that meant placing Annie in a position of danger.

"What if you're wrong?" was all she now said.

"I'm not."

"But if you are."

"I told you. We'll start over. We'll go back to the beginning and we'll figure something out."

"What if you're right but she doesn't make her move tomorrow? If she decides to wait?"

"At least we'll be able to tell if we're on the right track and we can prepare ourselves. We can concoct another situation to trap her. The main thing is that right now she's alerted to nothing. She thinks she's holding the winning hand, but you're the one going in there with every advantage. Even if she doesn't try anything, you can get her to give herself away by drawing her out, by getting her to stumble over her guilt. That might be enough. Once she's aware of how much you know, she might not be so eager to go any further."

"But you think she will?"

"Yes, I do." He spoke softly, as those sure of their rightness often do.

"I'm afraid," she admitted, her voice tremulously belying the brave smile she tried to manufacture.

"I know, but don't be. I'll be there."

"You? What will you be doing?"

"Nothing unless I have to. Use that to bolster your spirits as you try to break her down. You've got to push her, Annie, push her hard so—"

"But where will *you* be?" Anne wanted to know. "Won't she see you?"

"Sweetheart, don't worry, okay? I'll be there, that's the important thing. And believe me, she won't see me. That health club has more halls and stairwells than a school." He grasped her hand in both of his. "I promise I won't let her hurt you, Annie. She'll have to get past me first before she can put a finger on you again."

This time Anne's smile was a bit less fragile. He pressed. "Will you do it? Will you go through with it?"

She stared at him, through him, and he wondered if

she were debating with herself or whether she was recalling the past months of terror and anguish and how a girl she knew, at least knew of, could be responsible. If he was right; if Anne Fletcher was the one, he believed he was also correct in discovering the cause. Jealousy, a destructive emotion at best; possibly deadly now. But jealousy as a motive made the pieces fall into place, crediting each action with a *raison d'être* that felt right to his logical mind. Yes, it was sick; it also made horrifying sense. If only Annie saw it the same way.

"All right," she whispered at last. "I'll do it."

"Annie, you'll—"

"But you promise you'll be there in case anything happens? You promise?"

He nodded vigorously. "I promise," and then he took her in his arms, and hoped she could not hear his heart pounding loudly with his own fear.

Later that evening, at about the same time that Anne N. Fletcher and Arthur Dumont were engaged in somewhat violent, definitely cathartic lovemaking, Anne Fletcher was also in bed, though alone. She was snuggled under her comforter, head propped against two pillows, her face smeared and shiny with a new $25-a-half-ounce French cream. In her hands was the microphone to her tape recorder; on her mouth was a tight smile of satisfaction; in her eyes, bouncing off them, in fact, were anyone there to notice, was a glint of triumph as radiant as a rainbow. She turned on the machine.

I am so close I can hardly bear it. I feel the beginning of me as if I were aware of the moment of my birth. Things are falling beautifully into place, as well they should. I've worked hard, sacrificed so much and it is only fitting that success finally be mine. Last night was a particularly sweet victory. Dear Arthur, how I've missed him. But of course he returned, it was as inevitable as everything else. It was odd how surprised he seemed at my conviction that he would come back to me, but I suppose he needed to tell himself that *she* was what he wanted while he fought his true feelings for me. He got a little strange there for a while, all those questions, and then in the bedroom. Well, I handled the book thing okay, I'm sure he has no idea. Too bad we didn't go to bed, I was looking forward to that. Next time will be better, I'm sure of it.

Oh, I feel so good, so full. She must be an utter wreck by now, a quivering jelly of anxious confusion. Getting her number changed was so foolish, as if that will stop me. There are other ways, so many other ways. Sending the pages under her name was a masterful stroke, nothing I've done has surpassed that. It'll be funny if Arthur manages to sell that stuff. I don't know what made me give it to him. I guess I wanted him to know that she doesn't have the market cornered on talent.

The push against the subway was also rather inspired, come to think of it. Just hard enough to scare her, not hard enough to hurt. And totally spontaneous, too. Who would have thought I had it in me! Too bad I don't have the nerve to really hurt her, I mean like permanently. Ah, then, *then* I would truly be rid of her. But I could never do such a thing. Well, never is an awfully strong word. I guess lots of condemned murderers have said they could never kill anyone, then, the right moment, the right words and whammo! But that doesn't have to happen. All I want, all I've ever wanted is what's due me, what I deserve. Because she's had it, it's been necessary to take it from her. She must be eliminated so that she can no longer interfere, no longer halt the progression, the *natural* progression of my life. And the way to eliminate her is for her to concede that there is no more future for her as she had envisaged it. She must accept failure. That will grant me control again.

I'm looking forward to tomorrow evening. Lunch would have been interesting, but too public. I had to cancel that date when I realized how easy it would have been for her to get up and leave. The health club is private and relaxing, the right atmosphere for her to confess her troubles and for me to then . . . what? Actually, I'm not sure what I want to say to her. It's not the matter of meeting her, talking with her to understand her better. Those things don't mean anything to me anymore. I don't want to wait any longer, I want tomorrow evening to signal her end. Her time is up, and I want the bargain sealed in person: her failure for my success. I'll get her to promise to change her name, and most important, I'll get her to promise to give up writing. She'll do this in exchange for my stopping what's been going on. I suppose that means I'll have to admit to certain things, not all of them, of course, that would be stupid, but enough to let her know that if she doesn't agree, things could get much worse for her. She must leave the health club with the clear understanding that she has to step aside or be thrown aside.

Tomorrow night, just a few hours away. And then, complete victory. Soon, soon, dear diary, I will put you away, replaced with a typewriter whose keys will sing with my words. I thought it would have happened already. I thought just imagining what she was going through would be enough to inspire me, but talent is a funny thing, you can't call on it just because you want it. No, I'm wrong, talent has nothing to do with it. That I've got, of course I do, an extraordinary talent. It's the motivation and the discipline. Well, a special talent needs a special abundance of both, that's all. Tomorrow. Tomorrow the writing will flow. And then it will be the right Anne Fletcher, the only Anne Fletcher whose name will appear on the jacket of a book, who will have parties in her honor, who will have a man in love with her. I have only to wait until tomorrow.

Anne clicked off the machine, carefully placed it back in the drawer of her night table. Her smile was wider now, her eyes dancing with anticipation. She turned off the light, eager for sleep. The sooner it came, the less time between now and tomorrow.

258

Anne was sticky with perspiration before the first set of tennis was over. It had nothing to do with playing a hard game. She was scared, had been all day without Arthur's reassuring presence by her side. She called him three times for encouragement, the third time emphatically refusing to go through with his plan. But now here she was, playing tennis with a girl who might want to kill her. So far, Anne Fletcher seemed as sane as anybody Annie knew. They had met on time in the lobby of the health club, chatting about physical fitness and nutrition as they changed into their tennis clothes in the women's locker room. There had been nothing in the slightest manner peculiar or threatening, and she was beginning to doubt that there ever would be.

"Oops, sorry!"

Annie's attention was abruptly brought back to the game as a ball whipped against her bare arm. "My fault," she called back, "I wasn't concentrating."

They played a while longer, and then, after a strong volley that left her winded and losing the point, Annie waved for a break and loped up to the net.

"I think I've about had it," she said as Anne approached.

"You're good."

"No, you just played a soft game for me," she said with a grin.

"How about the whirlpool, or would you prefer a workout in the gym first or a swim?"

"The whirlpool sounds wonderful."

As they were going down the stairs to the locker room, Anne said: "You've changed your telephone number."

Annie stopped on a step. "How did you know?" she asked quietly.

"I tried to call you to confirm our date. Why'd you change it, too many crank calls now that you're famous?"

"No, I . . . uh . . . no. That's not why."

"Well, you'll give me the new number, won't you?"

Annie hesitated. "Sure, later, okay?"

"Whenever," said Anne, and with a smile the other girl could not see, continued down the stairs.

"Did you remember to bring a bathing suit?" Anne asked as she began to undress.

"Sorry, no, I forgot."

"No problem. I always keep extras of everything, that way I don't have to carry a heavy tote bag each time I come here. I've got plenty of towels, shampoo, an extra bathing cap, all sorts of things."

"Do we need to wear a cap?"

"It's not strictly enforced policy but management prefers it, especially in the swimming pool. It doesn't matter so much in the whirlpool."

"That's okay, I don't mind."

The girls changed into matching red tank suits, Annie feeling awkward with the enforced intimacy. "You *are* prepared," she said admiringly when Anne handed her a towel, washcloth, bathing cap, and a sample-sized bar of soap. "If I belonged I'd probably always forget something vital, like my sneakers."

"I thought you were very organized."

Annie's look was sharp, suspicious, then it softened. "Sometimes."

By eight-thirty according to the wall clock in the locker room, Annie was going down a few gray-carpeted steps to the coed whirlpool. She liked the feel of the cool white tile against her bare feet, and the strong smell of disinfectant in the air. There was something chaste, almost medicinal about the room that appealed to her. As she placed her things down on a bench near the door they had come in, she noticed there was another entrance to the room.

"Does that lead to the men's locker room?" she asked, pointing directly opposite from where they were standing.

"Yes. I'm going to lock both doors," Anne told her. "That way the cleaning people won't bother us."

Annie's heart fluttered with misgiving. What if Arthur has to get in? "How about other members? If they want to use the whirlpool, how will they be able to get in?"

"Nobody else will use it at this hour," Anne said. "Most everyone's gone by now. That's another nice thing about this place. All the doors lock from the inside so if you're here alone, you feel safe." She smiled, and Annie did not like the way her eyes remained hard green stones.

"What about the cleaning help?"

"They have a key to a special cylinder lock on the bottom of every door," Anne explained. "But they never use that before nine o'clock when the club officially closes, and then only if they have to, if someone's accidentally left a door locked from the inside. Great security, isn't it?"

Annie said nothing as the girl walked away. She was pretty, no denying it, and Annie easily could see why Arthur would be attracted to her. But hadn't he found her sullenness off-putting? No, sullen was not quite the

261

right word. There was something in her expression, particularly in the eyes, that was angry and unbending and brimming with frustration. She would not want to be on the receiving end of this girl's temper; Annie had a suspicion that it could strike with devastating viciousness. But that did not make her psychopathic, she reasoned with herself. Lots of people have volatile tempers, are hostile, frustrated, but they don't go around terrorizing people and adopting their tastes and pretending to be them. Anne Fletcher did not seem to be the kind of person who would do those things either, but there was so much proof, it was almost overwhelming. Well, she would soon find out how far the girl's guilt reached. Arthur had told her what subjects to talk about, topics that might trigger the jealousy or reveal her own knowledge and thus scare Anne Fletcher into action. But with the doors locked, how would he get in if—just if—something did happen? Stop worrying, she told herself as she saw Anne head back. What could happen in a whirlpool? There wasn't a weapon in sight, and a match of strength would probably be equal.

Both girls put on their bathing caps and walked over to the edge of the whirlpool. Anne dipped a foot in to test the temperature.

"See if that's okay for you," she instructed.

Annie stuck in a hand. "Feels fine."

They slid into the water, staying near the taps. Annie leaned back against the smooth, slightly raised edge, arms outstretched over the rim, and felt the weeks and weeks of tension ooze from her like sap from a tree. She closed her eyes briefly, tilted her head back against the cool tile.

"Feels good, doesn't it?"

"Mmm," she murmured, opening her eyes. "This was a great idea." It would take no effort to pretend nothing was wrong, she thought; to spend the time not probing and provoking, but only relaxing. She glanced at the other girl, then looked away, her eyes traveling to the door to the men's locker. With another little flutter in her stomach, she now saw that the doors were made of glass, the thick frosted kind that would blur and distort the vision of even a protective lover's vigilant eyes.

"How's your book selling?"

Annie was startled by the question, having almost forgotten she was not alone. Immediately, she was back on guard. "Okay, I guess. Won't crack any best-seller lists, I'm afraid."

"It must be very thrilling for you."

"Yes, it is." Keep your tone of voice light, natural. What did Arthur say? She suspects nothing, make sure you don't change that. "But you know what it feels like."

"I do?" Anne's face, moon-shaped under the unflattering bathing cap, reflected puzzlement.

"You're a writer."

"Well, yes, but I've never been published. Not like you've been." The words came out as an accusation, and Annie shivered despite the warmth of the water.

"You write novels too, don't you? I think I've read some of your work." Annie peered cautiously at the girl, saw the pink flush spreading on her cheeks. Had she gone too far too quickly? Was it really so smart to tempt her madness, if indeed Arthur was right?

"That's impossible," Anne said. "You couldn't have."

"Oh, but I'm sure I did. A love story, isn't it? Interesting style, kind of reportorial." Arthur had told her to say this, had rehearsed her, but still she was unprepared for the wave of sickening dread that came over her.

"I don't know what you're talking about," Anne stated harshly. Annie saw the way the other girl's chest was heaving with a more emphatic claim on air, saw the lips draw in on themselves, a pinch for self-control. She was hitting home.

"Well, perhaps I am thinking of someone else, although I'm sure Arthur said—"

263

"Arthur showed you those pages?" Anne said, her voice becoming strident with displeasure, and surprise. "Arthur Dumont?"

"That's the only Arthur I know," Annie replied, smiling innocently. "Didn't you want him to let me have a look? I'm sure he thought you did, to help you if I could."

"I didn't know you two were still seeing each other," Anne muttered, glancing away from the unwavering sable stare.

"Oh, sure we are. I must admit we've had a few obstacles put in our path, but we're still together. You wouldn't believe what happened once." She could feel her heart thwacking like a piece of taut elastic as she stalked harder, more earnestly. There seemed to be no blood left in her face, everything had drained downward, leaving her with a white, lifeless mask. "Somebody sent Arthur what amounted to a Dear John letter saying that I didn't want to see him anymore. Of course I never sent such a thing, but can you believe the sick mind behind it?" She shook her head. "Can you imagine such jealousy?"

A span of silence too short to be unusual, too long not to be noticed. "No." The voice was toneless, the eyes glassier. Spots of white now shadowed the mouth, and Annie's skin seemed to shrivel and turn raw as she was pierced with the first prick of genuine fear as she had come to recognize it. Her stomach jolted, and breathing became an exercise in pain. The back of her neck locked into a rigid pole. Her nipples puckered. Her thighs were turning liquid and fragile. Was her distress evident? Could the other girl now safely annul her own doubt and confusion seeing that Annie was a lady of straw? Perhaps, but she could not stop yet.

"Weren't you and Arthur—yes, oh gee, Anne," she said, her voice oozing embarrassment, "I'm sorry, I really am, I completely forgot that you and he—"

"We were nothing, and I'd prefer we didn't discuss him."

"Sure, I understand."

"I wonder if you really do."

Again silence, the only sound in the tile-insulated room the soft whirring of the water lapping against flesh. There was nothing comforting now about what they were doing; tension was a third body in the whirlpool; each girl felt its presence, its unpleasant, inescapable vibrations hitting at them as relentlessly as the eddying water. Annie wanted to leave. She was uneasy, unreasonably so because Anne Fletcher had done nothing unusual. But the voice, the mouth, those horrible hard eyes that refused to let anyone in . . . and her own corroded imagination were tricking her into fear. She was not able to play this game; if Arthur was right, there would have to be another way.

"I know what it means to have obstacles," Anne suddenly said, startling Annie. "You're lucky, you were able to ignore yours." She leaned forward, staring hard. "Did you ever feel that if you could just remove the obstacle, eliminate it, everything would change, you'd be in charge of your life again and . . . and succeed where before you failed?"

The words, the unexpected animation with which they had been spoken rattled Annie as if she had been given a surprise cue and the play would falter because she would fluff her lines. Had her little barbs and innuendoes worked so well and so quickly? Would she learn the real reason for this meeting now? Where was Arthur? Where *was* he?

"No," Anne answered for herself, studying her adversary with a slow, almost insolent look. "You don't really know about obstacles, do you? But you know about—" Abruptly she stopped, and in place of the intensity in her face was a feeble replica of conviviality. Annie felt her stomach contract with renewed apprehension.

"Tell me more about your book," Anne urged. "Has it been sold to paperback yet?"

Annie was reluctant to answer. Arthur had instructed her to try, as much as possible, to control the conversation: to ask the questions, introduce the subjects.

"Annie?"

"What did you call me?" The tone was brittle, crackling with incredulity.

"Annie. Isn't that odd?" Anne laughed, a thin sound devoid of everything but deception. "I don't know what made me say that. I guess you just strike me as an Annie." Another chirp of guile. "It doesn't bother you, does it?"

"I'd prefer if you called me Anne."

"Well, sure, no problem. I suppose Annie does sound a little unsophisticated for a famous writer."

"That's not why," she said stiffly.

Anne Fletcher shrugged. "Whatever you say. Now, about the paperback sale—did you make oodles of money from it?"

"It hasn't happened yet," Annie replied in that same tight voice. Arthur must have told her he calls me Annie, but why? No, he would never do that, she must have found out another way. And if she's found that out, isn't it possible she could have learned about a speaking engagement at college, who my editor was at *Glamour*; any of the things that have happened, all of them?

"That's a tremendously exciting part of publishing, isn't it?" Anne went on. "In juvenile publishing, I don't get involved with expensive auctions or anything. I'd love it."

"Have you thought about changing, getting into adult books?" Annie asked.

"Sure I've thought about it, but nobody's going to hire me at an executive level in an area where I have no experience, and I don't want to give up the few executive privileges I have now."

"I see your point, though it might be worth it if it means doing what you want to do." Annie was surprised to find herself actually enjoying the conversation. She had to be careful, she told herself; must not let her guard down, not for a second. This girl who seemed so pleasant, this girl might be waiting to hurt her.

"I'd rather be involved in reprints when it's my own book, anyway," Anne was saying.

"But while you're working, it's nice to be doing something you like."

"I suppose," Anne said with such disinterest as to banish the issue. "What about your book? What do you think you'll get for it?"

"Not that much. It's a first novel and it's had only a modest sale. I can't see it breaking any records."

"You have the best agent in the business. He'll make sure you get a lot."

"Well, he is working on a film deal now that may up the price," Annie admitted with a smile.

"A film deal?"

Annie did not hear the quick intake of breath as the other girl echoed her words, and there was no other indication given. As she seemed to innocently bubble on about the thrilling prospects in her future, Annie alertly watched Anne Fletcher edge closer, standing almost in front of her. But there was only a look of interest on her face, genuine attention to what Annie was saying. True, even the poor imitation of friendliness had vanished, but that did not strike Annie as peculiar nor did it disturb her; in a way she was glad it was gone for it had been a façade she could not believe. There was no way of imagining, therefore, what was going through Anne Fletcher's mind as she moved nearer and nearer. No way of knowing that she was suddenly, without warning, reminded of something she carelessly had said only the night before: *The right moment, the right words.*

And then, in flashing microseconds, the mask of interest became prominent white spots around a sliver of mouth, a pulse throbbing in the temple, a vein taut in the neck, eyes so opaque that reality bounced off them. It happened so quickly, so surprisingly that Anne N. Fletcher, watchful and wary as she had been, could not have been prepared for this moment, for Anne Fletcher herself was not. But how much could one person take? How much should one person have to take? Those were the questions ravaging Anne Fletcher's tormented mind as the girl in the matching tank suit, the girl with the matching name, chattered on about success.

Arthur opened the door to the tennis court only long enough and wide enough to spot Annie returning a hard serve and to see that the two girls were the only players. When the *ping-plop* of balls on wood stopped, he moved silently on Adidas sneakers over to the steps leading to the men's locker room. He was not sure where they would go from here: would it be to the gym to work out, or to the swimming pool, or was that bitch going to give Annie the royal treatment—had she arranged for a massage at this late hour? He doubted it. Maybe the sauna and steam room, or the whirlpool. He would have to check everything out, dammit, and possibly lose precious time leaving Annie unguarded. It was a risk he could not avoid.

He waited five minutes by the wall clock in the men's locker room, time for the girls to change and get where they were going. The place was almost deserted; only he and one other man were there, and that man was on his way out. When the allotted five minutes were up, Arthur took the carpeted steps two at a time. From the main floor, the lobby floor, he still had to climb another set of stairs to get to the gym. An open, doorless expanse, this could be tricky, he knew, for if they were there, they would undoubtedly see him, and his explanation would have to be totally convincing.

But they were not there; only three people were, two of them instructors who ignored the man dressed in street clothes. Arthur slipped down the steps, back to the locker room, down two short flights. He looked at his watch; another minute gone and he still had not found them. Now the coed swimming pool. Empty. Only the sharp stench of chlorine and the muted sound of the water filters. He stopped for a few seconds, trying to determine where next to go, to put some logic into his decision. He could not get into the sauna or steam room, the women had their own as did the men. If they were there, Annie was without protection. He had not thought of the possibility that they might be *forced* apart, he realized with disgust. All right then, the whirlpool. At least he could gain entry there.

With his heart speeding, his mouth dehydrated and sour as if he were on a drug, he bounded back up one set of stairs to the door that led to the whirlpool area. He peered through the glass door and thought he could make out two figures in the whirlpool. He cupped one hand over his eyes to cut off glare from the overhead fluorescent lighting, and leaned in closer. The glass was obstructing his vision. The glass! He had completely forgotten that the doors were made of thick squares of frosted, translucent glass! Even the motion of the water was grotesquely distorted into wide, slow ripples instead of pulsating whirls. But what did that really matter? he asked himself, urging his heart to stop its hard pumping, his mind to think clearly, calmly. At least he had found them, and nothing could happen. He was right there, and the whirlpool was the safest possible place, no fancy equipment, no strange, heavy machinery to use as a weapon. He just wished he could make out which girl was Annie. From what he could tell, they were wearing identical bathing suits, tank suits, and through the shadowing of the glass, they seemed red. And they both had on those confounded bathing caps, those rubbery white things that reminded him of surgeons' caps, or worse, shaved heads with a pleat on top.

He stayed close to the glass panel, his eyes riveted on the two bodies. It was so difficult to see, to make out what was going on, but he could have sworn one of them moved, yes, one of them was standing up now, closer, almost in front of the other. Dammit, they looked absolutely identical. He should be able to determine them by their bodies, but the glass made nothing seem the way it was. Wait a minute, wait a minute, what was that? Jesus H. Christ! It's happening, it dammit-to-hell was happening!

In the time lapse of a breath, he saw the hands of one girl come up and around the neck of the other, pushing, pushing and twisting until the knees sank lower, until the head was next to the water taps. He saw the other arms flailing helplessly, saw the space between the head and the metal taps narrow, and he gasped and his mouth opened in a silent scream as the head was banged down against the shiny silver metal. Frantically, his hands went down to the doorknob. *It would not turn!* The sonofabitch door was locked! He rattled it, furious with his impotence, his utter stupidity for having put her in such danger. He began to pound on the glass door, to kick at it, but the sound died within those thick frosted slabs. His heart seemed as if it would burst from his chest when he saw the body slump into the water, hands still waving about. And then the other body was climbing out of the whirlpool, standing over the edge, watching Annie die. That had to be Annie, he knew she was the one in that pool and he could not do a thing about it. But there was only four feet of water there; she couldn't drown in that. Not unless she was stunned into unconsciousness. *He* was going to die, though; he could feel it; his heart was pumping perilously fast and there was this pounding in his head as if hammers were driving pointed nails into it from all sides. His palms slid down the glass; they were slick and wet from beating on it, from the sweat of fear.

Wait, wait, she's moving. Oh, thank you, thank you, Arthur silently prayed as he saw the form in the water struggle up for air, saw her twist her body around and reach for the edge of the pool, reach further for the ankle above her. But the other girl was too swift; she moved her foot, used it to push the body back down in the water. She's too weak, Arthur's mind raged, she won't have the strength to fight. That knock against the metal . . . loss of oxygen . . . get up, Annie, come on, get up!

And again he saw the body push upward for air. Every struggle was his struggle; every bite for breath became a piercing gulp into his own lungs. His head throbbed with the pain of her blow; his own body strained with the effort she was now making to climb out of the whirl-pool. Helplessly, he again turned the knob, hit on the glass. And screamed, not silently this time but loudly, so loudly that he could feel the stringy muscles in his throat stretch and pull. A part of him knew how useless his actions were: management had wanted noise control and had all the walls lined in the same thick carpeting as the stairs.

Suddenly, he stopped, transfixed by the distortion before him. Both girls were on their feet on the side of the pool. *Both* girls, and now he could not determine which one had been struck. He did not know which was Annie! He saw arms moving as if to reach out and grab and then both red suits were in motion, running, it looked as if one was running over here, to the door. He pounded so hard his knuckles stung, and as the body neared the door, he could make out the round circles of horror her eyes and mouth had become. But the body kept going. "Annie, be careful, be careful!" he yelled to the girl in the lead, not sure that was she, not sure it was not. The tiles had to be slick, he thought, dangerously slick. And her feet were wet and she was wobbly, weakened. Now here was the other one, her pace not as quick but more surefooted because of that. Oh no, she was almost on top of her, almost there. She wasn't going to give up, she was not going to stop this madness.

Then Arthur saw the first girl lose her footing, as he had predicted. She was running near the edge of the whirlpool, too near the edge, the other girl was closing in from behind. Arthur's eyes dilated wide with paralyzing disbelief and bile rose into his mouth in a nauseating wave as the first girl's legs slipped out from under her, as she fought for balance and then fell, thudding to the stone tile, landing hard on her back, her head cracking against the inflexible surface. Tears streaming down his face, merging with his sweat, both fists battering the wall of glass, Arthur stood by helplessly, staring at the lifeless form.

"ANN-IE!" Arthur roared. "ANN-IE! ANN-IE!" And he screamed and he screamed as his head and his hands beat futilely against the glass.

The red flash of the ambulance light filtered through the gray gauze drapes to wash the lobby of the health club in a bloodlike glow. Arthur watched as the stretcher was borne out by two attendants, the white sheet, so final, so immutable, making his skin get goose bumps. He sat on the gray and purple tweed couch reserved for visitors, feeling guilty about his comfort as the men carried the body heavy in death. Those who were still in the club at nine o'clock had been stopped from leaving by the arrival of a cruising patrol car whose occupants had been first to answer the 911 Arthur had phoned in. The two policemen were in the small office used to entice new members, taking down statements from those who had heard nothing, seen nothing. Except for the hapless lady from Trinidad who had the cleaning detail for the evening, and who had been frightened to her core by what sounded like a bleating animal in the area off the whirlpool. It had been she who had found Arthur; who had, after much gesticulation that made less sense to her than the terrible sound and sight of the man's tears, used her special key to the cylinder lock to open the door. Her statement would be of more interest to the police than that of the two instructors and one member still in the club at closing.

As the front doors shut behind the stretcher, Arthur felt a tremble travel through his arm. He looked at her.

"Are you okay?"

Annie nodded, unable to speak. Haltingly, he reached out with his free hand and with his fingertips, gently stroked the tender lump over her left ear where the metal of the whirlpool tap had made contact. He could feel the fresh crust of dried blood. "That hurt?"

She shook her head, and he took his hand away, back to his lap where it plucked like an old lady's crochet needle at the twill of his pants.

He had no right to know such relief, he was thinking. A girl was dead and he, though numb, though weary beyond any conception he had ever had of the word, felt a relief that nipped at euphoria. How different from the fear and dread that had churned in his belly and poisoned his brain as he rushed through the doorway that was at last opened, his sneakers squeaking obscenely on the tiles, to get to the one kneeling body, to the other body lying so still, the head at a grotesque angle of death. And then standing there without the glass perverting his vision, seeing the face so dear to him. Seeing her hand, shaking and weak, lift off the bathing cap, her brown, her *brown* hair without a touch of auburn tumbling around the high cheekbones, not rounded ones; gazing with excruciating compassion into sable eyes that were filling with tears. He could never tell her what he had felt at that moment, the joy that coursed through every pore, that he could taste in his mouth like the sweet runny center of an imported chocolate. It had been no time for rejoicing; there probably never would be. His pleasure was something he would have to keep to himself, like other secret sins.

He had led her out of the area, up the stairs into the lobby where he had called the police. The cleaning lady had never ventured close to the bath, not after glimpsing Annie's face. She had followed them to the lobby, had sat waiting as Arthur patiently instructed her to. The body had been left unguarded.

And now the lady from Trinidad was giving her statement, and Arthur and Anne N. Fletcher knew it would soon be their turn. He worried that she would not be able to talk rationally, that hysterics would rob her of the poise to speak lucidly.

"Arthur?"

It was the first word she had spoken since the ordeal had ended. He could not help the small smile that erupted on his face; he was so glad to hear her voice again.

"Feeling better?" he asked.

"Arthur, she's dead, isn't she?" Annie whispered, saw his brief, sad nod of affirmation. "I was so scared, I didn't know what was happening."

"Shh, don't think about it," he said, squeezing her shoulder.

"But I have to think about it, the police, they'll . . . oh Arthur, could I have saved her, did I . . . *let* her die?" she stammered, her eyes luminous as they pleaded for him to exonerate her.

"Annie, there was nothing you could do, nothing anybody could do. She was dead the instant she fell. She cracked her skull."

Annie said nothing, seeing only that terrifying run around the slickly tiled room, the sudden stop; hearing that ugly, vicious sound of a head landing on something hard, deadly.

"She wanted to kill me, Arthur," she muttered. "You were right. She wanted to kill me."

"I know, and you don't know what it's doing to me because I put you in such danger," he said wretchedly.

"You were there just like you promised."

"Some help I was. Do you have any idea of the torture

I was going through? I couldn't even tell which one of you was the victim."

"It was so awful, so horrible," she gasped, her body suddenly beginning to shake with the tears she had been holding back. "I wasn't going to hurt her, Arthur, really, I wasn't. I just wanted to stop her, that's all. When I finally managed to get out of the water, I tried to reach for her, hold her so she would talk to me, so maybe I could help her. But she didn't understand." Her voice kept catching on sobs, swallowing words in great gulps of air.

"Annie, please . . ." He had to calm her, get her to leave the nightmare behind, but what could he say, what soothing words existed to erase death?

"That's why she's dead now," Annie went on as if she had not heard him, "because she thought I was going to hurt her, the way she was trying to hurt me. That's why she began to run. All I wanted to do was stop her until you could get there, but when she started to run, I had to follow her, I had to make her stop. Oh, Arthur, now she's dead. Dead." And she buried her face into his shoulder, tears taking over.

Finally, the trembling of her body began to subside, and the sobs turned into childlike sniffles. She gazed up at him. "You know what I was just thinking? I can't believe it but I know it's true."

"What's that, sweetheart?" he asked, caressing her head, lightly brushing the hair away from her face.

"Arthur, what if she hadn't been killed by that fall? What if I *had* to kill her?" She stared at him, eyes glistening with tears and with the shock of new self-knowledge. "I might have done it, Arthur. I really would have. If she hadn't fallen, if she had gotten to me again, I might have *had* to kill her to save myself, and Arthur? I think I would have done it."

The whispered confession, so awesome to Annie in its self-revelation, did not disturb or startle Arthur for he

276

was thinking the exact same thing. "I know," he quietly said. "So would I." He saw her eyes hood over with doubt. "It's true. In that second of choice, that quick moment when survival is all that counts, Annie, I swear to you, I would have killed her, too." He looked away a moment as he absorbed this truth about himself.

"But it never came to that, did it?"

He shook his head. "The fall killed her. Believe me, nothing could have been done to save her. But she really killed herself," he added.

"No, she—"

"Annie, she was a sick girl, very sick. Who knows how little it would have taken to push her over the edge. Maybe something you said tonight set her off, something you never could have foreseen, and she was ready to kill you for it. Or she came prepared to hurt you. It doesn't really make any difference. If it hadn't been tonight, it would have been another time, but it would have happened. You've got to see that. She was jealous, Annie, insanely jealous. She was driven by that jealousy, it distorted her view of herself the way that glass door distorted my vision earlier. That's what really killed her, Annie, her jealousy."

Annie's brows creased into a frown as she absorbed what he was saying. "It's so sad," she mumbled. "So sad to want to be what you're not. She might have been very good at something, why did it have to be what I am that she wanted so much?"

"Annie, don't do this to yourself. It's—"

"Extraordinary, really, when you think about it," she went on, her voice expressionless, her eyes seeing back to that body on the clean, white tiles. "To hate me so much that she thought destroying me would be good for her. That's what she said, you know, about removing an obstacle. She saw me as an obstacle to her own success. But I never did anything to her. I didn't even know her. Extraordinary, isn't it?"

Nearly ten days went by before Anne was able to hear the ringing of her telephone without heart pounding, palms sweating. Ten nights before she could sleep uninterrupted by vicious visions, without turning to Arthur for protection instead of warmth and love.

Then, two things happened in quick succession. At Arthur's request, she went to the police station and heard the tapes the police had found in Anne Fletcher's apartment. A few days later, the paperback auction was held for her book, and she found herself with $50,000— and fresh guilt. In her mind, she knew she held no responsibility for the other girl's madness or death. In her heart, she felt otherwise. Had she but told Arthur of meeting her; had she understood better the chilling ramifications of jealousy; had she not been so trusting or proud or any number of things, none of it might ever have happened. She tried to pretend that everything was the same again, but at odd moments—while Arthur would be talking to her, while she would be reading, in the shower, walking to the supermarket, getting her mail —she would hear the tapes, see the face on the tile floor, and she would shiver with fright and guilt. She had to do something to free herself, but she did not know what. Arthur did.

They were lingering over coffee and brandy in the wood-paneled, brass-fixtured dining room of a charming country inn a few miles north of Pawling, New York. Arthur had suggested they make use of the beautiful spring weather forecast for the weekend by getting out of the city. Their room was storybook, with a king-sized four-poster bed, a worn, multicolored rag rug, a vast window with a window seat overlooking a swan pond. Anne loved it, felt herself far removed from the recent nightmare.

"This is wonderful," she said now. "Shall we go antiquing tomorrow or walking or bicycling or—"

"All," Arthur decided. "We'll do it all."

Annie grinned. "I was hoping you'd say that."

There was a momentary silence between them, then Arthur, a new seriousness in his voice, said: "Annie, I want to talk to you about something."

"Sounds important," she quipped.

"It is."

She stared at him, could feel herself tighten with dread. He had learned something new about *her*

"We've been seeing each other how long now, eight, nine months?"

"I guess, something like that," she answered with confusion.

"We spend just about every night together, right?"

"Well, yes, I suppose, since . . . since . . ."

"Since whenever," he supplied. He leaned forward and grasped her hands. She saw the urgency in his eyes, how whatever he was about to say was difficult for him, and vitally important.

"What is it, Arthur?"

"I think we ought to live together," he announced quickly. "I think you ought to move into my place and we'll try—" He abruptly stopped, pulled his hands away. She was shaking her head, grinning, poorly stopping herself from breaking out into laughter.

"I just ask you something I've never asked another woman," he said, appalled, "something I've *rehearsed*, dammit, and your warm and sensitive reaction is to sit there and laugh at me." His voice was harsh with disbelief, his lips and jaw tight in an effort at self-control.

"Oh, I'm sorry, sweetheart," Annie said hurriedly, seeing his hurt. "I'm not laughing at you, I'm laughing at *me*."

"I didn't hear you say anything particularly amusing," he retorted.

"I thought you were going to tell me—oh, it doesn't matter. I just wasn't expecting *that*, that's all."

He did not speak immediately. When he did, the anger in his eyes had been replaced by an agate-hard determination. "You thought I was going to say something about Anne Fletcher, didn't you?"

"Arthur, please, let's not—"

"No, Annie, we're going to talk about it, now and for the last time."

She looked away from him. "Can't we—"

"It's been a month, one month, Annie. I knew it would take time. Christ, do you think it's been easy for me?"

She glanced up at him, startled, as if just now remembering that he, too, had shared the terror.

"That's right, Annie, I've had my own demons to live with. I'm the one who came up with the foolhardy plan that cost one person her life and almost another. But I'm not going to blame myself forever. Living with guilt is not living, and I won't do that to myself or to you. You must stop, Annie, you have to let it end."

"I don't feel guilty," she mumbled, her eyes down at her napkin.

"Oh no? Then why do you lie awake nights?" He saw her surprise. "Sure, I know about that. I see you lying there, staring out into the darkness, and I know you're reliving every moment and blaming yourself for it."

"Arthur, please, I don't want to discuss this anymore."

"You have no choice," he stated almost brutally. "I thought the tapes would help, but they didn't do a thing to shake this sense of responsibility you have for what happened. I thought getting back to work on your new book would help, but you haven't gone near your typewriter."

"I can't," she protested.

"*Why*, Annie? Why can't you believe the tapes? Why do you refuse to go on with your life? You can't bring her back or erase what happened or even stop someone else from being jealous. Don't you understand? Don't you see what you're doing?" His voice was gravelly with intensity. "You're letting her win, Annie. If you're responsible for anything, it's for giving her more success in death than she had in life. She's stopping you from being who you are, doing what you're best at, just as she wanted. She's getting away with it, and I love you too much to sit by and let it happen. I won't let her win, Annie, not without a helluva fight."

She sat there, motionless, wordless. Her eyes went through him, seeming to glaze over in stunned perplexity. *Giving her more success in death than in life. Letting her win. Letting her win.*

Seconds ticked by as the sense of his words echoed in her mind, pierced and penetrated that soft core of throbbing emotion that had not let her accept the truth, accept reason and logic. She began to feel as if she were returning from a journey, coming home—to reality, to herself. How stupid, how blind she had been. Arthur was so right. She *was* guilty, of perpetuating the nightmare, of walking into the last trap. Well, not any longer.

She refocused on him, wanting to quickly eradicate the tense anxiety on his face. "It will never go away completely," she confessed quietly.

He nodded. "I don't expect it to. It won't for me either."

Her mouth slowly widened into a smile, and she reached for his hand. "In that case, there's just one more thing I'd like to say." She was smiling fully, her eyes bright with love. "Would you move into my place instead of me into yours? I really can't stand your furniture."

———

About the Author

SUSANNE JAFFE is vice-president and editor-in-chief of a mass market paperback publishing house. This is her first novel.